Ruthless

Ruthless

Shelia M. Goss

www.urbanchristianonline.com

Urban Books, LLC
97 N18th Street
Wyandanch, NY 11798

ISBN 13: 978-1-60162-680-6
ISBN 10: 1-60162-680-0

First Mass Market Printing November 2014
First Trade Paperback Printing January 2012
Printed in the United States of America

10 9 8 7 6 5 4 3 2 1

Distributed by Kensington Corp.
Submit Wholesale Orders to:
Kensington Publishing Corp.
C/O Penguin Group (USA) Inc.
Attention: Order Processing
405 Murray Hill Parkway
East Rutherford, NJ 07073-2316
Phone: 1-800-526-0275
Fax: 1-800-227-9604

Ruthless

A Novel

Shelia M. Goss

Acknowledgments

Readers, I want to thank you for supporting my "notorious women" of the Bible series. I've chosen women like Delilah and Bathsheba, who, from their mere appearance, caused the downfall of several great men. But when you dig a little deeper, you realize the men had choices, just like we all have choices in our life. It's up to each individual to weigh their options before acting or reacting. Our decisions can lead to life or death.

I thank God for His grace and mercy. Without Him, none of this would be possible for me.

I can't do a dedication without mentioning my parents, who inspired me to be the best I can be: Lloyd (1947–1996) and Exie. To my two brothers, Lloyd F. (Jerry) and John, whom I love dearly.

A special shout-out to my Cedar Hill Baptist Church family and to relatives who help spread the word about all my books: Hattie Hogan

Acknowledgments

Jones, Nicolette Hogan, Demetrius Hogan, Mary Jean Foster, and Dorothy Hodges.

Thanks again to Joylynn Jossel and my agent, Dr. Maxine Thompson. I would also like to thank my publisher, Carl Weber, and everyone else at Urban Christian.

Kemmerly Beckham, Carla J Curtis, Kandie Delley, Peggy Eldridge-Love, Sharon "Shaye" Gray, Linda Dominique Grosvenor, Deborah Hartman-Fox, Sheila L. Jackson, Shelia Lipsey, Michelle McGriff, Angelia Menchan, Brock Anderson, Kevin Gill, A. Andrew Minix, and Augustus Shepherd, thank you all for your words of encouragement.

Thanks to all who have shown their support to me over the years. I don't have space to list everybody, but here are a few names: Emma Rodgers; Mrs. Til (Jokae's Bookstore in Dallas); Abiola Abrams; Vincent Alexandria; Black Pearls Keepin' It Real Book Club; Charlotte Blocker; Gwyneth Bolton; Tina McKinney Brooks; Crystal Brown-Tatum; Renata "Dee" Carter; Jennifer Coissiere; Cassie Coleman; Yasmin Coleman (APOOO Book Club); Ella Curry (EDC Creations); Jamise Dames; Desiree Day; Terrance Dean (*Hello Beautiful*); Essentially Women; Eleuthera Book Club; Brenda Evans; Pat "Sister Betty" G'orge-Walker; Yolanda Gore; Bettye Griffin;

Cynthia Harrison; LaShaunda Hoffman (*Shades of Romance* Magazine); Troy Johnson; Yolanda Johnson-Bryant; Live, Love, Laugh and Books yahoo group; Lutishia Lovely; Rhonda McKnight; Alfreda McMillan; Mindful Thinkers Book Club; Darlene Mitchell; Michelle Monkou; Celeste O'Norfleet; Debra Owsley (Simply Said Reading Accessories); Onika Pascal; V Anthony Rivers; Tee C. Royal (RAWSISTAZ); Brian W. Smith; Sherena Smith; Stacy-Deanne; Dee Stewart; Olivia Stith; Joyce Swint; Marietta Underwood; Tanisha Webb; Tu-Shonda Whitaker; all my Facebook and Twitter friends; and the list goes on and on.

If your name wasn't mentioned, it's not that I forgot about you. I just ran out of room. Thank you, _____ (fill in your name). I appreciate you all.

Shelia M. Goss

Prologue

David King used the borrowed hotel key and rushed into the corporate suite of Uriah Richards, his employee, to retrieve his forgotten cell phone. While meeting with Uriah to discuss a business proposition, David had absentmindedly laid the phone down and had forgotten it. He thought of it only when he needed to make a phone call. "There it is," he said out loud as he picked up his iPhone from the coffee table and placed it in his black tuxedo jacket pocket. His bladder needed relief, so he decided to make a pit stop in the bathroom before returning downstairs to the DM King Media annual corporate party.

The sound of the shower caused him to pause. The bathroom door was ajar, and he could see the silhouette of a woman's body as she showered. David knew he should have turned around and made a quick exit when he heard the shower, but his feet were planted in one spot. His mind wouldn't will him to move.

He watched as the water slid down her flawless chestnut brown skin. David was not a Peeping Tom, but her hourglass figure held him captive. He observed from a distance as she exited the shower and dried off with the white, fluffy towel. David had been all over the world, but never had he seen a woman as beautiful as the one whom he now laid eyes upon.

Her radiant jet-black hair cascaded down her back and accented her perfectly oval face. She seemed unaware that she had an audience as she sprayed on perfume. The sound of the hotel phone ringing broke David's trance. He slid out of the hotel suite without the mystery woman ever knowing she had company.

Chapter 1

Sheba rushed out of the bathroom to answer the phone. The sound of her husband's voice was on the other end. "Uriah, I told you I'm coming."

"Hurry up. I want you to meet my boss before he leaves."

"Give me ten more minutes. I'm getting dressed now." Sheba sat on the edge of the bed and finished drying off. She had worked up a sweat from shopping, so she wanted to take a shower before changing into the new dress.

"I don't know why you had to get a new outfit. Now you're late. There was nothing wrong with the dress you had."

Sheba loved Uriah, but they had two different views when it came to money and spending it. She loved the finer things in life, and he was a tightwad. She had hoped that with him getting the new job, he would stop tripping about the amount of money she spent.

"You want me to make a good impression with your new boss, don't you?" Sheba asked. She removed the sheer hosiery from its package and put it on as they talked.

"Yes, of course."

"Then trust me. When you see me in the new dress, you'll be glad I bought it."

They ended their call. Twenty minutes later, Sheba, dressed in a floor-length silver gown with a slit, cascaded into the hotel ballroom as if she was the queen of the ball. Men and women stared at her as she stopped to scan the room, in search of her husband. She was aware of her natural beauty, so she automatically ignored their glances.

She noticed a hand waving in the air. It was Uriah. She walked in his direction. The slit moved to the rhythm of her pace and showed her well-toned legs as she walked. The man standing with Uriah turned around to face her. His eyes seemed to pierce straight through her. Since he was a public figure, she recognized him immediately. He was the well-known David King. The CEO of DM King Media and Uriah's new boss.

She flashed her one-thousand-kilowatt smile and graciously walked up to where Uriah and David stood. Uriah reached his hand out for her, and she grabbed it. He kissed her on the cheek. Not once did she take her eyes off David. She could see why women flocked to David. He was a very attractive man. He stood at least six feet tall and had broad shoulders and naturally wavy brownish-red hair. He was what her friends would call a pretty boy.

"Mr. King, I want you to meet my beautiful wife, Bathsheba." Uriah smiled as he made the introduction.

Sheba held her hand out to David. "Call me Sheba. It's nice to meet you."

David's hand seemed to hold on to hers longer than necessary. "The pleasure is all mine." Without taking his eyes off Sheba, David said, "Uriah, you didn't tell me you were married to a model."

Sheba continued to smile. She was never one to be bashful, but something about David made her feel a little uneasy. "You're too kind, Mr. King," Sheba said.

"It's David, and I'm telling you the truth." He winked his eye.

Sheba could feel Uriah's hand on the small of her back. "Well, David, thank you for the compliment."

An awkward silence fell among the three of them.

David finally broke the silence. "Uriah, don't forget there are two settings for you and your lovely wife at my table. Dinner will be served in about fifteen minutes."

"Yes, sir," Uriah responded as they watched David leave to go speak with someone else.

Uriah led Sheba to a table near the front of the room. He held out her chair. She took a seat and waited for him to sit before saying, "So how did I do?"

"You were great. Thank you for coming with me."

"Now, you know when you told me the meeting was in Dallas, I would have no problem taking off work. I love shopping in Dallas."

"I know. Maybe I shouldn't have told you. I hate to get next month's credit card statement."

"Dear, you're making six figures, so why shouldn't I be able to splurge every now and then? Besides, I have my own money. I didn't work my butt off to be an RN for nothing." Sheba tilted her head and recalled the hard work it took for her to achieve her goal to become a registered nurse. She'd worked many long hours at one of the Shreveport, Louisiana, area hospitals before getting her license.

"But most of your money goes toward your spending habits. For once, I would like to buy myself something," Uriah complained.

"Don't I always buy you something?" Sheba asked. She rolled her eyes. "Here we go again. Arguing over the money I'm spending. This argument is getting old."

"Let's talk about this later. I don't need you embarrassing me in front of my coworkers, and especially my boss." Uriah turned his back to Sheba and started talking to the man sitting on the opposite side of him.

Sheba looked up and across the table and into David's hazel brown eyes. He flashed a smile. She glanced away. Uriah's actions had upset her. She wanted to leave but knew how important this event was to him, so she chose to put her feelings aside and pretend to have a good time.

Dinner was served. Sheba remained quiet throughout dinner. She spoke only when spoken to.

Uriah placed his hand on her thigh under the table and squeezed it. He leaned closer to her. "I'm sorry," he said. "Forgive me?"

With a half smile forming on her face, Sheba responded, "Fine."

"I can tell you're still mad at me."

"We can talk about this later, Uriah."

"Dance with me. Maybe that'll make you feel better," he said.

"I don't feel like dancing," Sheba replied. She loved to dance, and the song that was playing was one of her favorites. Uriah knew she could be stubborn, so why he had chosen to upset her now, she didn't know.

"Just one song. I want everyone to see what good dancers you and I are."

Sheba made the mistake of looking into her husband's eyes. She was a sucker for his puppy dog eyes. Looking into them, she couldn't resist giving him what he wanted. She pushed her chair away from the table. "Come on. One dance."

Uriah led them to the dance floor. Although it was a mid-tempo song, he pulled her closer into his arms. "You know you're the prettiest woman here tonight, don't you?"

"Tell me anything to get back on my good side."

"Baby, you know we're trying to save up for another house. That's why I want you to curb your spending."

"It's not like we can't afford the things I buy." She held on to his arm as he dipped her.

"For now, let's forget about all of that and just enjoy each other," Uriah said.

Sheba pushed the conversation to the back of her mind. The next song was an old-school number by Kool & the Gang. She snapped her fingers and moved from side to side like her husband. She turned her body around, and when she looked up, David stood near the dance floor, watching them with a sly grin on his face.

Chapter 2

David's date for the evening was a tall brunette named Majorie Logan. "I wish you would look at me like you're looking at her," Majorie whined.

David stopped staring at Sheba, the beautiful woman who captivated him the moment he saw her in the shower, and gave Majorie his full attention. "What, Majorie? You got my attention. You want to dance, too? Come on."

Before she could protest, David pulled Majorie onto the dance floor. She could dance, but her body didn't seem to have the smooth rhythm of Sheba's. David found himself stealing a glance in Sheba's and Uriah's direction. To his disappointment, they were no longer on the dance floor.

After finishing out the song, David grabbed Majorie's hand. "I think I'll sit this next one out."

Majorie kept up his pace. When they became stationary, she said, "David, this has been fun, but I know when it's time for me to bounce. Good luck." She got on her tiptoes and kissed him on the cheek.

"Majorie, you don't have to."

She placed her index finger over his lips. "Shh. No need to apologize. I'll have your driver drop me off at home."

David escorted her outside. "Bye, Majorie," David said.

"Good-bye, David," she responded right after entering the limousine.

David waited until the limousine had driven away before returning inside. He got a glance of a silver dress going toward the restrooms. He would know that body anywhere. He looked around for Uriah. Uriah was nowhere in sight. Instead of going back to the ballroom, David went in the opposite direction and headed toward the restrooms.

He pulled out his iPhone and sent Uriah a quick text message. He wanted Uriah to keep some of his investors entertained until he returned. Once he received confirmation back from Uriah that he'd received his text, David placed his phone back in his inside jacket pocket.

A young lady who worked for the hotel walked in his direction. When it appeared she was going into the restroom, David stopped her. "Can you tell the woman that's in there that someone's waiting for her outside?"

"Sure," the young lady responded.

David slipped her a crisp one-hundred-dollar bill.

The young lady looked at him. "Do you need me to do anything else?" she asked.

"No, that will be all," he responded.

A few minutes later Sheba exited the restroom and looked around. She paused when she saw David. "Is everything okay? Where's Uriah?"

David responded, "Uriah's fine."

Sheba sighed. "I thought something was wrong. Are you the one who sent the girl into the bathroom for me?"

"Guilty as charged," David admitted. His hand flew up to his chest in a bashful manner.

"Why? Where's my husband?" Sheba's forehead wrinkled.

"He's handling some business for me right now, so he's occupied." A mischievous grin was plastered on David's face.

"Fine. I'm about to head back and wait for him at our table."

"Why don't you walk and talk with me for a minute?" David asked as he walked closer to her.

Her floral fragrance filled his nostrils as he inhaled her scent. He had to stop himself from reaching out to her. He placed his hands in his pockets as they walked to the opposite end of the hotel.

"Uriah's one of my best employees. Hiring him was one of the best decisions I ever made."

"He enjoys working for you."

"That's good to hear. He's done a great job overseeing my Shreveport affiliate."

"I will have to let him know to keep up the good work."

David opened the door leading to the balcony. "After you."

"Maybe I should get back," Sheba said as she stopped in front of the door.

"Uriah's still busy. Enjoy the view."

Sheba stood and thought for a second and then followed David out onto the balcony. The other people on the balcony went back inside the hotel. David watched Sheba from the corner of his eye as she leaned on the rail. They both stared in silence at the beautiful view of downtown Dallas .

David eased near Sheba and said, barely above a whisper, "Sheba, I have to be honest with you. I find you to be a very attractive woman."

Sheba turned to face him. "I'm also happily married. And I do stress the word *happily*," she said.

"You didn't look too happy at the dinner table earlier. I could tell you two were having some type of disagreement," he said.

"That's what married couples do. We sometimes disagree. It doesn't mean we're unhappy, though."

"What if I told you I could make your money problems go away?" David had overheard Uriah speaking with Sheba earlier about their finances. David knew he was crossing the line, but he had to have Sheba.

"Cool. That means I can tell Uriah that you'll be giving him a raise." Sheba batted her long black eyelashes.

David laughed. "That's not exactly what I meant."

"Well, what exactly did you mean, Mr. King?"

Before David could respond, his cell phone vibrated in his pocket. "Hold that thought." He glanced at the phone. "That's one of my Hong Kong buyers. I need to take this call."

"Good-bye, Mr. King," Sheba said as she quickly retreated from the balcony, leaving David alone.

David wanted to protest, but duty came before women. That had always been his motto, and he wasn't going to disregard it, no matter how much he wanted Sheba. David spent the next thirty minutes putting out fires at his Hong Kong office. Once he was satisfied that the vice president of operations could handle the rest, he ended the call.

When he returned to the ballroom, Sheba was nowhere to be found. "Uriah, where's your beautiful wife?" he inquired, after approaching his employee.

"She was feeling tired, so I told her I would meet her in the room."

"Thank you for talking to those investors for me. Look for a bonus on your next check," David said as he patted Uriah on the back.

"Thank you, Mr. King."

David remained in the ballroom until everyone had left. He didn't feel like going home to his empty mansion, so instead he checked into one of the executive suites. He poured himself a glass of apple juice and sat back in the huge plush chair in the living room area. He leaned back and closed his eyes, not to sleep but to meditate.

"Lord, I know that your word says in Proverbs six not to 'Lust not after her beauty in thine heart; neither let her take thee with her eyelids.' Well, Lord, it's too late. Bathsheba Richards has gotten under my skin, and I don't know what to do about it."

David heard a whisper. "Yield not to temptation."

David's eyes popped open. The room was empty.

Chapter 3

"Ever since we got back from Dallas, you've been acting a little funny," Uriah said to Sheba over dinner the Monday following their weekend trip to Dallas.

"Baby, we had a full weekend. The shopping, the partying. I'm not as young as I used to be." Sheba wasn't tired physically, but mentally. She had been debating what to do about David. Ever since the night he led her onto the balcony, she hadn't been able to keep him off her mind. She knew he'd wanted to do more than just talk. She'd been prepared to turn him down, but he didn't seem like the type of man to take no for an answer.

Uriah stuck his chest out. "I know it's hard to keep up with big daddy and things. I gave you a full workout this weekend, so maybe we need to put you on some vitamins."

Sheba pushed David out of her thoughts and laughed. "Big daddy, I don't need any vitamins.

At thirty-one, I look better than those twenty-year-olds."

Uriah licked his lips. "Yes, you do, baby. Well, I just wanted to make sure my baby was doing okay."

"Baby, I'm fine. Just regretting I switched shifts with one of my coworkers."

"I don't like you working graveyard."

"It's only for this week, and then I'll be back on my regular schedule," Sheba assured him.

After dinner Sheba dressed for work. She was barely through the hospital doors when one of her coworkers and longtime friends pulled her to the side. Annette Johnson said, "Yesterday we had a patient admitted, and you're not going to believe this."

"What?" Sheba asked.

"She looks just like your mother. I looked at her chart, and you both have the same last name."

"Did you ask her if she knew me?" Sheba asked.

"Well, not exactly. She's unconscious. Someone shot her, and she lost a lot of blood. Right now the doctor's aren't sure if she's going to make it."

Sheba's heart rate increased. "I need to see her."

Annette waited outside as Sheba entered the ICU room. The patient had a visitor. The teary-eyed woman never looked up. The woman said to Sheba, "Please tell me you came bearing good news."

"I'm sorry. I just stopped by to see her," Sheba said. Sheba picked up her chart, and there it was in black and white. The patient had her maiden name. Even with all the tubes hooked up to her body and a swollen face, Sheba knew this had to be the woman her mother had been looking for all of Sheba's life.

"You know Delilah?" The woman glanced up. She looked as if she had seen a ghost. She peered at Sheba and then down at Delilah.

"I think she might be my sister," Sheba blurted out.

"She never told me she had a sister." The woman stared at Sheba in disbelief.

"She didn't know. I just found out myself. I've been looking for her for two years now." Sheba stood near the bed and couldn't take her eyes off Delilah.

"Well, apparently, you didn't look for her too hard. She's been right here in Shreveport." The woman had stood up and was now on the opposite side of the bed.

"I'm still not sure she's my sister, but she has to be. Too many coincidences."

"I can't believe the resemblance."

"Are you one of her friends?" Sheba asked.

"Yes, I'm Keisha." Keisha's face softened.

"Keisha, I'm Bathsheba, but everyone calls me Sheba."

Just then a police officer walked in the room. The blond-haired police officer said, "We were checking to see if the patient was conscious. We're still trying to find out who did this to your friend, Mrs. Graham."

"It's Ms. Graham, and I think I know who did it," Keisha responded.

"Let's step out of the room and give them their privacy," the officer stated.

"It's okay. I'm supposed to be working, but I'll stay here until you get back," Sheba said to Keisha.

Keisha and the officer stepped out of the room and closed the door. Sheba could see them through the glass window. She walked near the bed to get a closer look at Delilah Baker.

"Even with all the bruises, you look just like Mama," she whispered to the woman who could be her sister. "Too bad Mama died last year, before I could find you." The noise from the machines filled the room. Sheba went on to say, "She loved you. She had to give you up because her parents wouldn't let her keep you. She tried to find you when she turned eighteen, but no one would tell her where you were."

Sheba looked up, as if to the heavens, and said, "Mama, I found your little girl."

Delilah's eyes fluttered open, and the alarm on one of the machines went off. Sheba did what she was trained to do as a registered nurse. The door to the room flew open as some of the other hospital staff came in to assist.

A doctor yelled, "Her pressure is dropping. Someone give me the defibrillator stat."

One of the nurses yelled, "Bathsheba, this isn't your unit. What are you doing here?"

Sheba stuttered, "Sh-she's my sister."

"Let us handle it from here," the ICU nurse said.

Sheba moved to the side and said a silent prayer. She couldn't lose Delilah. She was her only link to her mother. "Please, God. Please spare her life."

The beeping noise from the machine sounded normal again. The doctor said, "Did you say you were her sister?"

"Yes. Well, I think I am," Sheba rambled. "Long story. But what can you tell me about her condition?"

"It's been a little touch and go for the last twenty-four hours. She needs your prayers, and we'll work on her from this end." He patted Sheba on the back, then left the room.

The ICU nurse remained behind. "Sheba, I'm going to stay in here and monitor her. Are you still going to handle your shift, or would you like to call someone to take your place?"

Sheba opted to take her shift. She called Uriah on the elevator ride up to her floor. "Can you believe it?" Sheba exclaimed after she had explained to Uriah what had transpired.

"It's amazing, if it's her," he responded.

"I think it's her. I think the lady in that hospital room, hanging on to her life, is my sister."

"Baby, before you go get emotionally attached to this woman, I think you should make sure."

"Even with a swollen face, she looks like my mama." Sheba felt herself shaking. "Seeing her lying there brought back memories of seeing Mama those last days in the hospital bed."

"Maybe you should take off work today," Uriah suggested.

"No, I'm determined to finish my shift."

It wasn't long before Sheba wished she had taken off, because she could not concentrate. Her mind was on the woman who could well be her long-lost sister.

Chapter 4

David's meeting with his Hong Kong investors ended on a high note. The legal papers had been signed, and he was well on his way to becoming the owner of one of the largest television stations in the region. He sat back in the brown leather seat on his private jet as it glided through the sky, headed back to the United States.

He watched as his staff celebrated their triumph by popping the cork on a bottle of some expensive champagne. David's plan to become global was quickly becoming a reality. If only he could get his personal life in check.

David had been married a couple of times. Each time, the marriage ended in divorce. His two ex-wives had married him mostly for the lifestyle he provided them, but David didn't seem to mind, because they were eye candy and catered to his every need. Once they stopped catering to him, David found a way to get rid of them. Both of his ex-wives had got nice divorce settlements, and since they shared children, they received generous child support payments. Due to David's busy schedule, he rarely spent time with any of his children, but he made sure they were well taken care of. Neither his kids nor his ex-wives would ever be accused of living the life of paupers.

David loved beautiful women, but none could compare to the visions of Sheba that seemed to be permanently implanted in his mind. She was the wife of one of his directors. A man he trusted and admired. Uriah was the only man on earth that he actually envied.

"Mr. King, I just received a message from one of my contacts in Afghanistan. Now is the time for us to make our presence known in the region," said Wade Martin, one of the members of David's staff.

"Wade, who do you suggest we send over to set up the satellite office?"

"Sir, I can give you an answer by the end of the day." Wade turned on his laptop and began to work.

David, tired from lack of sleep, closed his eyes. He would listen to Wade's suggestion, but in the end, he would make the final call. Opening up a satellite office in the Middle East was something that hadn't been done by any of his American competitors. His would be a first. Triumph swept across David's face in the form of a smile just before he drifted off to sleep.

David had a hands-on approach. Although he hired people who were good at what they did, in the end, he made the final business decisions. David started from humble beginnings. His family lived on a farm in Grand Cane, Louisiana. His father's employer took a liking to David and hired him to work at his locally owned newspaper after school. He also allowed David to meet some influential people and introduced him to the world of the rich. Although David's father provided for his family, and neither David nor any of his brothers went hungry, David wanted more. Seeing how some other people lived sparked his desire to do more. He would do whatever he could to make life better for his family.

David worked hard to keep his grades up and received a full scholarship to attend Louisiana State University. David had a double major in business and technology. When the owner of the newspaper in his hometown died, his kids were quick to sell the paper. David took out a loan and purchased it. Before long, he was acquiring newspapers that had found themselves in financial trouble across the region.

He used his technology experience and brought the newspapers up to date, taking advantage of the new era—which included the Internet. Not satisfied with just acquiring newspapers, David branched out into other media, adding television stations to his roster. David's company soon became DM King Media, and the rest, as they say, was history.

David's eyes flew open when the plane hit a bout of turbulence, waking him out of his slumber. The pilot's voice sounded over the intercom. "We're trying to go above the storm clouds, so please make sure your seat belts are buckled. We should be around them in about five minutes."

David's staff did as they'd been told. David knew he would not get any more sleep. The five staff members were all seated and buckled up. Wade sat with his laptop on his lap, still working diligently.

David was very careful about his inner circle. Each one of the people here served a purpose. Being in the type of business David was in, he had to feel like he trusted the person he hired, or else theirs would be a short-lived relationship.

Several people had been trying to undermine him and buy him out, but he would not sell any part of his company. He would revamp the way he did things before he would sell to his competitors. His goal was to never lay off folks, but if during the reorg, it was inevitable, he made sure they were given nice severance packages to tide them over until they could find other jobs.

His employees thought David was a fair and generous boss, but they also knew that he could be shrewd and that he expected his employees to be dedicated and to work just as hard as he would in their positions. Because of the level of respect David paid his employees, they didn't mind putting in the hard work and hours it sometimes took to keep David appeased.

"You can now unbuckle your seat belts. It should be smooth sailing from here on out," the pilot said over the intercom.

David released his seat belt and went over to his desk. He hit a button, and the computer monitor eased its way up. His business mind was always working, so he spent the rest of the flight planning his next move in the Afghanistan market. It would take some doing, but if it was done right—and with the right officials palmed American money—he would be able to get his satellite office set up.

"Wade, do you have any names for me?" David asked.

Wade got out of his seat and took a seat near David. He opened up his notepad. "I've narrowed it down to Blake Mitchell, Simon Crenshaw, and Miguel Nardin. I had one other person, but he's been with the company only a year, so I'm not sure if you want to consider him for such an important project."

"Who else do you have in mind?" David asked out of curiosity.

"Uriah Richards. He's taken the station in the Shreveport, Louisiana, market from the last spot to number one in less than a year."

"I'm well aware of his achievements, but I think Simon would be the best choice. Let me think about it."

Wade got up and went back to his seat.

The mention of Uriah's name caused David to think about Sheba. He licked his lips as his mind recalled the sight of Sheba in the shower. He wanted Sheba. He called Wade back over to him. "Call Simon and tell him to meet me at the Shreveport office tomorrow morning at ten."

"But he's in the New York office, and we're landing there to refuel."

David ignored Wade's comment. "Tell Uriah to be expecting us. But do not tell either one what the meeting is about. Understood?"

Wade had a puzzled look on his face. "Yes, Mr. King."

"Fine. Then it's all set. After I meet with those two gentlemen, I'll have my final decision. Thanks, Wade, for all of your help."

David turned off the computer and left Wade sitting there. He retreated to the private area of the jet. David used the last part of the plane ride to meditate. He kneeled down at the foot of the bed, closed his eyes, and recited one of his favorite passages from the Old Testament. "The Lord is my shepherd. I shall not want. He maketh me to lie down in green pastures. He leadeth me beside the still waters. He restoreth my soul. He leadeth me in the paths of righteousness for his name's sake."

David opened his eyes, hoping his mind would be free of Sheba, but instead she filled his thoughts and caused a spirit of lust to overcome him. David, normally a man in control, was losing control.

Chapter 5

Sheba spent the majority of her time at the hospital. If she wasn't working, she was holding prayer vigils in Delilah's room. It had been three days since Sheba had learned of Delilah, and she had been praying fervently for her full recovery ever since.

Uriah couldn't understand her need to be at the hospital when she should be home, resting. She was at home now only to shower and planned to return to the hospital. She was startled when she heard the bedroom door open.

"Sheba, baby, you need to sleep. I came back to make sure you got some sleep," Uriah said as he dropped his briefcase down and walked up to her.

The towel around her body fell to the floor as she flew into his arms. She didn't realize how much she missed having his arms around her until now. She drew upon his strength and allowed herself to be carried to the bed.

"Uriah, I need to be there when she opens her eyes. I want her to know she's not alone."

"Baby, she's not going anywhere. Even when she opens her eyes, she'll be right there. What good are you going to do her if you're exhausted? What good are you to your patients if you're walking around like a zombie?"

Sheba realized Uriah had a point. She hadn't slept much these past few days. She would do as her husband suggested. She would sleep, and later on she'd go in an hour before her shift started. "I love you. Love you for always thinking about my needs," she said.

"I love you, too, Sheba. I don't want to live my life without you. It's my job as your husband to make sure you take care of yourself."

Uriah bent down and kissed Bathsheba lightly on the lips. The taste of his lips stirred something within her. She forgot about being tired as Uriah discarded his clothes. Seconds later, they were enjoying a morning love session.

Once they were both physically satisfied, instead of cuddling like Bathsheba wanted, Uriah sat up in the bed and said, "I'm going to shower and then head in to work. I have a meeting with my boss and one of the other directors from New York."

"Really? It must be important for him to be flying into town."

"I'm hoping it doesn't mean a reorg. Some of the directors have had to lay off some folks."

"Let's hope not." Sheba followed Uriah to the shower.

"Baby, you know I won't be able to shower with you in there with me," Uriah said.

"Who said anything about showering?"

Uriah and Sheba spent another thirty minutes enjoying each other. Afterward, Uriah rushed and got dressed, while Sheba sat on the bed and watched.

"I'm going to tell David why I'm late," Uriah teased.

"Do that. You know he wants me, right?" There, she'd said it. She'd put it out there to Uriah.

"What man doesn't? Although I married you because I love who you are, Sheba, a man would have to be blind not to see your beauty."

"Well, I'm not a piece of meat, and it irks me sometimes how men like to gawk."

"You handle it well, baby. As far as David is concerned, he's around beautiful women all the time. I'm sure he was just admiring the master-piece that I call my wife." Uriah bent down and gave her a quick peck on the lips.

"What do you want for dinner? That's the least I can do, since I haven't cooked for you all week," Sheba said.

"With Mr. King coming into the office, I'll be there late, so I'll grab something."

"Looks like I won't see you until tomorrow." She felt disappointed but understood how important Uriah's job was to him.

"I might swing through the hospital tonight, if you like."

"No need to. I promise to come home in the morning. If there's an emergency, I'll call you."

"Do that." He leaned down and kissed her one more time.

She blew him a kiss as he exited the room. Sheba was asleep before her head could hit the pillow. The sound of the alarm she had set on her phone alerted her that she had two hours to get dressed and ready for work. She hadn't planned on sleeping that long, but apparently, her body had needed it.

She checked her phone to see if she had any missed calls. She had several from friends and one from her husband. Before returning any of the calls, she showered again, with the hopes of it giving her more energy.

Feeling rejuvenated, Sheba dressed for work and headed to the hospital, planning to check on Delilah first. Before getting out of her car, she dialed Uriah's cell phone but got his voice mail. "I'll be in Delilah's room, and I can't have my cell phone on while in the ICU. I'll try to call you before my shift starts. Love you."

She hung up the phone and waited for the shuttle to take her from the employees' parking lot to the hospital. Keisha was sitting near Delilah's bed when Sheba entered her room. Sheba was curious about what had led up to Delilah's shooting, and Keisha was the only one with answers to her questions.

"The doctor said she's doing better today. She opened her eyes up but closed them," Keisha informed her.

Sheba picked up her chart and read it. "Yes, she's doing much better according to the notes here."

Keisha's phone rang. "I must get this. This is my boss."

"You know the phone signals can interfere with the equipment, so you're not supposed to have your cell phones on in this area," Sheba lectured.

Keisha ignored her and answered her call. She walked out of the room to get some privacy.

Sheba walked over to Delilah's bed. "Your friend is something else," Sheba said. "Anyway, how are you today, sis?" Sheba laughed out loud. "I wanted to meet you, but not like this. You might not believe this, but I need you just as much as you need me. We'll never have to be apart again. I love you, Delilah."

Sheba laid her head down on the bed. Keisha walked back in the room. Sheba sat up and dried the tears on her face.

Keisha said, "I'm sorry about earlier. I know that I wasn't supposed to have the phone on, but I called in to work."

Sheba shrugged her shoulders.

Keisha took a seat. "Besides you, Delilah hasn't had any other visitors."

"I've been so caught up in this uncanny re-union, I forgot to ask you why that is," Sheba said.

"Well, there are some things about Delilah that you don't know. Things that I'm sure she's not proud of."

Keisha seemed to want to talk, and Sheba wanted to know more about Delilah. She took a seat in the other chair.

"She'll probably kill me for telling you these things, but I'm going to tell you, anyway," Keisha said.

Sheba's mouth fell open in shock as Keisha told her about Delilah's past.

Chapter 6

David watched Uriah and Simon as they held a healthy debate over the state of affairs in the business world. David admired both of the men that sat before him. Both had attributes that would benefit his company. Deciding who would head the Afghanistan office hadn't been easy.

Uriah removed his cell phone from his pocket when it rang. He excused himself from the dinner table. When he returned, he said, "Sorry. I needed to take that call. That was my wife, and we've been playing phone tag."

"How is your wife?" David asked, hoping not to sound too enthused.

"Honestly, not too well. She's been working hard since we got back from Dallas and seeing about someone at the hospital during her off-hours."

"Do you need to go see about her? If so, I understand," David said. He was really concerned about Sheba. He wanted to ask more questions but didn't want to raise Uriah's curiosity.

"I might need to. She sounded a little distraught."

David pulled out several hundred-dollar bills. "Simon, I'm going to leave you to take care of our bill. My driver can drop you off at the hotel." David faced Uriah and said, "I'll ride with you so you can go check on your wife."

"Mr. King . . ." Uriah said nervously as he stood up.

"I told you to save the Mr. King for when we're in the office. Tonight I'm David."

"David, you don't have to go with me. I appreciate it, though."

"I know I don't have to. I want to. She's your wife. You're concerned about her, so your concerns are my concerns. Why are we wasting time? We need to go check on your wife."

Uriah stopped protesting, and David followed him to his car. David could tell Uriah was a little uneasy about him going.

"Uriah, I know this is an unusual situation, but I like you. I want to know more about you, outside of work."

"Not much to tell. I like what the average guy likes. I love my wife. Sheba and I have been married for almost ten years now. There's nothing I wouldn't do for that woman."

"I love your dedication and devotion to your wife." David didn't lie. He did admire that.

"Sheba can be a handful at times, but she's also a sweetheart. She motivates me to do better."

"Every man needs a woman like her in his corner," David said.

"If they should be so lucky. I just hate that she's allowing this stranger room in her heart."

David listened curiously as Uriah explained to him about the woman who Sheba suspected was her sister. "You know she could easily get a DNA test, which will confirm the truth."

"I've told her that, but she won't listen."

"Maybe I can talk to her for you," David suggested.

"David, this is a personal matter, so I don't expect you to help me out."

"You're more than just an employee. If talking to her will help you, I'll do it."

"Maybe she'll listen to you, because she sure won't listen to me," Uriah said.

Fifteen minutes later, they had parked and were walking into the hospital. It had been years since David had entered this particular hospital. The last time he'd visited, he was going to say his final good-byes to his father. That had been over fifteen years ago. Now here he was, in a place to which he'd vowed never to return.

He followed Uriah to the elevator. Uriah said, "She works on the tenth floor. We'll try to catch her in between her rounds."

David tapped his foot. The ride to the tenth floor seemed to take forever. He didn't realize he was holding his breath until the doors opened and Uriah exited. He exhaled. Sheba stood near the nurses' station with her back toward them. They hadn't seen each other since the night on the balcony. One of the other nurses got Sheba's attention and pointed in their direction. Her smile filled up the room when she saw Uriah, but when she looked past her husband and saw David, the smile faded.

David had hoped she would look past his boldness from that night, but from her reaction, she hadn't forgotten or forgiven him for making a pass at her.

Uriah and David approached her.

Uriah hugged her. "Baby, are you okay?" he asked.

She avoided his question. Frowning, she asked, "What is he doing here?"

"This is Mr. King, remember?" Uriah responded.

David extended his hand. Sheba shook it. "I heard about your sister and wanted to see if there was anything you needed."

"Oh, how sweet. I think," Sheba said. She turned and said something to one of the ladies behind the desk. "I'm going on a quick break. If you need me, call me on my cell."

"That guy looks awfully familiar," the nurse said.

"He's just Uriah's boss," Sheba responded. She left the nurse to ponder her thoughts. "Follow me," Sheba said as she walked near Uriah and David. She led them to the empty waiting area.

Sheba pulled Uriah to the side. "Baby, I'm okay. You didn't have to come all the way down here," Sheba said, while holding Uriah's hand.

Uriah tilted her hand up and kissed the back of it. "You don't have to go through this alone."

Sheba squeezed his hand. "Thank you, baby, for always being there."

David strained his ears to listen but could only hear bits and pieces of their conversation.

Sheba asked, "Why is he here with you?"

"We were at dinner, and he insisted on coming. What was I supposed to do? Tell him he couldn't come?" Uriah responded.

David pulled out his cell phone to make himself look busy. He went through his messages as he continued to eavesdrop.

After speaking with Uriah, Sheba addressed David. "David, thank you for coming with Uriah, but it wasn't necessary. He overreacted. I'm fine."

Uriah wrapped one arm around her waist and kissed her on the cheek. "I can't help but worry. You're my heart."

David wanted to puke. Seeing Uriah express love for the woman of his desires was beginning to make him sick. Sweat started flowing from his forehead. He couldn't explain what was coming over him when it came to this woman.

Sheba asked, "Are you okay? You seem a little flushed."

"I'm fine. Probably jet lag. When I left Dallas, I flew to Hong Kong. I just got back this morning," David explained hastily.

Uriah said, "Sit. Sheba, check his vitals. Make sure he's okay."

Sheba eyed Uriah curiously. "He doesn't need me to check him out." She looked at David and added, "He said he's fine."

"I want to make sure. You're a nurse. Do what you get paid to do."

"He's not my patient," Sheba said.

"Sheba, please. Do it for me." Uriah pleaded with his eyes.

"Fine. Mr. King, follow me. There's a vacant room down the hall. I can check you out in there," she snapped.

"Thanks, baby," Uriah said. He faced David. "David, you're in good hands."

"I know I am," David mumbled under his breath as he followed Sheba down the hall.

Chapter 7

Sheba cursed under her breath the entire time she walked to the empty patient's room. She didn't know why Uriah felt the need to check on her, and then, on top of that, he brought David. She checked the room to make sure it was empty. "You can have a seat over there. I'll be right back."

David did as she told him. He started to unbutton his shirt. "I'll be waiting."

"You can leave your shirt on. Just roll up your sleeve, and I'll be back to take your blood pressure."

David smiled and stopped unbuttoning his shirt. He sat as instructed, and Sheba went in search of a blood pressure cuff. She returned with it and a thermometer. "Open up," she said as she placed the disposable thermometer in David's mouth. "Now, hold out your left arm for me."

He extended his arm. She rolled up his sleeve some more so that she could wrap the black piece of cloth around his arm. She could tell he worked out from his nice biceps. Once she had the cuff secure, she squeezed the ball and watched the gauge. "Your blood pressure is a little high. When was the last time you saw a doctor?" she asked.

He mumbled something. She couldn't understand him, because he still had the thermometer in his mouth. She removed the thermometer.

"Your temperature is normal. Now, what were you saying?" she asked.

"I get a regular checkup once a year."

"Well, nothing to be alarmed about, but your upper number is on the borderline of putting you in the high blood pressure category. I'm no doctor, so I suggest you follow up with your primary care physician."

"Yes, ma'am. I appreciate you looking out for me." David smiled and stared at her with his piercing eyes.

"You're good to go. Again, I appreciate you coming with Uriah to check on me, but as you can tell, I'm fine."

"That you are." David looked at her with lustful eyes. "I think we have some unfinished business to discuss." David reached for her hand.

Sheba felt the electric current that seemed to flow from his body to hers. She didn't pull back, although she knew she should. "The only business we have in common is sitting out there in the waiting room." She withdrew her hand from his.

"Touché," David responded.

"Uriah's my heart, and I won't jeopardize our relationship for anyone. Is that understood?"

David saluted her. "Yes, ma'am. You're dedicated to your husband, and I commend you for that. Uriah's one lucky man."

"I'm lucky to have him, and so are you."

Surprisingly to Sheba, David changed the subject. "You know he wants you to get a DNA test on the woman you said is your sister."

Sheba laughed. "You two have become real chummy. He's sharing our personal business—or should I say my personal business—with you. I don't know if I should be mad at him or you."

"Neither. He's only concerned about your well-being, and I would be, too, if you were mine." David stressed the word *mine*.

Sheba felt a knot in her stomach. Being around David alone made her feel uneasy. She had to get them out of this room. The magnetic pull she felt for him at this moment was not right. Not when she had the man of her dreams waiting for her. Besides, her mind should have been on Delilah, the sister that had an aura of drama surrounding her. She hadn't had time to think about all the things Keisha had told her about Delilah. She had to get out of this room and away from David before she suffocated. She rushed to the door, opened it, and searched for her husband.

"Baby, he's fine," she said as she walked up to Uriah, who was standing by the window in the waiting room.

"That's good to know." Uriah pulled Sheba into his arms.

Uriah didn't notice the smirk on David's face, but Sheba sure did. She squeezed Uriah as if she were holding on for dear life. Sheba's cell phone rang. She pulled away from her husband and answered it. She listened to the caller a moment before saying, "I'll be right there." She faced Uriah. "I have to go. I'm fine, okay, baby?"

"Let me get David to his hotel. Call me later, when you get a chance." Uriah gave her a quick peck.

"Will do." She walked away without saying good-bye to David.

She went to make her rounds, and instead of taking a break afterward, she made a detour to Delilah's room. Keisha had long since gone home. She sat near Delilah's bed and recalled some of the things Keisha had told her. Delilah had gotten caught up in a scandalous affair with one of the local ministers, and all hell had broken loose at Delilah's church and in the community because of it.

Delilah was something else. No wonder the police didn't know who tried to kill her. It could have been a number of people. It seemed she had a hard time making friends but had no trouble making enemies. Maybe Uriah was right. Maybe Sheba should get a DNA test. Sheba was a peaceful person, well, for the most part, but drama seemed to follow Delilah wherever she went.

Sheba was in deep thought and didn't realize she had company at first. She almost fell out of her seat when she looked up into David's face. "What are you doing here?" For the second time in one night, she found herself asking that question.

"I told Uriah to go on home. I'm waiting on my driver to come pick me up."

"That was an hour ago. Shreveport is not that big that he couldn't have been here to pick you up by now."

Before David could respond, Sheba felt a touch on her hand. She looked down. Delilah had reached out and touched her hand. She looked into the eyes of her sister for the first time.

Delilah started coughing. Sheba jumped up. "It's okay. I'm here. Don't try to talk," she said. She looked in David's direction. "Go get a doctor, quick."

Delilah had regained consciousness and seemed to be alert.

"Thank you, Lord," Sheba said out loud several times.

David returned to the room with a doctor. Sheba moved to the side as the doctor examined Delilah.

"You're our miracle lady," he said to Delilah.

Delilah looked at the doctor and then at Sheba. Delilah coughed a few times. Her voice was low, but Sheba could make out the words. Delilah wanted water.

Sheba handed the doctor a cup of water with a straw. He held the straw while Delilah took a few sips. "Thank you," she said, barely above a whisper.

The doctor examined Delilah some more. "Ms. Baker, you had us concerned about you for a minute. I think you're in for a full recovery."

"Thank you," Delilah whispered.

The doctor looked in Sheba's direction. "That lady over there has been here every day."

"Doctor, I'm grateful for all you've done," Sheba said, with tears of joy in her eyes.

"You're the voice I heard in my head, aren't you?" Delilah's eyes looked in Sheba's direction.

Sheba responded, "Yes. I'm your sister."

Chapter 8

David stood nearby and watched the exchange between Sheba and the patient. Even with all the tubes and Delilah's swollen face, he could see the resemblance. From appearances alone, the woman who went by the name Delilah was Sheba's older sister. Still, he hoped Sheba would get the DNA test just to remove any doubts.

He felt like an outsider, but his feet were planted. He was not going anywhere anytime soon. He moved so the nurse who had entered the room could get by.

"Can you two step outside?" the nurse asked, speaking to him and Sheba.

David led Sheba into the hallway.

"She's going to be fine. Praise the Lord," Sheba repeated over and over.

"Yes, praise the Lord," David said.

Sheba stopped and for the first time seemed to remember he was there. "Do you go to church?"

David wished people wouldn't automatically assume the worst about him. David was a God-fearing man who knew from whence his help came. He knew without God's blessings, he would not have obtained the riches he had over the years. David communicated with God daily. David had an anointing on his life. He knew it, and his dad, who was no longer with him, knew it.

"Without God, I am nothing. I don't go as often as I should, but the Lord knows my heart," David responded.

"I'm surprised. You seem a little too arrogant to think highly of anyone but yourself," Sheba said.

David pouted. "My feelings are hurt. I'm confident, that I admit, but arrogant I'm not. God could take all I have with a snap of my fingers."

"You're right about that. I'm glad to know my husband is working for a God-fearing man."

"Yes, that he is. You asked me earlier why I was still here. Well, since we're on the subject, I went to the chapel. I prayed for your sister. I prayed for you."

David could see her eyes watering. Tears streamed down her face. David didn't know what to do, so he did what was natural. He placed his arm around her. "It's going to be okay."

"Thank you. I've been snapping at you. Here you are, praying for my sister. Forgive me, please."

David reached up and brushed her hair. He had been wanting to touch her hair from the moment he laid eyes on her. He inhaled the apple scent. "You're forgiven. Pull yourself together. Your sister needs you."

David handed Sheba a tissue, and she wiped her face. "I'm usually not this emotional."

"Most women are emotional, so your reaction doesn't surprise me."

"Well, I'm not most women," Sheba said as she headed back to Delilah's room.

"No, Ms. Bathsheba, no, you're not. You're an exceptional woman," David responded, out of her earshot.

It looked like his duty there had been served. He thanked God for answering his prayers and left the hospital. Two hours later he was fastening his seat belt on his private jet. Less than an hour after that, his plane was landing in Dallas.

Before going to bed, David said a quick prayer. Exhausted, he slept eight hours straight, something he rarely did. On average, he got five hours of sleep a night. The eight hours weren't dreamless.

In his dreams, he was holding Sheba in his arms and running his hands through her ebony tresses. He could still smell the apple scent, and when he woke up the next morning, he had a craving for a ripe red apple for breakfast.

A few hours later he was in his corporate building, overseeing a meeting in one of the huge conference rooms.

"Is there anything else anyone has to say before we disperse?" David asked as he sat at the head of the long, oblong table in the conference room.

He looked around the room at the staff of ten who sat around the table. No one said a thing. He continued, "Well, that's all I have for today. I will see you all later. Wade, could you please stay behind? There's something I want to discuss with you."

Wade, looking nervous, remained seated. Once everyone was out of the room, Wade said, "Yes, Mr. King?"

"I've decided who I want to go to Afghanistan."

"Do you want me to make the call, or do you want to?"

"Tell me what you think. I think Simon is the best for the job. However, he shouldn't go alone. Inform Simon that I want him to head the satellite office, but I want Uriah to go with him to assist. Those two together will have the office up and running in no time."

"But what about the Shreveport office? Who should we get to run it in Uriah's absence?"

"Uriah can do both. The bulk of the responsibility in the Afghanistan office will be Simon's, so I don't see why Uriah can't run the show remotely. Do you?" David leaned back in his chair while waiting on Wade's response.

Wade appeared to be in deep thought. "I guess it can work."

"Guess? I didn't get this far by guessing. I want you to be sure."

"Yes, Mr. King. It'll work. We'll make it work." Wade sounded much more certain this time.

"Good. Now, make those phone calls. When you get Uriah on the phone, transfer the call to my office phone. I'll be in there."

David got up and left Wade alone to make the phone calls.

"Mr. King, you have a visitor," Trisha, his secretary, said as he walked past her desk.

"In my office? You know I don't like people in my office when I'm not there."

Trisha opened her mouth to speak, but David had left her desk and was inside his office before she could say anything. David's blood pressure lowered when he saw his good friend Nathan McDaniel turn around.

"What's up, my man?" Nathan asked.

David gave Nathan one of their fraternity handshakes. Nathan and David had met in college and had been best friends ever since. Nathan was one of the few people David knew who would keep it real with him. Most people were too busy trying to kiss up to him to tell him the truth.

Trisha's voice came over the intercom. "Uriah Richards is on the phone for you."

"Put him through," David responded, then said to Nathan, "Man, give me a minute."

David took a seat and swiveled his chair around. "Uriah, how are things with your lovely wife?" He paused and listened to Uriah. "Yes, I heard the good news." Apparently, Sheba hadn't told Uriah that he was there when Delilah opened her eyes. He shifted the conversation to the job. "I wanted to tell you congratulations on your new position."

After a few minutes, David ended the call. He turned his chair around, and Nathan was looking at him suspiciously.

"Man, what are you up to?" Nathan knew David better than anyone, and David knew it was hard to hide something from him. He wasn't surprised that Nathan had picked up on David's ulterior motives.

"Nothing. I'm innocent," David said.

Nathan shook his head. "Thou protests too much."

Chapter 9

"You're going where?" Sheba shouted.

Uriah reached for her, but Sheba jerked her body away from his embrace. "It's only for a few months. I'll be going back and forth between here and Afghanistan."

"What am I supposed to do in the meantime? You have a wife. You have responsibilities here." She folded her arms. How could Uriah abandon her when she needed him the most?

"Baby, with the Internet, we can Skype. I'll be gone for maybe six months at first."

"Six months? That's like a lifetime. The longest we've ever been apart is three days. Count them." Sheba used her fingers to illustrate her point. "One." One finger popped up. "Two." She held up a second finger. "Three." She now held up three fingers in total.

"It's not as bad as it seems. Those six months will fly by." Uriah tried his best to convince her, but Sheba wasn't having it.

"So when are you supposed to be leaving?" Sheba asked.

"Monday morning."

"That's in two days. What's David's number? I can't believe he's taking my husband away from me."

"Baby, calm down. I'm not giving you his number. You'll make me lose my job."

"Forget your job. Any job that takes a husband away from his wife for long periods of time is no job worth having."

Uriah pulled Sheba into his arms. "Look at me," he said. She refused to. He placed his hand on her chin and tilted her head up so she was looking into his eyes. "Look at me," he repeated.

Sheba rolled her eyes. "What, Uriah? Looks like you've already made up your mind."

"Baby, I'm doing this for us. You want the new house. You want to do all of the shopping. Well, me going to Afghanistan will only get us in the new house sooner. The bonus I'll be making for taking this transitional position will put me in the high six figures."

"I'm trying to be understanding. I do want the house, but it doesn't mean I'm happy about this. I love you, baby, and I don't want to stay in this house without you in it."

"It's only temporary. When we get the office set up there, I'll be coming back here. You know it's temporary because I'll still be overseeing the Shreveport office."

Sheba thought about it. He had a point. If he wasn't being removed from his Shreveport post, then the Afghanistan job was only temporary. Her gut told her that it wasn't a good move, but knowing that she would be in her big two-story house sooner and would not have to hear Uriah complain about her spending money pushed her reservations to the side.

Uriah went into the bathroom. Sheba picked up her phone and called her manager. "Uriah's leaving for Afghanistan. I need to take the next few days off," she explained. "I'll work doubles if I have to. It'll be six months before I see him again."

"I didn't know your husband was in the military," her manager said.

"He's not. His job is taking him there. I'm not happy about it, but it's something he has to do, or he might lose his job."

"Consider your time granted."

Sheba thanked her manager and then ended the call. She watched her husband reenter the room. He sat down next to her on the edge of the bed.

"I don't want our last few days together to be memories of us arguing," he said.

Sheba said, "They won't be. I just took the next few days off. Ironically, the day you leave is the day I go back to my regular shift."

"Let big daddy make you feel better," Uriah said.

"No, baby. Let me make you feel better," Sheba said. Sheba wanted her husband to be fully satisfied so he would not be tempted by any women that he came across. Six months was a long time.

About an hour after their lovemaking, Uriah lay next to her, snoring. Sheba remained wide awake. She rubbed his arm. She loved the feel of his arms around her as she slept. She would miss it. She knew she could be a handful at times, but she loved her husband.

They had met while in college and had been practically inseparable ever since. They had been surprised to learn they both were from Shreveport and knew some of the same people. Getting married young wasn't in Sheba's original plans, but how could she say no when Uriah proposed to her? He was everything she felt she needed in a man at the time. She loved him with all her heart. Her mother adored him, too.

The only regret she had was that she and Uriah had never had any kids. It wasn't that they hadn't tried. She'd stopped taking birth control pills over five years ago. A part of her hoped that maybe he would plant a seed in her before leaving for Afghanistan. She rubbed her stomach as she thought about Uriah fathering a child.

"I love you, Uriah," Sheba said before drifting off to sleep.

The next morning, Sheba was awaken by the gentle nudge from Uriah. "Breakfast in bed, sleepyhead." He smiled.

Sheba did a morning stretch. "It smells good." She sat up as Uriah presented her with a tray holding some of her favorites. Grits, scrambled eggs, and turkey bacon. "All of this for me?"

"You've always loved my breakfast."

"That's because that's the only meal you can cook, my dear," Sheba teased.

He laughed. "While you're eating, I'm going to take my shower."

Sheba got up and washed up and then returned to eat her breakfast. Uriah's cell phone rang while he was still in the shower. Thinking it could be an important call, Sheba answered it.

"Maybe I have the wrong number," said the female voice on the other end.

"Who were you trying to reach?" Sheba asked. She was quickly losing her appetite.

"Is this Uriah Richards's number?"

"Yes, it is."

"Good. This is David King's secretary. He wanted me to connect a call with Mr. Richards."

Sheba was relieved. For a second, she thought something else was going on. "You can put him through."

"Thanks. Hold on a second."

"Uriah," David said.

"No, this is Sheba, and I have a bone to pick with you."

Chapter 10

David was surprised to hear Sheba's voice on the other end. She got on David's case about sending her husband out of the country. "Sheba, I thought you would be glad that I was giving your husband an opportunity to make more money."

"But did you have to send him to Afghanistan? Don't you have another office you want to open up in New York or somewhere? Anywhere but Afghanistan."

David doodled on the notepad in front of him. Did he want this woman so bad that he was sending her husband into enemy territory? If he were truthful, the answer would be yes. Simon was more than capable of handling business there without any assistance. All he had to do was make a phone call and Uriah would not be going anywhere.

"Sheba, this is nothing personal. It's business," he lied. David heard Uriah's voice in the background.

Sheba said, "Here's Uriah. You owe me."

"I plan to pay up, too," David said mischievously right before Uriah got on the phone. He spent the next few minutes following up with Uriah about some plans of his that he wanted to see implemented when he got there. "If you have any questions, I'm only a phone call away," David said.

"Mr. King, thank you again for this opportunity."

"No problem. When you come back, I may end up losing you to another company, because you'll be able to demand your price." David laughed.

"Mr. King, I'm loyal to you. You don't have to worry about me leaving to go anywhere else," Uriah assured him.

"That's good to hear. I'll talk to you once you get settled in Afghanistan."

David ended his call with Uriah. He closed his eyes for a brief moment. Psalm 69:5 crept into David's mind. *O God, thou knowest my foolishness; and my sins are not hid from thee.*

David could pretend with Nathan, but he knew God knew everything. Even though he knew it was wrong to send Uriah away, David pushed the thoughts of canceling Uriah's trip to the back of his mind. *What's done is done.*

Trisha chimed in on the phone. "You have a call from NBN News. There's been a leak about your deal in Hong Kong."

"Tell them I'm in a meeting, and then get Wade in here pronto." David hit a button under his desk, unlocking his door.

A few minutes later Wade walked in, looking flustered. "Trisha told me."

"Who let this leak? Some heads are about to roll."

"Mr. King, the leak didn't come from my office. I promise you that. I've been handling this directly myself."

"Now that it's being leaked, I have no choice but to make an official announcement." David hit the intercom button on his phone. "Trisha, I need you to work with Wade and get a press release typed up."

"This trade agreement between us and the news affiliate in Hong Kong isn't such a bad thing," Wade said, trying to assure him.

"No, it isn't, but I decide when news is told. We have a leak in-house, and I need to find out who. When I do, he or she better hope I show mercy."

Two hours later David had to exit his own building by the back door because reporters were camped out in front. David enjoyed the riches of his success but hated some of the things that came along with his rise to power. Not having privacy and being hounded by nosy reporters were among them.

He also hated to be called the black Trump. He was his own man. If anything, he wanted them to call him a man of God. That was who he was imaged after. Not some man who happened to catch a lucky break and make millions.

David's driver eased through the alleyway and out into the Dallas traffic. He had eluded the reporters, and David was happy to have avoided them once again. He had a dinner function to attend later on that night. It would give Wade time to prepare a statement and send it out to the press.

He dialed Wade's cell phone number. "Wade, how's that press release coming?" he asked as he flipped through a business proposal he wanted to go over before Monday.

"I just e-mailed it to you. I'm waiting on your approval, and then I'll get it out to everyone," Wade said.

"Great. Hold on." David downloaded the press release while Wade was on the phone. He read it. "Sounds good. Send it."

David was home only long enough to shower and dress. His three-piece, custom-made suit fit his body perfectly. He called his date for the night, Heather, to let her know he was on his way to pick her up.

David made a few phone calls while his driver drove to pick up Heather. He was still on the phone when they pulled up to her address. He sent the driver to her door. He could tell by the frown on her face that she wasn't too happy about it. His eyes scanned her body and hoped that he could replace her frown with a smile later that night.

David ended the call. "Heather, thanks for agreeing to be my date tonight."

"I want you to know that I'm tired of being your arm candy. When are we going to take our relationship to another level?" Heather asked and then rambled on and on.

David thought about the rise of his stock with the news of his new Hong Kong deal. He thought about how Heather would look naked but snapped out of those thoughts when he heard his name called several times.

Looking irritated, Heather said, "Wipe that smirk off your face. I swear you have a one-track mind."

"I'm guilty as charged," David said. David loved the Lord, indeed, but had never professed to be a saint. Women were his weakness.

"If I didn't want to see my picture in the paper tomorrow, I would tell your driver to take me back home," she announced.

"If I didn't want to be seen with the prettiest woman in Dallas, I would tell my driver to take you back home," David said.

David knew flattering Heather would work. She had to be one of the vainest women he knew. That was another reason why she could never be more to him than the role she now played: eye candy and an arm piece for when he needed a date to events such as these.

She had a reputation of being a gold digger, but she would never get her claws on his money. He had two ex-wives and was not really looking for a third. Sheba's face appeared in his mind out of nowhere. No matter how much he tried, thoughts of Sheba crept into his mind.

"Maybe you can make up for being rude to me. You could buy me that new sports car I want," Heather said.

"We'll see," David responded. After tonight, Heather's number would be deleted from his phone contacts. She was becoming too needy and clingy. If she waited on him to buy her a car, she would be waiting a very long time.

Chapter 11

The day after Uriah's big announcement, Sheba insisted that he go with her to meet her sister. Uriah wasn't too enthused about going, though.

"You're going to be gone for six months. I want her to meet my husband." Sheba knew throwing on the guilt would make him do what she asked.

They walked through the hospital doors together. Delilah had been moved off the critical list, so she was now in her own private hospital room.

"I told you I was coming back," Sheba said as she and Uriah entered the hospital room.

"So what you said yesterday wasn't a dream?" Delilah asked. The tubes were no longer in her, except for an IV, but her face was still swollen, and a bandage was still wrapped around her head.

"I'm afraid not. We're sisters."

Uriah cleared his throat a few times.

Sheba said, "Delilah, I want you to meet my husband, Uriah."

"You are what?" Delilah asked as she tilted the bed upward with the control button.

"It's Uriah," he said as they approached the bed.

"I can barely 'member Bathsheba," Delilah snapped.

Uriah eased away from the bed and took a seat.

Sheba said, "Call me Sheba. Everybody else does." Sheba sat in the chair near the bed.

"This medicine is wearing off, so my senses are coming back to me. Explain to me how we're sisters. This is a little overwhelming, to say the least."

Uriah said, "Maybe this isn't a good time. Sheba, the woman is trying to recover from a gunshot wound. Give her some time to heal."

"I'm recovering," Delilah said. "But I want to know. She can't just drop this news on me and then not give me details."

"She's right," Sheba interjected. "I need to tell her what I know so she'll understand how I know we're sisters."

"That still remains to be confirmed," Uriah said.

Delilah stared at Uriah. In a sarcastic manner, she said, "You don't know me, and you don't like me already. Brother-in-law, don't be like that."

This was not going the way Sheba had hoped it would go. She said, "I'll tell you what I know."

Delilah's eyes were now back on Sheba's.

Uriah shifted in his seat. "Maybe, I should leave."

"No, baby. I want you to stay," Sheba said to her husband. She proceeded to tell Delilah the story of how she had ended up being separated from their mother. "Our mother had to give you up for adoption because our grandparents wouldn't let her keep you."

"But she kept you," Delilah snapped.

"By the time she had me, she was living on her own. She had you at fourteen and me at seventeen."

"But she should have left. She didn't have to give me up. I never got adopted. I went from foster home to foster home. In fact, I was told my mama was dead. The woman who I thought was my mama wasn't my mother, after all." Delilah's eyes teared up.

Sheba reached out to her and squeezed her hand. "I wished things could have turned out differently for you. Our mother did try to find you, but the social workers she contacted wouldn't give her any information. She even put her information out on this Web site so if you were to ever come looking for her, you would be able to find her."

"But I didn't know she was my mother. How could this be? My whole life has been one big lie."

Sheba could see the pain in Delilah's eyes. She wished she could erase it. All she could do was help her get through this. "I didn't mean to make you upset. Maybe we should continue this conversation another time."

Delilah snapped, "Maybe we should. I'm kind of tired right now." Delilah closed her eyes and didn't open them back up.

Uriah stood up and then motioned for Sheba to follow suit. She remained seated. Uriah tilted his head toward the door.

Sheba finally took the hint and stood up. "Delilah, I'll be back. You're not going to get rid of me that easy. We're family. And we're going to get through this together. We're all each other has."

She heard Delilah mumble something under her breath, but couldn't make out the words.

She and Uriah exited the hospital. As soon as they were in the car, Sheba went off on him. "You could have been nicer to her."

"I was nice. She's the one who got on the defensive."

"She's been unconscious. What do you expect? Then I drop the news on her that we're sisters. Come on, Uriah. I've never known you to be heartless." Sheba couldn't stand to look at Uriah right now, so she looked out the window as he drove.

"What do you want for dinner?" he asked.

She ignored him.

"Baby, let's not play the silent game. I will be leaving the country soon. Let's not fight."

Sheba knew he had a point. She loved Uriah but couldn't understand why he couldn't show the same compassion as she did when it concerned Delilah. She would try to forget what had happened back at the hospital. They had only two more days together, and they would make the best of it.

Sheba took his hand, and their fingers interlocked. "Love you, even though you can be stubborn," Sheba said.

"Don't mean to be. I just don't want you to end up hurt."

"I won't be. I promise you that," she responded. She squeezed his hand.

He pulled their hands up and turned hers over and kissed the back of it. "I'm going to miss you so much."

"I'm going to miss you, too." Sheba turned her head away so Uriah couldn't see the tears flowing down her face. She used her free hand to wipe them away.

She didn't want to admit it to Uriah, but she was scared. She was scared that if he went to Afghanistan, she might never see him again. Right now she blamed one person, and that person was David King. She had convinced Uriah not to join the military years ago, but for what? He was still being deployed overseas in a sense. The next time she saw David, she vowed to tell him a thing or two about himself.

Chapter 12

David decided to take an impromptu trip to the Horse-shoe Casino in Shreveport. Although he hadn't decided whether or not he would spend the night, he rented one of the executive suites to change his clothes in.

He had planned on calling Uriah to make sure he had everything he needed for his trip, but instead, he opted not to. While relaxing before going to the hotel's casino, he picked up the local paper. One of the articles caught his attention.

Police are still trying to find the suspect who shot Delilah Baker. If you have any information on who committed this crime, please contact Crime Stoppers.

David picked up his cell phone and called his driver. "There's been a change of plans. I need you to meet me back up front."

An hour later David's driver dropped him off at the hospital. David went to the ICU but learned that Delilah had been moved to a private room. Upon arriving at her room, he caught the tail end of a conversation.

A woman dressed in burgundy hospital scrubs said, "Ma'am, we're sorry, but the insurance you had is no longer valid. We're going to need to move you to another room."

"But I've been paying my insurance. I worked for William Trusts Company," Delilah responded. "I'm no longer working there, but my insurance should still be good."

"Ms. Baker, if you had signed up with COBRA, then we could keep you in this private room, but because you didn't, we will need to move you."

David made himself known. "Ms. . ." He squinted his eyes to read her name badge. "Ms. Lindsay, I'll take care of her bill."

"Who are you?" Delilah asked.

"I'm King. David King," David told Delilah, then turned his attention to the hospital administrator. "I'll take care of all her charges."

Delilah eyed him curiously.

David gave the hospital administrator all the information she needed. She felt very satisfied because she couldn't believe that David King, the media mogul, was talking to her. "Can I have your autograph? My friends will never believe this."

"You can, but on one condition," he said.

"Anything," she replied.

"It must not become public knowledge that I'm taking care of her bill."

"Of course. We here keep everything under strict confidentiality," she assured him.

David knew about the HIPAA law, but he also knew people. Laws were meant to be broken, or else folks wouldn't break them.

David wrote something special on a blank sheet of paper and signed it. "Just in case your friends don't believe you, I'll give you one of my business cards." He handed her one of his gold-trimmed business cards, which contained only his office information.

"Wow. Thanks, Mr. King," the hospital administrator said.

"It's David. Now, remember, this is between me, you, and Ms. Delilah over there." He nodded toward Delilah.

"Yes, sir. My lips are sealed. Thanks again."

David, assured that for now his secret was safe, held the door open for her. After she was gone, he walked over to Delilah's bed and took a seat. "No need to thank me," he said.

"Why did you do that? You don't know me," Delilah said.

"Not yet. But hopefully, we'll get to know each other better."

"No one has ever put themselves out there like that for me." Delilah seemed stunned.

"You didn't ask to be in this situation. I don't see why you shouldn't be afforded the best health care."

"Don't get me started. I have money in the bank, but the time I've spent in here is going to wipe that clean. I don't know how I'll ever repay you," Delilah said.

That was the opening David had been waiting for. "Actually, I do. I need a favor. And you're the only one who can help me."

"From me?" Delilah pointed at herself. "I don't know you. I know who you are. You're David King, but I don't know you. How can I help you?"

"I was here the night you came to. The night Sheba told you she was your sister."

"You're Bathsheba's husband. Wait a minute. The man she introduced me to was named Ur something. I would have remembered if it was you."

David laughed. "Her husband's name is Uriah. I'm their friend."

"Okay. Fine. Now that's been established. How can I help you?"

"You're feisty, aren't you?" David asked. His eyes sparkled.

"That's one word to describe me," she responded.

"I can trust you, can't I?" David asked.

"It depends. What am I going to get out of it?" Delilah asked.

"I think a paid hospital bill is a good down payment on more to come, if need be." David eased his chair closer to the bed.

"Spell it out. A man like you comes to a woman like me only for one reason. Being that I'm not looking my best and I am not in the best of shape right now, I don't think sex is what's on your mind."

David could tell that Delilah and Sheba were cut from the same cloth. Although Sheba wasn't as brazen as Delilah, they were definitely sisters. Both spoke their mind. He admired that in a woman. He didn't like women who bowed down to his every command. Well, he did, but sometimes he welcomed a challenge.

"Delilah, you and I can be the best of friends."

"I have very few friends, Mr. King."

"Forget the formalities. I think we're way past that, so call me David."

"David, one thing I've learned since being shot is that life is precious. Time is precious. So spill it out. Tell me exactly what you want from me."

"I want you to convince your sister to give me a chance. I want her and need her in my life." There. He'd said it. David had actually let someone else in on his plan.

Delilah shook her head. "Let me get this straight. You just told me they were your friends, but now you want me to convince my married sister to give you a chance?"

"That doesn't sound right coming out of your mouth, but I guess if that's how you want to look at it, then yes, that's what I want you to do."

Delilah laughed. "You're telling me that multimillionaire—correction, Mr. Billionaire David King—needs my help to get a woman. Please. With all the cheddar you got, you can get any woman."

"Any woman, except for Sheba," David confessed.

Delilah thought for a minute. "Who knows? I might be able to help you out," Delilah said as a sly grin came across her face.

Chapter 13

Tears streamed down Sheba's face, although she had told herself she was not going to cry. "I'm going to miss you so much," Sheba said over and over as she and Uriah embraced at the private airport terminal.

He wiped her face with one of his hands. He then kissed her cheek. "These six months are going to fly by."

"I hope so. It's going to be lonely at home without you."

"We're going to be talking every chance we get," Uriah said.

"I know." Sheba pouted.

Uriah reached into his pocket and took out a box. He opened it. "Wear this and know that you're always close to my heart."

He removed a gold necklace with a half of a heart pendant that had the words *My better half* written on the back and placed it around her neck.

He unbuttoned his top button. "See? I'm wearing the other half."

Sheba wrapped her arm around his neck. "I love you, Uriah."

"I love you, too, Bathsheba."

The stewardess approached them and said, "Mr. Richards, the pilots are ready to take off."

The stewards turned toward Sheba and smiled. "Mrs. Richards, he's in good hands," one of them assured her.

Sheba forced a smile. "I guess this is good-bye."

"No, baby, it's 'See you later.'"

Uriah kissed her passionately before walking away to get on the plane.

The moment Uriah stepped foot on the corporate jet, the floodgates opened again for Sheba. Tears slid down her face. She stood at the terminal window and watched the plane fly away. A sinking feeling came over her. Although he wasn't going to war over in Afghanistan, it was still dangerous there for American workers. Life for her Uriah would never be the same. She could feel it in her gut.

Fortunately, she had to go into work. She was supposed to be there for the seven o'clock shift but had let everyone know she was going to be late. She could have taken the whole day off, but she knew she would need a distraction. She wasn't ready to go back to her empty house.

Upon arriving at work, she was handed a bouquet of flowers by one of her coworkers. She sniffed the bouquet of colorful flowers. "Uriah, you think of everything," she whispered when she glanced at the card, which read, "I miss you already. Love you, pumpkin." He hadn't called her pumpkin in years. That was the little pet name he had given her when they were in college.

"I have another delivery," said the floral deliveryman as he walked up to the nurses' station. He handed the bouquet of flowers to Sheba.

"What room?" Sheba asked.

The deliveryman read what was on his order. "These are for Bathsheba Richards."

Thinking Uriah had truly outdone himself, she was excited. Uriah was going overboard by sending two bouquets of flowers in one day, Sheba thought. But she loved flowers, so she wouldn't complain.

"Thank you," she said as she reached into her pocket and handed him a tip. She removed the card from the plastic stick. Disappointment swept over her face when she read the card. *Hope you can forgive me for sending Uriah away. He'll be back to you soon. Your friend, David.*

She tore the card up. David was no friend of hers. She stopped one of the LPNs. "Give these flowers to Ms. Frierson. She was just saying she wished someone would send her some flowers."

"Who do I tell her they are from?" the LPN asked.

"Tell her it's a thank-you from the staff for being such a great patient." Sheba wanted to get rid of the flowers. She could have thrown them away, but she felt her patient would benefit a great deal from receiving them.

"But she is such a disturbance."

"I know, but maybe she'll think twice before giving us a hard time if we butter her up," Sheba said.

"I doubt it, but I'll take them to her."

"Please do. I'll be running some reports in the back office if you need me," Sheba said before walking away.

After running her reports, Sheba decided to take a break. She made a beeline to Delilah's room. She hadn't seen her since she and Uriah had stopped by two days ago. She'd wanted to give her some time for things to sink in. Her door was ajar, so she walked right on in.

"Good to see you're sitting up," Sheba said as Delilah shifted herself on the side of the bed.

"They started me on therapy today. Looks like my limbs don't want to agree with me, so I'm having to learn how to walk again."

"Do what your therapist says and you'll be walking in no time. If you like, I can come to some of your sessions."

"Oh no. It's embarrassing enough. I don't need an audience." Delilah shifted her legs and got back in the bed. She pulled the white covers over them to ward off the cold.

"I'm here if you need me." Sheba took a seat.

Delilah laughed out loud. "I still think it's funny that after all this time, I find out I have a sister."

"I wish Mama was here to see our reunion."

"My feelings are still a little twisted about your mom."

"If only you had met her, then maybe you could see how much she really did love you."

"Well, I only have your word on it."

"That's something I wouldn't lie about." Sheba tried not to get an attitude, but she wouldn't stand for anyone saying anything negative about her mom. In her opinion, she was the best woman who had ever lived. She wouldn't have harmed a fly.

"Tell me more about our mom. What was she like?" Delilah asked.

Sheba's eyes glazed over as she told Delilah about their mom, Elizabeth. "She was always doing something for people in the neighborhood. If she saw a need, she did her best to fulfill that need. If she couldn't, she would find someone who could."

"You make her sound like a saint."

"If she wasn't, she was close to it."

"Then why didn't she look harder for me? I was in the system. I could have been found."

"Our mom, God rest her soul, was generous, but life dealt her a bad hand. Money was never her friend. Don't get me wrong. We never went hungry, but she didn't have a lot of resources. She dropped out of school her senior year, when she got pregnant with me."

Delilah asked a few more questions before saying, "Sheba, I can't promise you anything. I've led a hard life. I tried to change my life, but some people won't let you. Look at me. I changed my lifestyle and still ended up here."

Sheba wondered if the things Keisha had told her about Delilah were true. Maybe one day she would ask, but for now, she would keep her questions to herself. Sheba wasn't a saint, so who was she to judge?

"Let me tell you a little more about our mama. She was nice and sweet, but she wasn't a pushover," Sheba said.

"Sort of like myself, I see," Delilah commented.

Sheba raised her eyebrows. *That remains to be seen.*

Chapter 14

"What do you mean, they don't have clearance to land in Afghanistan?" David was livid. He thought his team had cut through all the red tape.

This mission had been planned for almost a year. Now he was being told that his men might not be able to land in Afghanistan. David had invested too much money in opening the Afghanistan satellite office, and he didn't want anything to get in the way of his ultimate goal. David's goal was to expand his media business globally. Having an office in Afghanistan was the next step toward building his global empire. And he needed to make this happen if he was going to keep Uriah away from Sheba.

Wade came back on the phone. "Okay, the pilot said they got clearance to land now. I had to call someone at the State Department."

"Do whatever you have to do! Keep me informed," David said as he slammed down the phone.

Why was all of this happening? He hoped this wasn't a sign of things to come. He needed this satellite office to be set up with the least amount of problems. David wanted to spread freedom of speech throughout the world. That was one of the reasons why he had acquired newspapers and television stations in other regions of the world. David had succeeded in getting governments to agree to sell to him, while others had failed. One thing most governments had in common was greed, an insatiable appetite for the mighty dollar. As bad as the economy was, the mighty American dollar still held its own in all regions of the world.

Thanks to some good business decisions and lots of prayer, David had been blessed financially, which, he hoped, would enable him to reach his goal of broadcasting around the world. DM King Media's name was known not only in the United States but worldwide. Although he had the respect of his peers, they knew that when it came to business, David was cutthroat. He did whatever he had to do within reason to get what he wanted.

His employees especially knew this. No one wanted to cross him. If they did, they would have to withstand his wrath. When David was mad, there was no telling what he would do. He tried his best to meditate daily to keep that side of him dormant. Every now and then, he would lose control, but his strong prayer life would draw him back in and bring him back to a peaceful state of mind.

He was glad Wade was able to handle the Afghanistan situation. David poured himself a cold drink. He leaned back in his chair and looked outside to view the Dallas skyline. He could have easily built his building in one of the surrounding suburbs, but he wanted to be in the heart of downtown Dallas. He wanted to be in the downtown so everyone could see DM King Media no matter which direction they were coming from when they entered the area.

Trisha's voice rang over the intercom. "You have a call from Mrs. Richards."

David smiled. "Put her through. And, Trisha, we have a long week ahead, so if you want to leave for today, you can. But I want to see you here around seven thirty in the morning, instead of eight."

"Thanks, Mr. King."

Trisha connected the call. David took a quick sip from his drink, then said, "Hello, Sheba. How are you?"

"I would be doing much better if my husband was here with me," she responded.

Sheba's voice sounded like an angel's from the other end, an upset angel's, but her voice was sweet nevertheless, David thought. "I thought the flowers would help smooth things over, but I take it those didn't work."

"I'm not one of your little floozies. You can't buy my affection."

"That's why I like you. You're cut from a different cloth."

"And another thing, if you think trying to buy my sister's affection is going to help you get closer to me, you have another thing coming."

David swiveled his chair around. "What do you mean?" He hoped Delilah hadn't betrayed him and told Sheba his plans. If so, she would regret it.

"She told me you are paying her hospital bills. Although it's generous of you, it's not necessary. I will make sure her hospital bills get paid."

David laughed. "Let's get real. Her bill is already in the thousands. I'm paying Uriah good money, but I doubt very seriously he wants his entire year's salary going to paying for your sister's medical bills."

"What Uriah and I do with our money is our business."

"Calm down, Sheba. I only did it because I wanted to release the pressure for Uriah. I would do it for any of my employees."

There was a long pause on the other end of the phone. Finally, Sheba broke the silence. "Sorry for going off on you like that. Thank you. I appreciate what you're doing for Delilah."

David wanted to rub her nose in it, but he had to handle her delicately to get what he wanted. "You're welcome. If you need anything else, don't hesitate to call me. In fact, let me give you my private number so you can call me direct."

"I don't want your number."

"What if you need to reach Uriah and can't? I can always reach him."

Sheba paused, as if she was thinking about what David had said. "Give it to me. But wait. I need to find some paper to write it down on."

David recited his personal cell phone number and home number. Their call ended afterward. David saw another trip to Shreveport on the horizon. He went online and looked up the phone number of the hospital where Delilah was staying. He called the hospital and asked to be transferred to Delilah's room. Once she was on the line, he said, "For a moment, I thought you had given me up to your sister. That was a good move, telling her about my generosity."

"I had to tell her something because her nosy behind read my chart. She knew I no longer had insurance."

"I'm in a generous mood. What's your bank account number? I want to make you a quick deposit."

"David, as I told you before, I'm not for sale."

"Then why did you agree to help me?"

"I don't care too much for my brother-in-law, and he doesn't exactly like me, so why not?"

She had a point. Fortunately for David, Uriah and Delilah's newfound relationship was off to a rocky start. "Delilah, I think I like you."

"Most men do."

David laughed. "You're something else. I still need your information. When you get out of the hospital, you're going to need money to live on, so consider this a friend helping out another friend."

"I must be doing something right, with rich friends like you." Delilah laughed.

David ended their call. He said out loud to himself, "And knowing a woman like you will help me get the woman I want."

Chapter 15

It had been two weeks, seven hours, and five minutes since Sheba had had any physical contact with her husband. They had been Skyping several times a week and communicating via e-mail daily. Every morning—which was actually night where he was—they found time to chat. It had taken them both time to adjust to the ten-hour time difference.

Sheba turned on her computer and logged into Skype. After a light exchange with Uriah, Sheba said, "Are they treating you okay over there? It looks like you've lost some weight."

"I'm fine." Uriah shifted in his chair.

"You don't look fine," Sheba responded.

"I'm still on our time zone, so my sleep pattern is still a little off, baby."

"I miss you so much. I'm so bored without you here." Sheba tapped her pen on the desk.

"Stay out of trouble. You know how you are when you get bored."

"Let's see. There is a sale going on at Kohl's."

"Sheba, we're supposed to be saving money, remember?"

"You're getting a bonus for being over there, and you did say I could do more shopping, remember?" Sheba flashed him her Colgate smile.

"Yes, I did, baby. Just don't do too much damage, okay, sweetie?"

"I won't. I promise."

"I'm serious, Sheba. This money is extra, but I don't want it all going to credit card bills."

"It won't. Besides, Kohl's sends me these coupons, and I'll be saving at least twenty percent on my purchases."

Uriah laughed. "Baby, you're something else."

"That's why you love me, right?"

"You know it."

Their Skyping session was about to end when Uriah asked, "How is Delilah?"

Delilah had been a sore subject between the two, so she was surprised he asked about her. "She's fine. She'll be getting out of the hospital soon. I was thinking about having her move in here."

Uriah frowned. "Maybe you should think twice about that. You don't know anything about that woman. It's not wise to have her come live in our house."

"She's my sister. She has her own house, but she'll still need medical care, and I am a nurse, or have you forgotten?"

"Baby, all I'm saying is, I've talked to some people, and there are rumors about Delilah that don't put her in a favorable light. What if she is like folks are saying she is? Do you really want that type of woman around you?"

Sheba threw her hands up in the air. "Delilah is not as bad as people make her out to be."

"So you think."

"Before this gets out of hand, let's end this discussion about Delilah."

"Promise me you won't move that woman into my house," Uriah said.

Sheba crossed her fingers. "We'll talk about it later."

"No, Sheba. Promise me now."

Sheba shook her laptop. "Baby, I think we have a bad connection. Love you."

"I love you, too. But—"

Sheba hit the switch on the power cord so the computer would turn off. She had no intentions of listening to Uriah. He had left her alone, and she could use this time to get to know Delilah better. Besides, with him being in another country, he would never find out Delilah was there, anyway. She had made up her mind. She would ask Delilah to move in with her. And stay until at least the doctor gave her a clean bill of health.

She called the hospital. When Delilah picked up, Sheba said, "Delilah, you're moving in with me when you get out of the hospital, and I'm not taking no for an answer."

"You weren't going to get one from me, either, because I was just sitting here wondering how I was going to take care of myself once I got home. I have money in the bank, but I can't afford a live-in nurse to take care of me. But since I have a sister who is a nurse, I might as well take advantage of the resources around you."

"You're something else," Sheba said.

"That's what they tell me." Delilah laughed.

Sheba hung up with Delilah and went about cleaning up her house. She took extra time in the guest bedroom to get it ready for Delilah. She later went grocery shopping to ensure Delilah would have everything she needed while she was at work.

Sheba's cell phone rang while she was unpacking the groceries. Delilah was on the other end of the phone. "The doctor just signed my release papers. Is the invitation still open?

Sheba responded, "Yes, of course. I'll be there in about thirty minutes."

Sheba thought she had a day or two to get ready for Delilah, but fate had intervened and she was being released today. Fortunately, she had cleaned up and gone shopping. After unpacking the groceries, she grabbed her keys and purse and headed to the hospital.

An hour later, she and Delilah were seated in her car, heading toward Sheba and Uriah's place. "Do you mind swinging by my place so I can get some clothes and stuff? Besides, I need to check on my house," Delilah asked Sheba.

Sheba was hesitant, but she turned her car around and took the I-49 ramp to get on the interstate. "Are you sure it's even safe to go back to your house?" she asked.

"I'm not letting anyone scare me. The only reason I even agreed to go to your house is because I figured it would give us both a chance to get to know each other better."

Delilah's words touched a soft spot in Sheba. Sheba smiled. "Well, now that I've found you, I don't want to lose you to another bullet."

"I spoke to the police, and they are doing everything they can to find out who shot me."

"Do you remember anything?" Sheba asked.

Delilah's voice trailed off as she spoke. "I had just left the church and was thinking about the drama that had just taken place at church. But, anyway, as I was driving, I heard this voice, and it said, "Be not deceived. God is not mocked. For whatsoever a man soweth, that shall he also reap."

"Mama used to say that all the time. That's a scripture from Galatians six, seven. She recited it so much, I know it by heart."

"Well, I don't know who said it, but before I blacked out, those were the words I heard in my ear."

"Girl, that was the Holy Spirit talking to you."

Delilah adjusted her seat belt. "I wish the Holy Spirit would have talked to me sooner. Maybe I could have avoided that bullet."

"Fortunately for you, the doctors were able to remove the bullet and no more damage was done."

Delilah's hand flew to her face and landed on a huge scar. "I have this to remind me of that day."

"With a little cocoa butter and aloe vera, that scar will go away."

"I hope so. You know, if I don't have my beauty, I don't have anything."

"I used to think that, but Uriah's made me feel differently."

"You really love Uriah, don't you?" Delilah asked.

"Of course. If I didn't, I wouldn't have married him."

"Tell me more about you two. How did y'all meet? How long have you been married?" Delilah asked.

By the time Sheba reached Delilah's house, she had given Delilah the condensed version about her and Uriah.

"You have a nice house," Sheba said when she pulled up into the empty driveway.

"Thanks. Now, if I can find my keys. . ." Delilah fumbled through her purse. "Bingo."

"Don't move. You can lean on me, and I'll help you up the stairs." Sheba got out and went to Delilah's side of the car.

One of her neighbors walked over. "Delilah, is that you?"

"Yes, it's me, Ms. Mabel."

Ms. Mabel was an older woman who looked to be in her sixties. "Child, I didn't think I was going to see you ever again. I've been meaning to come see you up in the hospital, but with my arthritis and being blind in one eye and can't see out the other, I couldn't drive up there to see you."

"That's okay, Ms. Mabel. I know you prayed for me, right?" Delilah said as she leaned on Sheba.

"Wasn't a day gone by that I didn't send up a special prayer for you. God is good. He answered my prayers. Just look at you." Ms. Mabel raised her hands up and looked up toward the sky.

Sheba helped Delilah up the stairs. They left Ms. Mabel outside, still talking.

Delilah said, "She'll be on the phone in a few minutes, calling everybody in the neighborhood. She's the neighborhood gossiper."

"I can tell," Sheba responded as the two laughed.

Chapter 16

David was thrilled to get the call he had been waiting for. Delilah's voice boomed through the room. He was in the middle of his morning workout, so he had her on speakerphone. "My sister has allowed me to stay with her while I recuperate. I don't know how long I will be here, so if you're going to make your move, I suggest you do it soon, so I can at least be around to get in her head."

"I'm leaving for New York in the morning. I wish you would have called me sooner. I could have been there tonight."

"That wouldn't have gone over too well with her. Let me work on her for a few days. When do you think you can come through?" Delilah asked.

David stopped working out and picked up his iPhone. He scrolled through his calendar. "I'll be in New York, and then I'm flying to Milan. I'll be back in the States on Wednesday."

"You go, boy. I see why you're the king."

"And you know it," David responded.

Nathan walked in the room but remained quiet when he saw David hold up his hand.

"Do what you do. You got my number. Just call me when you're on your way, and I'll do the rest."

David ended his call.

Nathan said, "Hey, man, you're a hard person to catch up with."

"Trying to keep a roof over my head," David replied.

"You mean, a couple of roofs. You got property in every state."

"No, man, not in every state. Twenty-five of them, but not every."

Nathan threw his hands up in the air. "See? That's what I'm talking about. You need to hook a brotha up with a job so he can share in the wealth."

David knew Nathan was joking. Nathan was doing well on his own. His wealth didn't compare to David's, but as the pastor of one of Dallas's mega churches and the author of over ten *New York Times* best-selling books, Nathan was far away from the poorhouse. He was a sought-after speaker and had traveled the world. He repeatedly showed up on the *Forbes* and the

Black Enterprise millionaires' list as one of the top paid authors in the United States.

"Who was that woman with the sexy voice?" Nathan asked as he took the liberty of getting himself a bottle of water from the small refrigerator in David's office.

"That's Delilah," David said as he went back to lifting weights.

"Is she as sexy as she sounds?" Nathan asked while sitting down with his drink.

"Just as sexy as her sister."

"Do I know her sister?" Nathan asked.

"Not yet, but you will. Remember Sheba, the woman I was telling you about?"

"The one married to one of your directors?"

"Yes. Delilah is her sister."

"Well, what is her sister doing talking to you?"

"She's helping me out with something."

Nathan finished his water and placed the empty bottle on the coaster on the table. "Man, you're playing with fire."

"After I get Sheba where I want her, the first thing I'm going to do is tell her not to trust her sister. Because as much as I want Sheba, Delilah shouldn't be scheming behind her back."

Nathan laughed. "Man, you're a trip. What do you call what you're doing? You're scheming behind her back. In fact, you sent the woman's husband to Afghanistan. Come on, man. Afghanistan. I hope she's worth it."

David slammed the weight down on the floor. "Why do you always have to be so judgmental?"

"As your friend, it's my role to keep you on the straight and narrow." Nathan looked David directly in the eyes.

"As my friend, I need for you to mind your own business."

"I wish I could do that. Remember when we were in college?" Nathan asked.

"What does that have to do with anything?"

"Oh, I don't think you do. Remember when I walked up to you and told you that God wanted to do great things in your life, if only you would submit to Him?"

"Yes, I remember. I started going to church more because of you."

"Well, David, you must have forgotten what else I told you."

David tilted his head from side to side as he tried to recall the conversation Nathan was referring to. "I honestly don't remember what else you said."

"God sent me to you that day. I had no intentions of coming to the student union. I was napping when I heard God tell me to seek you out. The description I got of you in my head was eerie. That was one of my most vivid visions. So when I saw the light-skinned black man with curly red hair sipping on a cola like in my vision, I knew you were the one."

"Oh yeah, I remember now. I thought you were just kidding."

"No, man, I was serious then, and I'm serious now. God sends me visions. We've talked about some of them before."

"I know. God speaks to me, too."

"He would speak with you more if you would stop and listen."

"I listen." David wouldn't look Nathan in the face. "Well, most of the time."

"Are you listening now?"

David didn't say a word.

Nathan stood up. "You don't have to answer me. This is between you and God."

"Then see your way out of my business."

"Don't shoot the messenger," Nathan said as he retrieved another bottle of water from the refrigerator. "I got a date, anyway, so I'll catch you later."

"For a preacher, you sure go out on a lot of dates," David said.

"I'm trying to find a first lady, because I'm tired of the single women coming to church with their dresses getting shorter and shorter and their blouses cut lower and lower."

"Man, I need to be coming to church more often if that's the case."

"Yes, you do, but you need to be focused on the word, not the women."

"Then what's the fun?"

"Lord, what are we going to do with him?" Nathan said as he looked up toward the heavens.

After Nathan left, David thought about his own life and his weakness for women. Would God forgive him for what he had set in motion?

Chapter 17

It had been almost a week since Sheba moved Delilah temporarily into her and Uriah's home. Now she was beginning to think Uriah was right. Delilah wasn't the easiest person to get along with. In fact, she could be quite demanding. Sheba ended up having to do another round of grocery shopping, because Delilah was picky about the things she ate.

"You would think someone opening up their home and refrigerator to you would make you a little more grateful," Sheba blurted out.

"Well, you're the one who invited me here. Remember?" Delilah snapped back.

Sheba rolled her eyes and mumbled under her breath, "I'm not going to let you get under my skin today. I promised myself that."

"Well, I can just call Keisha and have her take me home, since I'm such a bother." Delilah reached for her purse to look for her cell phone.

Sheba picked up the cell phone on the counter and waved it around in the air. "Is this what you're looking for?"

"Yes. Now, if you'll pass it to me, I'll be out of your hair shortly."

Sheba disobeyed. "Look. I'm sorry. I'm missing Uriah. You're quite demanding, and my nerves are just shot, okay?"

"Well, don't take it out on me. I'm just an innocent victim of your wrath."

Sheba raised her eyebrows. "Innocent, you are not."

"Okay, I admit, I can be a little demanding." Delilah held her fingers inches away from each other.

"You can lie to me, but you can't lie to God," Sheba said as she handed Delilah her phone and then took a seat on the couch, next to her.

"Lord, forgive me for lying. I know my little sister is doing all she can to make me comfortable."

"Thanks. Sometimes all a person needs is to feel appreciated." Sheba thought about the scant attention she felt her husband was giving her. He had missed their last two chat sessions due to work.

"How long is your husband supposed to be gone?" Delilah asked.

"Five more months. I don't know if I can take this. We've never been apart more than a few days."

"What are you going to do when you get that itch?" Delilah asked.

"Itch? If I'm itching, I better be taking my behind to the doctor."

Delilah laughed. "No, silly. I'm talking about the urge. The urge to do what grown folks do."

"Pray. Read my Bible. Bug you. Something to get my mind off it."

"David seems to be interested in you. It wouldn't hurt to see what he's about. Maybe Uriah's not here because you're supposed to be with another man," Delilah said without blinking.

"The only reason why David is interested in me is because I'm off-limits. If I was single, he wouldn't look at me twice. I don't have time to be a pawn in a rich man's games. Besides, I love my husband too much."

Delilah pouted. "Well, who said anything about you falling in love with him? I'm talking about getting your groove on. I'm sure with a body like his, he can work it."

Sheba laughed. "If you're that interested in David, maybe you should make a move on him yourself."

Delilah looked away. "He's not my type. Only one of us can be the center of attention, and he's too arrogant for me."

Sheba swung around to face Delilah. She placed one of her legs under the other. "I said I wasn't going to say anything, but since you're all up in my business, I'm curious. Is it true you had an affair with that preacher and that's why you were shot?"

"Li'l sis, don't believe everything you hear. I know none of those Holy Rollers would risk spending the rest of their lives in jail for shooting me."

"But that's not the question I asked you."

"Would you look at me differently if I told you that yes, I did?" Delilah bit her bottom lip. "Samson Judges tried to convince the church that it was my fault that he and I had an affair. I didn't make Samson do anything. He slept with me because he wanted to. I made a mistake. I was foolish enough to think he cared for me. I thought he loved me. He led me to believe that he did, anyway."

"Something tells me you're not as innocent as you would like for me to believe, but if that's the story you want to go with, then so be it." Sheba tilted her head to the side.

Delilah batted her eyes. "Surely, you're not calling me a liar."

"Well, if the shoe fits."

"None of my shoes fit anymore. My feet are still swollen up." Delilah glanced down at her feet and laughed.

"How I wished our mother was here to see the two of us."

"She would be proud of one and not so proud of the other." A sad expression crossed Delilah's face.

Sheba patted Delilah on the leg. "You're a beautiful woman. Yes, you made some mistakes. Who hasn't? Lord knows, I've made plenty. I used to envy you because you were her first."

"Really?" Delilah looked at Sheba in disbelief.

"Yes, really. Mom talked about you so much that sometimes I was jealous."

"You have nothing to be jealous about," Delilah said.

"Tell a teenage girl that."

"I must say us Baker girls are some bad mama jamas."

"No, you didn't say 'Bad mama jamas.' You're only three years older than me, and you sound so—"

"Old school," Delilah interrupted.

"Yes, old school." They both burst out laughing. Sheba's phone vibrated in her pocket. She looked at the caller ID display. There was a message from Uriah. "Look, I need to go chat with Uriah, but we'll finish this sister session later."

"Tell my brother-in-law I said hello," Delilah said.

"Okay." Sheba knew she had no intentions of delivering the message. Uriah still didn't know Delilah was staying at their home, and she planned to keep it that way.

She went into their home office and turned on the laptop. While it was booting up, she checked the mirror on the desk to make sure her hair was in place. She had put on some light makeup earlier. She logged on to Skype. It took a few minutes for their connection to be established.

The first thing out of Uriah's mouth was, "I'm sorry I had to cancel the last two times."

Sheba didn't like how Uriah looked. He had bags under his eyes, as if he hadn't slept in days. "What's going on?" she asked.

"I can't disclose everything going on over here, but let me just say that it's different than what I thought it was going to be."

"Meaning?" Sheba asked.

"The people are eager to learn, but going out of the compound can get a little dangerous. One of my coworkers got injured because the truck in front of him blew up. I was supposed to be in that truck, so that sort of freaked me out."

"And you're just now telling me this? Uriah, I don't care what you do, but you see about getting transferred back here. That job is not worth you losing your life."

"Calm down, Sheba. See, that's why I didn't want to tell you. Only reason I'm telling you now is because it'll probably be on the news, and I didn't want you to hear about it from someone else."

All Sheba saw was red. "Uriah, either you talk to David King or I will. I need you home with me."

"I'm not going to do it, and you promise me, you won't, either."

Sheba wouldn't promise. As soon as they disconnected their Skype call, she would find David's number and call him. No amount of money was worth Uriah risking his life. She would give up getting another house if it meant having her husband back with her safe and sound.

Chapter 18

David went straight home. He had planned on working some before going to bed, but he drifted off to sleep. His was a light sleep, and his eyes popped open when he felt his personal cell phone vibrate. He answered it without looking at the number on the phone display. "This better be good."

"Is that how you answer all your calls, Mr. King?" Sheba said.

"Who is this?" David was now fully awake.

"I'm your worst nightmare if you don't bring my husband home."

"Sheba, is that you?"

"You know who it is. Stop playing games with me. I told Uriah that if he didn't ask to be transferred back here, I would call you myself, and since he's too chicken to call you, I did."

David laughed. He loved her spunk. Knowing she was upset made him want her more. "Sheba, Uriah's there because he wants to be there. He could have turned down my offer."

"Nobody defies King David. Whatever you ask, they do," she said mockingly.

"Let's put an end to this. I'll call him on the three-way, and you can see for yourself. Hold on." Before she could protest, David clicked over to his other line. He dialed the number he had saved for Uriah. "Uriah, how are things going?"

"Fine, Mr. King," Uriah responded.

"I have your wife on the phone. It looks like we have a slight problem," David said, then clicked a button on the phone. "Sheba, are you there? I have Uriah on the phone with us."

"Baby, what did you say to Mr. King?" Uriah quickly questioned his wife.

"Don't 'baby' me. I told you if you didn't call him, I would. Now, David, tell him he can come home."

"Uriah, it's your option, and it's not going to affect your job," David told him. "If you want to come back and run the Shreveport office, come home and I will send Richard or someone else out there with Simon."

Uriah didn't hesitate to say, "Mr. King, there will be no need for that. You sent me out here to do this job, and I will. I will not leave until your plans have been implemented."

"But, baby," Sheba said.

"Sheba, I hate that you got Mr. King involved in our little issue, and, dear, I will have to ask you to lose his number. If you have a problem with my job, call me. Let me deal with it. Okay?"

"Yes, dear," Sheba said, barely above a whisper.

"Now that you two lovebirds are straight, I'm going to end this call and get back to sleeping."

David disconnected the call and threw his phone on the bed beside him. He closed his eyes, and Sheba's face invaded his thoughts. He drifted off into a deep sleep. In his dreams he and Sheba had met under different circumstances. In his dreams Sheba became his wife. In his dreams Sheba bore his first child. It all seemed so real in his dreams that when his alarm buzzed and woke him up the next morning, he wanted to go back to sleep and back to his dreams. David started his day off by praying and reading scriptures. He had gotten out of the routine and needed to feel close to God, so after praying, he picked up his Bible and turned to Psalm 3. *I laid me down and slept; I awaked; for the LORD sustained me. I will not be afraid of ten thousands of people, that have set themselves against me round about.*

David felt that the scripture spoke volumes in his life. Wade had given him some bad news over the weekend. Someone was secretly buying up some of his stock. They had not been able to discover who the culprit was as of yet, but David was sure they would soon find out. He would always have the majority of the stock shares, but he didn't want anyone else to have enough shares to be able to veto any of his decisions.

David's phone rang the next morning, waking him up. The song he had preset on his phone indicated it was Nathan calling. Whenever the ring tone of Marvin Sapp's song "He Saw the Best in Me" played, David knew it was his friend Nathan. "Nathan, I'm surprised you're calling me on a Sunday morning."

"I need you, man."

David could hear the desperation in his voice. "What's wrong?"

"I need you to sing a solo."

"What? No. Now, you know I don't sing anymore."

"You should. Please. Just one. It's by special request. Remember Jonathan Heard? Well, he's dying of cancer, man, and he's in town. He asked me if I could get you to sing. Please. He might not make it to another service."

Nathan really knew how to lay the guilt on David. After thinking about it, David responded, "I'll be there. But I'm not staying for the entire service."

"Now, David, you have to stay and hear the Word. God has a word for you today."

David sat up in bed, ignoring Nathan's comment. "Since it's after nine, I better get dressed so I can find me a seat."

"Don't worry about that. I'll make sure a seat is saved for you. The ushers will direct you to the front."

"You've thought of everything, haven't you?"

"Almost everything."

David could imagine Nathan wearing a smirk on his face. He ended their call, got up, took a shower, and then put on one of his tailor-made suits. He opted for a black and gray pin-striped one and his gold, wing-tipped, matching shoes.

He decided to give his driver the day off. He jumped in his silver Jaguar and headed to Church On the Way, where Nathan was the senior pastor. David had always wanted to ask Nathan why the church's name was Church On the Way, but never had.

David eased his car into the first available parking spot he could find. Several people seemed to recognize him as he entered the church, but they wouldn't approach him. Instead, he heard people murmuring about him.

"Sir, this part of the sanctuary is full. We're asking everyone else to go to the balcony," the slim usher said to David as he searched for a seat.

"My name's David King, and I'm here as a special guest of Pastor McDaniel," David said in a calm voice.

"Oh my goodness. I can't believe I'm actually talking to *the* David King. Why didn't you say something? We have a seat saved for you up front. I'll personally escort you."

"No need to. Just point me in the right direction, and I'll find it."

The usher pointed to the right side of the sanctuary. "Just tell Ms. Simmons, the usher up front, who you are, and she'll show you exactly where your seat is."

David walked down the aisle. It had been months since he had actually taken the time to attend anyone's church. He was usually either in another city or flying in from another city. Although he didn't attend church on a regular basis, he felt like he had a close relationship with God.

Ms. Simmons showed him to his seat. When he looked up toward the pulpit, Nathan acknowledged him with a huge smile. David was glad he'd come. It was the least he could do for their dying classmate.

Nathan introduced them both. The congregation clapped. When Nathan asked David to render a solo, the congregation was shocked. Few people knew that David could sing. They knew David only as the king of media.

The pianist rose from the piano bench, and David sat down on it. He took a few seconds to get reacquainted with the piano keys and then looked in Jonathan's direction. "This is dedicated to my friend Jonathan and anyone else who may be going through the storms of life," he told the congregation.

From the moment David started playing and opened up his voice, the congregation was mesmerized. There was not a dry eye in the church after David sang his rendition of the Twenty-third Psalm.

David felt the presence of God, and it took him a while to remember he was in the presence of others. Once his song was over, he graciously went back to his seat.

Nathan said, "It's going to be hard to preach after that heartfelt selection."

"Amen," was heard around the room.

"But the Lord has a word for you today. A word that will hopefully make some of you change your wicked ways." Nathan looked directly at David.

Chapter 19

Sheba had never been so embarrassed in her life. Uriah could have handled the phone call with David differently. David wasn't lying. Uriah actually wanted to be where he was. All this time he'd been telling her that he wished he could be with her, but his job was actually his first priority.

Fine. She was tired of sitting around the house, being Delilah's maid and waiting eagerly by her cell phone for calls from Uriah. She was going shopping, and Uriah had better hope he had enough money to pay the bill when it arrived. She retrieved his gold MasterCard from underneath the socks in his dresser drawer.

He didn't know she knew about his hiding spot. Yes, she had found it some time ago, but she'd vowed never to use the card unless it was an emergency. Her sanity was an emergency.

Delilah was lying on the couch, reading one of her books she had lying around.

"Delilah, I'll be back. I'm going to the store."

"Can you pick me up a book? I'm enjoying the New Day Divas series. One of the characters reminds me of myself."

"I should have all the books already. Just check my bookshelf."

"I did, and you're missing the latest one."

Sheba realized she had been so wrapped up with missing Uriah that she had slacked off on her book purchases. "I'll swing by the store and see if they have it."

"If they don't, let me know so I can order it from Amazon," Delilah yelled.

Four hours later, Sheba returned to the house, carrying several department store bags. She had so many bags, she had to make two trips to the car to bring them all in.

Delilah walked in her bedroom. "I hope you have something in there for me."

"I did see a cute outfit I thought you would like," Sheba said. She rummaged through one of the bags. She held up a purple satin blouse and black jeans.

Delilah inspected them. "Thanks, sis. Did you remember the book?"

"I sure did." Sheba found the bag with the books. "I also found books by other authors you might like."

Delilah removed some of the books. "I haven't heard of some of these, but if they are anything like the book I'm reading now, I can't wait to read them."

"We can both read them and discuss them later," Sheba said.

Delilah read the back of one of the books. "Oh, before I forget, your hubby called you."

Sheba froze. "Did he leave a message on the answering machine, or did you answer the phone?"

"I answered. I thought it could be you calling or something."

"What did he say?" Sheba stopped unpacking the bags.

"He thought he had the wrong number at first, but I assured him, he didn't."

"And . . ." Sheba's heart rate increased.

"He wanted to know what I was doing at his house and why you weren't here."

"Did he sound upset?" Sheba asked.

"He wasn't upset until I told him that I had been here for a few weeks, and that it wasn't my fault he didn't know what was going on in his own house." Delilah placed the book she held back in the bag.

"Did you have to be so mean about it?"

Delilah said, "Are you keeping secrets from your husband? I wasn't aware he didn't know I was here."

Sheba went back to removing the items she'd bought from the bags. "Mind your own business. What goes on between me and Uriah is our business alone."

"I'm just saying, sis. You act like y'all have the perfect relationship, but if you're keeping secrets, what's perfect about that?"

Sheba tried to control her rage. She clenched the bag tighter. "Look, Delilah, Uriah and I are just fine. No, he didn't want you here. You want to know why?" Sheba looked Delilah in the eyes. "He doesn't trust you. He believes all the things people have been saying about you."

Delilah crossed her arms. "Well, there's no love lost here. I don't like your husband, either. So him and I have something in common."

"You don't know him to not like him."

"Sis, I don't have to spend years with someone to know I don't like them. There's no law that says we have to like each other, anyway."

"You put me in an awkward position."

"I didn't ask to come here. You invited me. If me being here is causing problems with your husband, don't blame me." Delilah didn't flinch.

Sheba rolled her eyes. "I just wished you hadn't answered the phone. I was going to tell him eventually."

"I'm feeling much better, so I can get my stuff and go if you like."

Sheba felt torn. She didn't want to anger her husband, but she didn't want Delilah to leave, either. "No. Uriah's miles away. He should be happy you're here with me so I won't have to be in this big old house all by myself."

"Exactly. I don't know why he's tripping."

Sheba's phone rang. "It's Uriah," she said out loud to Delilah. She sat on her bed, in between the bags, and answered the phone.

"You went behind my back and moved your sister in, anyway. How could you defy me like that, Sheba?" Uriah asked.

"I'll let you have your privacy," Delilah said as she left Sheba alone to deal with Uriah's wrath.

"Calm down. It's no big deal. At least I'm not home alone. Be glad about that," Sheba reasoned.

"I don't trust her, and you shouldn't, either."

"Baby, don't get me started on trust. I trusted you to do what was right for us, but you haven't. You're there and I'm here."

"Sheba, I don't know what your problem is, but you need to get it together. I'm dealing with enough stress. I shouldn't have to worry about my wife."

"Worry about your wife? You act like I'm out there whoring around. Delilah's my sister, and it's not my fault you have a problem with her," Sheba yelled.

"I want that woman out of my house," Uriah snapped.

"Are you coming home?" Sheba asked.

"I'll be home in four months."

"Then, she's staying as long as she needs to." Sheba hung up the phone.

She looked up into the face of Delilah, who was standing in the middle of the doorway, with a sneer on her face.

Chapter 20

David sat at the table with Nathan and Jonathan and enjoyed a dinner with two old college friends. With them, he could be himself. No one was trying to impress him, hoping he would do something for them. He didn't get to hang with Nathan as much as he liked.

The occasion saddened David, however, because this could well be the last time he saw Jonathan alive. His friend's normally two-hundred-pound frame was now a mere one hundred and twenty-five pounds. He admired Jonathan for the strength he showed, despite knowing that the cancer had spread to all his vital organs.

"David, thank you, brother, for singing for me today," Jonathan said.

"Anything for you."

"I wanted to see my two old buddies before I left this side."

Nathan said, "This is a time to rejoice. You're going home to be with our Father."

David smiled, although he felt like crying. "Yes, to your home going. Save a place for me."

They each held up their glass and toasted.

Two days later, while in between meetings, Nathan called David on his private number. "He's gone, David. Jonathan's gone."

David ended the call as tears flowed down his face. He called Trisha. "Cancel my calls for the next few hours."

He got on his knees at the foot of his desk and prayed fervently. "Lord, please take this pain away. I know Jonathan is in a better place, because he's now in your presence. He's left behind a wife and two children. Lord, be with them and protect them as they deal with their loss. Thank you for letting me spend time with him before he departed this world. It is our selfishness that makes us want our friends and loved ones to be with us forever.

"Lord, please ease the pain for his loved ones. Let them know that you will never leave them or forsake them. Lord, I cry out to you and ask you to have mercy on me, as I know that lately I've not been doing what you would want me to do. Lord, I've failed you, and I ask that you show mercy on me. Please forgive me, Father, for I can't control this thing inside of me that won't let me stop lusting after another man's wife. Amen."

David wiped the tears from his face with the handkerchief in his pocket. He stood up and then sat down in the chair behind his desk. He swiveled the chair around and stared out the window. He was in deep thought. The sound of his private phone line ringing broke his trance.

Nathan's voice was on the other end. "Just calling to check on you."

"I know we were expecting him to die. Just not this soon."

"Our time's not God's time," Nathan said.

"It's still hard. I know he's in a better place."

"He's no longer in pain."

"That's what I keep telling myself. If his wife needs anything, and I do mean anything, let me know. I'll take care of it."

"I've checked with her. Fortunately, Jonathan had a nice life insurance policy before he got diagnosed, and he kept the policy up. Financially, she should be fine."

"I'm still going to set something up for his kids. That's the least I can do."

"That's nice of you. I'm sure she'll appreciate it."

David hung up with Nathan and called his banker. After allocating funds to Jonathan's kids, David went back to his normal routine. After putting in a twelve-hour day, he left to go home to his empty house.

Here he was, one of the richest men in the world. He could have any woman he wanted, yet he yearned for one woman. The one woman who seemed to be off-limits. A woman who was another man's wife.

Thinking about the loss of Jonathan put more things in perspective. Life was too short not to get what he wanted out of it. He wanted Sheba, and as the clock ticked, he knew time was of the essence. Who knew how much time he had left? No one did, so he had to make the rest of his time on earth count.

David picked up the phone and dialed Delilah's cell phone number. "Delilah, I'll be in Shreveport tomorrow. Will Sheba be off?"

Delilah responded, "Yes, I think so. I'll make sure she's home."

"Good. See you then. And please don't let her know I'm coming."

David called Trisha at home. "Trisha, I'll be working out of the Shreveport office tomorrow. You can forward all important calls to my cell phone."

"Yes, sir. You were supposed to be meeting with the head of NBN tomorrow. Do you want me to reschedule it for another day?"

"No need to. Call them and have them meet me at eight, and I can still be in Shreveport by noon."

"Consider it done."

David got a restless night of sleep, handled his business the next morning at his Dallas office, and flew to Shreveport to check on operations there. After wrapping up business matters in the Shreveport office, he raced to his rental car, got behind the wheel, and headed to Sheba's house.

Chapter 21

"Somebody's at the door," Delilah yelled out.

Sheba rolled her eyes. Delilah was closer to the front door but didn't move from the couch. How did she expect to walk better if she didn't get her behind off the couch and move?

"You could have gotten the door," Sheba said as she passed by the living room door and peeked out the window. "David, what are you doing here?" Sheba asked as she yanked the front door open.

"I came to check on Delilah. I heard she was staying with you," he said.

"She is, but I know you didn't come all the way to Shreveport to see my sister."

"You must have forgotten that I have a company here. Now, are you going to let me in and let me see Delilah, or are we going to give your neighbors something to talk about because some handsome man is standing on your porch while your husband is away?"

Sheba wanted to wipe the smirk off his face. She moved over to the side and allowed him entrance. "You better be glad you're my husband's boss, or I would have slammed the door in your face."

"I love a woman with pizzazz."

"She's in the living room."

David remained standing in the same spot. "I've never been to your house before, so can you please escort me to your living room?"

"We don't live in a big mansion like you. Just walk that way and you'll see it." Sheba pointed. She brushed past David, and he followed behind her. "Delilah, you have company."

"I do?" Delilah swung her legs around and planted them on the floor. She quickly ran her hands through her hair. She tried to stand up but failed.

David rushed to her side. "Stay sitting. I just wanted to check on my favorite patient."

"I'm doing fine. I go to rehab three times a week, and my sister is taking great care of me." Delilah pointed in Sheba's direction.

Sheba said, "I'll excuse you two so you can talk. I need to go cook dinner."

"Why don't I treat you lovely ladies to dinner?" David asked.

"I'm really not up for getting out," Delilah said. "But you and Sheba can go right ahead."

"It's probably best that I don't leave her alone," Sheba quickly added.

"Nonsense. I'm a big girl. I can take care of myself. Besides, I'm going to need you to bring me a doggie bag, because any restaurant he takes you to is probably going to be an expensive one."

David looked at Sheba. "So what do you say? Can I treat you to dinner? It's the least I can do."

Sheba thought about it. David was right. He could treat her to dinner since he'd sent her husband across the globe. "You know what? I'm going to take you up on your offer. Give me twenty minutes, and I'll be ready."

"Great. That'll give me and Delilah time to talk." He winked at his accomplice.

Thirty minutes later Sheba followed David outside. "Surprised you're slumming it today," Sheba said as David held her car door open and she got inside the black SUV.

"What do you mean by that?" David was puzzled.

"No driver. You're actually driving yourself somewhere. I'm surprised you even know how to drive."

David didn't respond. He closed the car door and walked around to the driver's side. Sheba felt kind of bad for her rude behavior. She vowed to tone it down a little.

David started up the engine. "What do you want for dinner?"

"Italian. I love Italian."

"There's this Italian bistro near downtown that my employees have been talking about. Do you know where it is?"

"I sure do. We'll need to take I-Twenty and then take the Fairfield Avenue exit."

David followed her directions, and they were there in no time. Normally, patrons needed reservations, but David slipped the maître d' some money and they were seated immediately.

"Times like these are when I enjoy the fact that I have a little extra money," David said to Sheba.

They made small talk over dinner. They talked about the weather, the food, and the casinos. Sheba hated to admit that talking to David was like talking to any other person. She had this negative image about him in her head, and he was quickly erasing it. To her surprise she found he had a good sense of humor. He was no Mike Epps, but he made her laugh.

"Tell me who the real David is. Not the one the world knows, but when you're not at the office. The person that hardly anyone gets to see." Sheba stopped eating her dessert.

"What you see is what you get." David threw his hands up halfway.

"So you're this shrewd businessman who never turns it off? I've gotten to see a different side of you tonight. What else should I know about David?" Sheba asked.

"Like I said, what you see is what you get. I see something I want, and I go for it." David stared directly into her eyes.

"Do you always get what you want?"

"For the most part. Some things are easier to acquire than others." He winked his eye.

"I bet you were spoiled growing up, weren't you?"

"Never that. I worked hard for everything I have. Don't you see how hard I'm working now?" David laughed.

Sheba didn't. She picked up her glass of lemonade. The only thing in it was ice and a few drops of lemonade. She didn't care. She sipped on the straw until it started making noises. She needed something to quench the heat radiating from David's eyes that was meant for her.

"I'll be right back," Sheba said. She eased away from the table and rushed to the restroom.

She paced back and forth in front of the sink. Sheba wet a paper towel and held it to her neck to cool herself down. "Get a grip," she said to herself in the mirror.

What was she doing? David hadn't made a pass at her. They were only talking. So why did she feel like she was doing something she had no business doing?

Chapter 22

David knew women. He could tell Sheba's resistance to his natural charm was getting low. He would have to treat her delicately, though, because he didn't want her to retreat into that hostile shell she had built around herself. He needed her to feel at ease. To keep her guard down around him. For the most part, he needed to make sure the conversation stayed away from the one person that stood between the two of them: Uriah.

Sheba walked back to the table, looking calmer than she had when she left. He got up and held her chair out for her, and she sat down.

"Are you okay?" David asked.

"Just had to use the bathroom. I'm okay now," she responded.

"I've paid our bill. I also paid for someone to deliver Delilah a plate at your place."

"That's nice of you, but I could have taken it."

"The night's still young. I was hoping you would go with me to the Horseshoe Casino."

Sheba glanced at her watch. "Normally, I'm chatting with Uriah around this time."

"He's going to be busy tonight. There was a problem with one of the building permits, so Uriah's tied up right now. It's daytime over there, so it'll be a while before he will be available to talk to you."

"If I didn't know better, I would think you planned it that way."

"No, I'm about business. The last thing I want is problems," David assured her.

Sheba looked to be in deep thought. "Fine. Delilah can fend for herself. I need a night out."

David planned on showing her a good time. Fifteen minutes later he pulled up to the front of the Horseshoe Casino. He tipped the valet and took his valet ticket. "Let me show you how the high rollers do it."

He placed his hand on the crevice of her back as they walked inside the casino. The workers knew him by name as they were led into the poker room, where participants had to have at least a million dollars just to play at the table.

"Do you want anything to drink?" the waitress asked.

"Nothing for me," David said.

"I'll have a Cosmopolitan," Sheba responded.

David took a seat at the table. Sheba stood behind him. "Rub my head for good luck," David said.

"I will not. In fact, I'll just sit right over here until you finish." Sheba sat in a chair behind him and crossed her legs.

David noticed that his opponents were distracted by Sheba. He won the first few hands because they were not concentrating on the game. They were concentrating on her movements. David smiled. He hated losing, and Sheba was already bringing him some good luck.

"Sir, we're going have to ask your guest to leave," a member of the casino security said.

Sheba said, "But I'm not doing anything but watching."

"Yes, we know. If you're not going to sit at the table, you will have to leave."

David, not wanting to press his luck, cashed in his chips and left with Sheba.

Sheba said, "How rude! They were just mad because you were winning."

"I don't blame them. If I had been distracted by you and not able to play, I would have had you removed, too."

Sheba batted her eyes. "So you weren't distracted when I crossed my legs, exposing my long and lean thighs?"

"No, baby. 'Money before broads' has always been my motto. But now that I've made some extra money, you can expose those long, lean thighs you were flashing those guys." He chuckled.

"I don't think so," she responded with a frown on her face.

"We'll see about that. Follow me." David grabbed her hand and led her outside the casino and into the lobby of the adjacent hotel. He walked right to the front desk. He pulled out his Visa Black Card. "I would like to book one of your executive suites."

"How long?" the front desk attendant asked.

David looked at Sheba. "One night. We'll need it for only one night."

Sheba removed her hand from his. "What are you doing? You need to take me home."

"Shh. Unless you want to draw attention to yourself," David said.

Sheba remained quiet. The attendant handed David his electronic keys.

David grabbed Sheba's hand again. "Come on. We can talk in the room."

They got on the elevator, and David pushed the button for their floor. Sheba mumbled something under her breath, but David couldn't make out what she said. Some of the other people in the elevator were looking at her like she was crazy.

Sheba said, "I can't believe I let you talk me into going to your room."

David didn't respond as they stepped off the elevator. He used one of the electronic keys he'd been given to access the executive suite. "Come on. We can talk inside."

The plush room was fully stocked with food and drinks. "Have a seat," he instructed.

Sheba removed her shoes and sat down on the white couch. David sat beside her, and before she could protest, he picked up her right foot and began massaging it. She leaned her head back and moaned. "That feels good, but you shouldn't be doing that."

"I want to. You work hard. You need a man to take care of you."

"I have a man, or have you forgotten?" She removed her foot from his hand.

David leaned closer to her. "But he's not here now."

"And whose fault is that?" she asked.

David's plan to seduce Sheba was backfiring. He had to think of something quick. "Tonight it's all about you. What do you want, Sheba? Let me make your dreams come true."

Sheba looked disheartened. "I want my husband."

"I have a suggestion. Let's not talk about Uriah," he said.

"You asked me what I wanted. I was just answering your question," she snapped.

David knew only one way to shut Sheba up and to get her mind off Uriah. Before he could change his mind, he did what he had been wanting to do from the moment he met her. He kissed her.

Chapter 23

The moment David's lips touched Sheba's, she knew the dynamics of their relationship had changed. Instead of pushing him off of her, like a good wife should do, she welcomed his kiss. Her mind was telling her no, but her body couldn't deny the magnetic pull that held her captive in David's embrace.

Sheba felt as if she was having an out-of-body experience as she heard moans coming from her mouth as David's hands roamed over her body. Within minutes, David swooped her up in his arms and carried her to the king-size bed. She still had time to stop what was about to happen, but instead of turning away, she reached for David and allowed the passion that had been building up between them to take over. She gave into those desires and allowed David to please her in ways that Uriah never had.

Several hours later, naked and with David's arm wrapped around her waist, she stared into space. David slept beside her. She could hear his soft snores as she thought about what had just transpired. She had enjoyed David's touch. David had pleased her body as if it were a harp. It had sung to every stroke of his touch.

Guilt threatened to fill her mind, but she kept it at bay. If Uriah had been home, none of this would have ever happened. It was his fault that she was now sleeping in the arms of another man. It was only a coincidence that the man happened to be his boss. It wasn't her fault. None of it was. David and Uriah were to blame, as far as Sheba was concerned.

No, she would not let guilt over sleeping with David behind her husband's back get to her. Instead, she would let this be a one-time thing and would go on with her life. She had needed this, and now that David had gotten what he had been after, he should be satisfied, too. Two adults pleasing one another for one night.

Sheba closed her eyes, knowing that the things she told herself were only excuses. She had vowed in front of Uriah's family, her mother, and their friends, but most importantly, God, to honor her marriage vows. In one senseless night of passion, she had broken them.

Even if Uriah forgave her for the indiscretion, would God? Why did He send David into her life if this was not supposed to happen? Sheba tried to find other ways to justify her actions. None made sense to her, so she stopped trying to reason with herself. Instead, she finally succumbed to sleep.

She felt the light brush of David's fingers on her thigh as she woke up. "You're the most beautiful woman I've ever known," David said.

That was when Sheba realized that the dream she thought she'd had was not a dream. It was real. She had really slept with David, and here they were, still in bed, like two lovebirds. Two adulterers were what they were. With the light streaming in through the curtains, Sheba could see clearly. What had happened last night was a mistake. A mistake she didn't plan on making again. Justified or not.

She jumped out of bed. "Take me home," she said. She picked up her clothing, which was scattered on the floor, and headed to the bathroom.

David was on her heels. "Sheba, please don't do this. What we shared last night was special. Don't think negative."

Sheba turned and looked at David as he stood there, naked. She tried her best to keep her eyes focused on his eyes. "It was special, but we can't do it again. It was wrong. You know it, and I know it."

David reached for her, but she was quicker than him. She ran straight to the bathroom and shut the door. She clicked the lock and leaned on the door. "Lord, what have I done?"

She placed her clothes on the counter, showered, and used the expensive toiletries in the bathroom. When she exited the bathroom, she was fully dressed. She had left David naked, but when she returned, he was fully clothed.

"I showered in the other bathroom," he said as he stood up from the couch.

"I'm ready to go home now," Sheba said.

"Whatever you wish," he responded.

David was acting too calm for her. She thought he would try to talk her out of it. Maybe her initial assessment was right. He'd gotten what he wanted, and now he was satisfied. She just hoped that their one-night indiscretion wouldn't be discovered by Uriah.

When they reached the lobby, she bumped right into one of Uriah's cousins. "Hey, girl. What are you doing here? You heard from my cousin?" Renee asked.

Sheba stuttered, "N—no. He's been busy, but I'll tell him to call you."

"Do that, will you? I better go. My hand's itching, so that means I'm about to win me some money. Those slot machines are calling my name."

Sheba was glad that David had kept his distance. "Who was that?" he asked as they watched Renee walk through the casino doors.

"Uriah's cousin. Now, let's go, before we run into someone else I know," she responded, agitated.

Sheba felt paranoid. She kept watch in all directions and didn't stop looking around until the valet brought David his rental car and they were riding on I-20, headed toward her house.

"Look, David, what happened last night . . . Well, that can never happen again. Is that understood?" Sheba said sternly.

"Sheba, your wish is my command."

"So, you're not going to try to talk me into it again?"

"Nope." David kept his eyes on the road and never once looked in Sheba's direction.

"Oh, so I'm just another notch on your belt," Sheba said, fuming.

For the first time since getting in the car, David turned his head to look at her. "Sheba, you're special to me."

Sheba didn't believe him. All she wanted was to get back home safely and to be out of his presence. She had to, because something about David drew her to him, and she didn't want to feel that way. She wanted to hate him. She wanted to despise him, but she didn't. She didn't feel any of those things.

David pulled up into her driveway. He walked around and opened her car door. He walked her to the front door. While she searched for her keys, they stood face-to-face. Sheba could feel his breath on her face.

David said, "You're more than just a booty call to me. I love you." He then walked away, leaving Sheba to mull over those words.

Chapter 24

David beat the steering wheel one last time as he drove away. He had never planned to confess his feelings to Sheba. When the words "I love you" flew out of his mouth, he'd regretted them immediately. Where did those words come from? It had been years since David felt love for any woman. *Why this woman? Any other woman but her.*

He dialed Sheba's phone several times, and she finally answered. "Thanks for taking my call," he said.

"If I hadn't, you would have just kept calling," she said.

"You're right. I wanted to apologize for what I said."

"No apology necessary."

"Yes. You've made it perfectly clear that what happened between us was a one-time thing. I need to . . . Correction. I will respect your choice."

"Well, no harm. You were caught up in the moment, and those words just flew out of your mouth."

"I knew exactly what I was saying. I would repeat those words to you if I thought they would make a difference."

"David, don't. We both know that what happened shouldn't have happened."

David heard a shuffle from the other end of the phone. "What's wrong?" he asked.

"I think Delilah heard me. Look, I have to go. I'll talk to you later."

Before David could say anything else, Sheba disconnected their call. David called his pilot, and thirty minutes later he was turning in his rental car and boarding his plane.

"Mr. King, will you be wanting lunch, sir?" the stewardess asked.

"No. I'm fine. In fact, I think I'll go to my private area. Just knock on the door when we get ready to land," David said.

He buckled up in the chair next to the bed. Once they were securely in the air, he unbuckled himself and lay down on the bed with his face toward the ceiling. He wasn't sleepy. He just needed to rest his mind. Conflicting emotions fought each other as he dealt with loving Sheba and the guilt of taking another man's wife. There used to be a time when the words of Psalm 26 fit his life. *Judge me, O LORD; for I have walked in mine integrity: I have trusted also in the LORD; therefore I shall not slide . . . For thy loving-kind-ness is before mine eyes: and I have walked in thy truth.*

Recalling those verses now left a hollow feeling inside him. If God searched his heart now, He would find plenty to fault. Tears streamed down David's face as he came to terms with how he had allowed the lust of his loins to take over his senses. David loved women and had had plenty, period. No one would believe this, but Sheba was the first married woman he had slept with.

"Thou shall not commit adultery" was one commandment David had never broken.

"Lord, what do you want me to do? I've never met a woman like Bathsheba before. I tried resisting her, but I couldn't get her out of my system. Now that I've tasted how good it could be with her, I don't want to give her up. If I must, I will."

David cried out to the Lord in despair. He knew that what he was asking of God was not God's will. He silently recited Psalm 51:10–12, hoping God would hear his cry. *Create in me a clean heart, O God; and renew a right spirit within me. Cast me not away from thy presence; and take not thy holy spirit from me. Restore unto me the joy of thy salvation; and uphold me with thy free spirit.*

A week after Jonathan's death, David picked up Nathan on his way to Jonathan's wake. He made the mistake of telling him what had happened with Sheba.

Nathan berated David. "I told you to stay away from that married woman. Now look what you've done. God is not pleased with your actions."

David hung his head low. "I did everything I could to stay away from her, but I couldn't. You know how I am when I get an idea in my head. I have to see it through."

"Something tells me you didn't try hard enough."

"For those few hours I felt loved. I've never felt like that with any other woman."

"I would be clapping and cheering you on if she was single, but she isn't. You need to find a woman of your own. End of story."

David tuned out his friend as he went on and on about how wrong David was. David welcomed the sight of the funeral home. After they pulled in front of the building, the driver opened their car doors, and they went to pay their respects to

Jonathan's family. Neither David nor Nathan brought up Sheba on the ride back. Instead, they exchanged stories about their time with Jonathan.

"He was only forty-one," David said. "He had so much more to live for."

"When God is ready to call you home, it's time to go," Nathan said. "It was his time. Time waits on no man."

"That's for sure," David said. That was why he wanted to enjoy whatever time he had left, and he wanted to do it with the woman that he loved—Sheba.

The next day wails were heard throughout the sanctuary as Jonathan's home going took place. Nathan wasn't Jonathan's pastor, but he had been asked to preach the sermon since they were close friends. Nathan stood behind the podium and spoke with the fire of his Sunday sermons.

"Our brother Jonathan wouldn't want us down here, crying for him. In fact, if he was here today, I would hear him say, 'Dry those weeping eyes, for I'm in the presence of my Father.' So, children of God, dry those eyes and let's rejoice, because the angels of heaven are rejoicing because another saint has been called home."

David held back his tears and listened to Nathan. Two hours later David decided to skip the repast. It had been an emotional week. He needed time to decompress. He called his pilot and hopped on a plane to Miami. He would check on his office there but also planned on spending time on his yacht. Just him, the ocean, and God.

Chapter 25

Sheba and Delilah were enjoying a quiet evening at home. Sheba had just finished her shift at work. Delilah had surprised her with a home-cooked meal.

"Girl, these greens are good." Sheba poured more hot sauce on the greens.

"Us Baker women can cook inside and outside of the bedroom." Delilah laughed.

Sheba didn't find it funny. She still felt some guilt over what had transpired between her and David. "Did Uriah call the house? We've been playing phone tag on my cell phone."

"He did, but I didn't answer. I didn't want to cause any more problems."

"He knows you're here now."

"Well, I'm not talking about that. I'm talking about, what if he had asked me questions about the other night?"

Sheba stopped eating. "Why would he be questioning you about my whereabouts? I'm a grown woman. I can come and go as I please."

"I know that, but you know men. If I had answered when he called, he would have interrogated me with one hundred and one questions."

"For all he knew, I could have been at work. You could have told him that."

"So, you want me to lie for you, in other words?" Delilah had a smirk on her face.

"No, not lie, just stretch the truth."

"Well, I think God would look at stretching the truth the same as a lie, but then again, I could be wrong."

"Delilah, sometimes you make it hard for me to like you."

She laughed. "Don't be getting mad at me because you almost got busted for getting your groove on with another man."

"David and I were not getting our groove on."

Delilah's hands moved back and forth while she talked. "Knocking boots, or whatever you want to call it. Y'all were doing something, because you left at seven in the evening but didn't come back until ten o'clock the next morning."

Sheba tried to think of how she could lie her way out of this, but she couldn't come up with anything. She decided to face her dilemma head-on. "So what? What if I did spend the night with David? It's no big deal. Men do it all the time. The wife's out of town. He goes out, gets himself a little something, and pretends like it never happened."

"Do your thing. David's fine with a capital *F*. If you weren't my sister, I would have made my move on him a long time ago."

"You can have him. In fact, I can give you his private number so you can call him."

Delilah laughed. "Sheba, please. I don't do leftovers. He's too smitten with you to pay me any attention. If any man can overlook these double Ds, then I know he's really in love with his woman. David has eyes for one woman, and that's you."

"But I'm married. He can't have me."

Delilah snickered. "Sis, he's had you, and I bet you it won't be the last time."

That was a one-time thing. It'll never happen again. I guarantee it, Sheba thought to herself, rather than addressing Delilah's concerns.

Delilah went back to eating her food. Sheba went back to eating hers, but her mind wandered to the night she and David crossed the line. She could not forget how he made her feel, no matter how hard she tried. The sound of the house phone interrupted her daydream. She picked up the cordless phone. It was Uriah.

Delilah listened to her as she stammered during her conversation with Uriah. Once she had hung up, Delilah said, "Remind me not to do a crime with you, because you would have given us both up to the po-pos."

"Po-pos?" Sheba said.

"The police. Girl, you were stuttering so much, I thought you were Elmer Fudd. Look, what Uriah doesn't know won't hurt him. You said you don't plan on sleeping with David again, so woman up."

Sheba thought, *Delilah's right. I need to forget David and pretend like nothing happened.* Sheba knew that was easier said than done.

To reiterate how much she loved Uriah, Sheba took a few sexy poses with her cell phone camera and sent the images to him. She wanted Uriah to see what he had been missing while he was over in Afghanistan. A negative thought crossed her mind. What if one of the women overseas was servicing Uriah the way she had serviced David the other night?

She got livid. She called Uriah back after she sent him the photographs. "What are you doing?" she asked.

"Thinking about you," he responded.

"You haven't been sleeping with any of those women over there, have you?" she asked.

"Of course not. Baby, where is all this coming from?" he asked.

"Well, people have told me what goes on when their husbands go overseas."

"Baby, if I wanted to cheat, there are plenty of women in Shreveport who I could cheat with. I wouldn't have to go to a foreign country to do so," Uriah responded.

"I know. I just wanted to hear from you that you weren't." Sheba felt bad for accusing him now.

"What about you? You haven't been letting anyone dip into my pudding, have you?" he asked.

"Uh, of course not," Sheba lied.

"Better not. Big daddy will be home soon enough to take care of you, so don't be dipping out on a brother."

Sheba laughed. "Baby, you know you're the only man for me."

How had this become about her? Sheba hated that she had called Uriah back now. Now he would suspect that she had cheated on him. What was she going to do? Whatever it was, she had to do it.

"Did you get those pictures I just sent to your cell phone?" she asked.

"Hold on. Let me see."

She waited as he pulled up the pictures on his phone. He came back on the line. "My, my, my. I can't wait to get stateside so I can tap that."

"Uriah, watch your mouth."

"I miss you so much, and these pictures are not helping me."

"Well, you remember that when one of those floozies tries to throw herself at the rich American."

"Believe me, there's not a woman here that can rival you, babe. We got something special, and I'm not going to mess it up for a few moments of pleasure."

"Aw, that's so sweet. That's why I love you," Sheba said. She was smiling on the outside, but on the inside guilt was tearing her apart.

Chapter 26

Six weeks later . . .

Wade walked into the conference room. He was not his normal confident self.

David sensed the news he was about to hear was not good. He sighed, said a quick prayer, and offered Wade a seat. "Give it to me straight," David said as Wade sat down in the chair across from him.

Wade handed him a manila folder. "It took longer than I had anticipated to get this information, but I've confirmed it. It's Bo Shet that's buying up those shares."

David's fist hit the table. "I knew it. I knew I should have wiped his bank account clean when I had the chance, but out of respect for his father, Saul, I didn't."

"You didn't want Saul's heirs to be left with nothing," Wade reminded him.

"Exactly. Saul was a good man at one time. He just let greed get to him, and he ended up losing his businesses. Him selling me his companies helped ensure his heirs would have money."

"I wouldn't take this sitting down if I were you," Wade said.

"Oh, Bo has messed with me for the last time. I want you to get our attorney on this and pronto. There's no way I'm going to let him take what I've built into an international empire."

Wade rushed out of the room to do as requested. David opened up the folder and read each document one by one. With each page, his bright skin turned a shade of red. When he was done, he slammed the folder on the table, and one of his hands flew up to his forehead as his head pounded.

Saul Shet had been a broadcasting pioneer and had taken David under his wing when he first graduated from college. Over time Saul trusted him with more and more and taught David everything he should know about business and the world of broadcasting.

Bo was Saul's son, but he never had any interest in learning. He couldn't understand his father's interest in the young black man from Louisiana. David never let his skin color deter him from reaching his goals. When David got enough money to start acquiring newspapers, he left his position with Saul, and they became competitors.

David never disrespected Saul and would back away from a deal if it meant doing something that would make Saul look bad. When Saul's gambling habits became overwhelming, and he was on the brink of losing it all to creditors, Saul got word to David.

They arranged a secret meeting, and David walked out of it the owner of one of the largest media conglomerates in the Southern region of the United States. That was the beginning of David's rise to the top. After that acquisition, people started calling him King David. He gained respect from many in the business world, not only nationally, but abroad.

Shortly after David took the reins of Saul's company, Saul's two-seater plane crashed, with Saul at the controls. Many believed he crashed the plane on purpose. Bo accused David of stealing Saul's company and sending him into a deep depression, which resulted in him crashing his plane.

David had ignored Bo, but now he realized that maybe he had underestimated him. Bo needed to be dealt with. Although he was Saul's child, David would have to deal with him like he did the rest of his competitors: cut them off at the knees and let them fend for themselves.

David's personal cell phone rang, and he saw Sheba's number displayed on the screen. A smile swept across his face. "I'm surprised to hear from you," David said upon answering.

"It's me," Delilah said.

David was disappointed that it was Delilah, instead of Sheba. "How are you?"

"Doing fine. Wanted you to know that my sister has conflicting emotions. You must have put it on her."

"What we did is our business," David snapped.

"Excuse *me*. I thought you would want to know."

"Delilah, I appreciate it, but your sister has made it clear to me that she doesn't want to be bothered with me."

"Well, she doesn't know what she's saying. I think she likes you more than she's letting on."

David entertained the thought for a moment but then stopped. "Bathsheba has my number. If she wants to talk to me, she can call me anytime."

"You know Bathsheba's stubborn, so if you want her, you better put your game face on and make your move. You got Sheba to sleep with you, so everything else should be easy."

Was Delilah right? Did he really stand a chance with Sheba? What could he do to convince her to cut her ties with Uriah? David said, "I got a lot of stuff going on right now. I will have to call you back."

"Don't bother." Delilah disconnected their phone call.

Wade returned to the room. "Things are in motion. By this time tomorrow, he should be served papers."

"Bo, you think you're slick. Well, let me see you squirm your way out of this legal battle," David muttered.

Chapter 27

Sheba assisted Delilah with her suitcases and took them inside Delilah's house. "Sis, I'm going to miss you."

"Well, I could move back in with you if you want me to."

"I'm going to miss you, but every grown person that's not married should have their own space." Sheba laughed.

"Gotcha." Delilah hugged her.

Sheba's heart warmed. She was glad that she and Delilah were able to form a bond. "If you get scared or just want to talk, I'm here," Sheba assured her.

"Oh, you're not going to get rid of me that easy."

"I better go so I won't be late for work," Sheba said.

An hour later Sheba was sitting at the nurses' station. Annette slid in the chair next to Sheba. "Boo."

Sheba jumped. "Girl, don't be sneaking up on me like that."

"What's going on? You've been so busy with your sister lately that we haven't had a chance to really talk."

"It's all good. Delilah's back home now."

"Well, I heard they think they know who shot her."

"Really? I know a lot of her church members didn't like her, so I hope it wasn't one of them." Sheba looked around to make sure none of the other nurses could hear their conversation.

"This dude from the neighborhood named Luther supposedly. Something about some money she owed him."

"Wow. It's never that serious. I just dropped her off at home. Let me call and check on her." Sheba dialed Delilah's number while Annette looked on.

"Hey, li'l sis," Delilah said.

"Did you hear anything about them making an arrest?" Sheba asked.

"Yes. I was going to call you when I thought your shift ended. This joker I went out with once did it. According to the detective, his trifling behind shot me because, he claimed, I owed him some money."

"Well, do you?" Sheba asked.

"No, I don't owe him nothing but a good butt whupping for putting me out of commission for these last few months."

Delilah told Sheba about their one date and how he had insisted she pay $18.57 for her half of the meal. Sheba tried to refrain from laughing. Delilah was making it hard as she mimicked him as she described the parking lot scene in which he ran behind her car, trying to get her to fork over the money.

In between laughs, Sheba asked, "So how did they find out it was him? It's been three months since you were shot."

"That fool went around bragging about it. He had been drinking, and one of the people he told needed the money from Crime Stoppers, and they turned him in."

"Wow," was all Sheba could say. After a moment of silence, she added, "Sis, if you need anything, let me know."

"I'm good. Well, let me go check on my bathwater. I've missed my sunken tub."

When Sheba got off the phone, she filled Annette in on what Delilah had told her. Annette seemed fidgety. Sheba knew she couldn't wait to leave so she could go spread the gossip to anyone else who would listen.

The light flashed on the switchboard. All the LPNs were busy seeing about patients. Sheba grabbed her nurse's gear and headed to the patient's room. After making sure her patient was fine, she headed back to the nurses' station to sit back down.

"Oh my goodness," she said as she felt herself get dizzy. She leaned on the wall until she could gather her bearings.

"Are you okay?" a passing coworker asked.

"Yes, I'm fine. I need to eat something. I think I'm going to take my break early. Can you handle things around here?"

"Sure. I'll call you if we need you."

Sheba went to the cafeteria and grabbed a salad and juice. Her stomach was a little queasy, so she didn't want anything heavy. She still felt a little dizzy even after eating the salad. She ran into Annette on her way back to her station.

"Girl, you look bad. You must be coming down with something," Annette said.

"I hope not. I hate being sick." Sheba grabbed her stomach. "Excuse me, Annette. I need to find a bathroom."

Instead of getting on the elevator, Sheba rushed to the nearest restroom and found an open stall. She released the food she had just eaten into the toilet. Sheba felt like her insides were being torn out.

Annette handed her a wet paper towel to wipe her face and mouth. Sheba wasn't aware that Annette had followed her into the restroom. "Dear, I hate to tell you this, but you might not be coming down with anything, after all."

"It must be food poisoning," Sheba said.

"When was the last time you had a period?" Annette asked.

Sheba looked dumbfounded. "I just had one." Then again, she hadn't had one in over six weeks. "I can't be," she said out loud.

"You're in a hospital. You might want to confirm whether or not you're pregnant." Annette left her alone in the restroom to ponder that.

When Sheba said she couldn't be pregnant, she'd meant it. Uriah had been gone too long for her to be pregnant, and she'd had her menstrual cycle since he'd been gone. It had been six weeks since she slept with David, which meant that if she was pregnant, David King was definitely the baby's daddy. This could not be happening. How would she explain a baby to Uriah? He would never forgive her. She couldn't lose Uriah because of one slipup. Why did this have to happen? Why did she behave so foolishly? Neither she nor David had brought up contraceptives.

"Lord, what am I going to do?" she yelled.

Chapter 28

"We need to talk," were the words in the text message David received from Sheba's number.

He was in the middle of a huge merger and really didn't have time for unnecessary drama. She had made it clear she didn't want a repeat of their night together, so he had respected that and had left her alone. Had he forgotten Sheba and moved on to be with another woman? No. He'd poured all of his energy back into his business. Trying to keep the vultures like Bo at bay had been a full-time job on top of his other responsibilities.

When an hour had passed and he hadn't returned Sheba's text, David received a phone call. He answered on the third ring. "Sheba, let me call you back when I get out of this meeting."

"Please do. It's urgent," Sheba insisted before ending the call.

From that point on, David found it hard to concentrate. It seemed like everything was moving in slow motion. Each speaker went on and on about their point. Some of the questions asked needed to be asked, but David wanted things to hurry along so he could find out what was so urgent with Sheba.

Four hours later David walked out of the meeting and into the back of his waiting limousine. He called Sheba.

"It's about time," she said.

"I've been in meetings all day. How are you?" David asked as he poured himself a cold drink.

"Not good. Not good at all. How soon can you get to Shreveport? There's something I need to talk to you about, but I need to do it in person."

"Well, I'm in Los Angeles now."

"Dang. Well, I guess I better go ahead and tell you. Are you sitting down?"

"Uh. Yes."

"I'm pregnant."

"Congratulations. I think." David paused.

"Duh. Did you hear me? I said I was pregnant," Sheba shouted from the other end.

"I'm happy for you and Uriah. He'll make a good daddy."

"For someone with all those degrees and all that money, you sure are dumb. The baby's not Uriah's. It's yours."

David laughed. "Where are the cameras? I know this is a joke, right?"

"I wish. I'm late. My hormones have me going crazy, and this baby is making me sick to my stomach. Without a doubt, it's yours."

David rubbed the top of his head. "What are we going to do?"

"That's why I'm calling you. You helped me make it, so you're going to help me figure out what I need to do."

"I don't believe in abortions," David said.

"Neither do I." Sheba started crying.

David hated when women cried. He felt helpless not being able to be there to comfort her. "Sheba, calm down. It's going to be okay. We'll figure something out together. Just stop crying."

"Uriah's going to hate me. He's the only man I've loved, and he's going to hate me."

Hearing Sheba say how much she loved Uriah stung. David had to do something to fix it. He had got them into the mess by seducing her. If only he had thought to use contraception, they wouldn't be in this situation. What was he thinking? The only thing that could have saved them both was not sleeping together.

David ended the call with Sheba and called Nathan. "Man, I've messed up. You tried to warn me, but I've really messed up this time."

"What's going on?"

David told him about Sheba's pregnancy. "Go ahead and tell me, 'I told you so.'"

"I don't have much to say," Nathan responded. Even Nathan was speechless.

"What am I going to do?" David asked.

"David, I'm afraid this is out of my hands. You'll have to take this one directly to the Lord."

David ended his call with Nathan. He put his head in his hands. David had to think of something and fast. He'd forgotten to ask Sheba how many weeks along she was. His business cell phone rang. "Just the man I wanted to avoid," David said out loud before answering. "Hi, Uriah," he said after clicking the green on button.

Uriah said, "I thought you would be happy to know that stage one has been completed. We'll be ready to start implementing stage two in about two weeks."

"Two weeks," David repeated.

"Yes, Mr. King. In two weeks we can bring in the other set of contractors."

A lightbulb went off in David's head. "Great. Why don't you take the next two weeks off and come home? No need to make reservations. I'm sending the company jet to pick you up. Be ready to leave at eighteen hundred hours."

Problem solved. Uriah would be coming home. It would be up to Sheba to take care of the rest.

If she wanted to pass the child off as Uriah's, this would be her perfect opportunity to seduce him and get him to sleep with her.

Chapter 29

Sleep failed to come for Sheba as she tossed and turned, thinking about the predicament she found herself in. The phone ringing was a welcomed distraction from her restlessness.

David's voice rang out from the other end. "I sent one of our corporate jets to pick up Uriah."

"So my husband's coming home? Thank you." Sheba sat up in the bed.

"He's going to be here for only two weeks, so I need you to make sure you perform your wifely duties. That way he will never suspect the child you're carrying is not his."

"Oh, just get him here. I don't need instructions from you on how to take care of my husband," Sheba responded quickly.

"A part of me wishes Uriah knew you were carrying my child. I don't want my child growing up not knowing his father," David said.

"Uriah will make a great father. The child will not go unloved."

"He's a good man, and he doesn't deserve this. That's the only reason why I'm trying to make things right."

"Uriah is a good man, and it's your fault we're in this predicament," Sheba said.

"It's nobody's fault. We shouldn't have been so careless."

"There is no *we*. If you had just left me alone, but no. You had to have me. Now look at us." Sheba was wide awake. Talking to David troubled her.

David attempted to calm her down. "Sheba, I know things don't look good right now, but trust me. Just get Uriah to sleep with you while he's here, and he'll think the baby is his."

"When the baby comes early, what am I supposed to do then?"

"Babies come early all the time. No big deal," David responded.

Sheba was a nurse, and she could pull it off. David was right. If she could get Uriah to sleep with her, then her entire dilemma would be solved. Since she knew her husband found her irresistible, and she didn't want her marriage to end over the mistake that she'd made, she would do whatever it was she had to do to get him to sleep with her.

"When is he supposed to be here?"

"It'll be tomorrow sometime."

"Thank you, David. Thank you for bringing my husband home."

"Anything for you," he replied before disconnecting the call.

Late the following morning, Sheba was awaken by Uriah shouting, "Honey, I'm home." She rubbed her eyes a few times, because she thought she was dreaming. David had told her Uriah would be coming home, but could she trust him? The man standing in front of the bed was her husband. David hadn't lied.

"Uriah, don't wake me up if I'm dreaming," Sheba said sleepily.

Uriah rushed to the bed and swept her up in his arms. "It's me. In the flesh."

"Baby, I've missed you," Sheba said as they kissed each other and embraced each other. Tears ran down Sheba's face. She was thrilled to see Uriah. She loved him more than life itself. If only she hadn't slipped and slept with David, her world would be perfect.

"I missed you, too. Look what Papa brought you." Uriah got up, picked up one of many bags, placed it on the bed, and opened it.

Sheba removed the pretty silk cloth. "This is beautiful, but what am I supposed to do with it?"

"Find a seamstress and get a blouse or something made with it."

"Thanks. I think," Sheba said.

Uriah picked up some more bags and placed them on the bed. "Well, I wasn't sure how you would react to the cloth, so I bought you a few more items."

Sheba's eyes lit up even more. She removed custom-made jewelry and a few designer purses from the bags. "Baby, I love them. I love them all."

She hugged him again, and Uriah welcomed her hugs and kisses. "I knew you would."

Sheba, still snuggled up to him, said, "Believe me when I say this. I love the fact that you bought me all these things, but what happened to my husband?"

He pulled back and looked at her. "What do you mean?"

"I'm just surprised you bought me all this stuff."

"You're my queen, and you deserve it. You've put up with me being gone all these months. Besides, you're right. I'm making good money, so why shouldn't I splurge a little?"

"Thank you, baby. I love it all. Now I feel bad about the purchases I made last week."

"Don't worry about it. There's enough money in the checking account to cover whatever you spent."

Sheba couldn't believe what she was hearing. This was not Mr. Thrifty, not coupon-cutting, don't-spend-any-more-money Uriah. Did a spaceship come and kidnap her cheap husband and replace him?

Sheba pushed the bags out of the way and positioned herself on Uriah's lap. She kissed him passionately, hoping they could get reacquainted with one another's body. "I've missed you in more ways than one," Sheba said.

Uriah pulled away. "Baby, I need to take a long hot bath. Can you run me some bathwater?"

Sheba didn't want to stop. "That can wait. I want you now."

"I haven't bathed since yesterday. I'll just feel better if I take a bath."

Sheba got up. "Fine. I'll run you some bathwater, but when you get out, be prepared to put in some overtime."

Sheba went into the master bathroom, ran some hot water in the tub, and added a men's bath product, Twilight Woods, which she'd purchased at Bath & Body Works. He always liked to soak in it. Once the water was just right, she yelled out to Uriah to come in.

She admired his body as he removed his clothes. She couldn't wait to feel her husband again. "Baby, if you don't hurry up, you will have to skip the bath," she said.

"Give me thirty minutes, and I'll be good," Uriah assured her.

Sheba left Uriah alone in the bathroom.

While he was bathing, her phone rang. "Delilah, this is not a good time. Uriah just got home, and I'm waiting on him to come out of the bathroom now."

"I didn't know he was coming home. I thought he was supposed to be over there a few more months."

"It was a surprise. So, sis, I got to go." Sheba hung up the phone.

Uriah walked out of the bathroom, drying off. "Who was that?"

"Delilah," she responded.

"Oh. Well, I'm tired. I've been on a long plane ride. Wake me up before you go to work." He got in the bed, turned his back to Sheba, and pulled the covers over his head.

Sheba couldn't believe he had been gone for months and hadn't touched her yet. It was absurd. She didn't know if she should be sad or angry. She felt conflicting emotions. She wanted her husband, and he had just turned his back on her. Did he find out about David? No, he couldn't know. Sheba cried herself to sleep because she couldn't bear the thought of losing her husband due to her mistake of sleeping with David.

Chapter 30

David answered his personal phone. He wasn't expecting to see Sheba's number. "Is everything okay? You didn't tell him, did you?" David asked.

"Of course not. Hear that." Sheba got silent.

"No. I don't hear anything."

"Well, he's sleeping. Uriah's snoring like a bull train."

"After a round with you, I can understand." David flashed back to the one night he had had with Sheba. He knew he shouldn't, but he still had feelings for her. He still wanted her.

"We haven't slept together. He went straight to sleep."

"Sheba, he just got home. Give the man some time. You have two weeks."

"Well, something needs to happen and quick. Hold on. My stomach's not cooperating with me."

Sheba hadn't disconnected the call, so David could hear her puking from the other end. He was glad he wasn't around to view it.

"I'm back," she said.

"Are you okay?"

"I'll be fine. Just need to get through the first trimester, and then I'll be fine."

"If you need anything, don't hesitate to let me know," David said.

Their call ended. David was feeling an attachment to the baby, and it hadn't been born yet. How could he allow another man to raise his own flesh and blood? He thought about his kids with his ex-wives. David hadn't spent much time with his kids since divorcing their mothers. He had vowed that when he had the next child, he would play a more active role in his or her life. Uriah would be known as his child's father. This child wouldn't know David as his father. David wasn't too sure he could live with that.

David didn't get much work done over the next few days. He couldn't stop thinking about Sheba and Uriah. He wondered what they were doing. He found himself getting upset at the thought of Uriah touching Sheba. He had no right to feel that way. Sheba was not his, but it still didn't stop him from feeling like she was.

One afternoon David dialed Delilah's number.

"So how's life treating you?" she asked.

"Missing your sister."

"Me too. Since my brother-in-law's been back, she hasn't had time for me."

"It's only been a few days. Give them time."

"I don't know why he doesn't like me. He doesn't even know me."

"Why don't you go over and try to get to know him while he's here? I know your sister will probably love to see you," David said.

"You know what? You're right. We're family, so I'm going to get dressed and go over there right now."

"And can you do me a favor and let me know how they are doing?" David asked.

Delilah laughed. "Is there something else you want to tell me?"

"No, nothing at all. Just checking on my employee." David didn't want to reveal more to Delilah than necessary.

"Something's going on, and I'm going to find out," Delilah said.

"Call me back and let me know how they are doing, okay?"

"Fine, but if I find out you're keeping secrets, you and I will need to talk."

David disconnected their call without responding to Delilah's accusations. Delilah didn't need to know about Sheba's pregnancy, not yet, anyway.

Nathan called. David didn't answer. Ever since David had confided in Nathan that Sheba was pregnant, things had been strained between the two. Not because of Nathan, but because David didn't want to feel condemned. He knew he was the cause of the problem, but he would not take 100 percent of the blame. What Nathan and even Sheba had failed to acknowledge was that Sheba could have told him no at any point, but she didn't. She participated and gave herself to him willingly. He did not force her to. She was just as responsible for what happened as he was. He was tired of being the fall guy, and he would no longer be the fall guy.

David called Sheba. She didn't answer but returned his call a few minutes later. She said, "You can't call me like this. What if Uriah had answered my phone?" Her voice sounded tense.

"I would have told him I was trying to reach him. I got everything covered."

"Well, be careful."

"So how are you two lovebirds?" David asked.

"Although it's none of your business, we still haven't had sex."

"Say what? It's been a few days. What's going on over there?"

"You tell me. We had an argument about Delilah, and it's caused a rift between us. He claims he can't get it up because of the strain between us."

"Well, I suggest you kiss up and apologize and do whatever you need to do to get him to sleep with you, or you and I both are screwed."

"I'm trying, but he's not budging."

David remembered at that moment that he had sent Delilah over there. He had to stop her. He needed Uriah to forgive Sheba so they could sleep together. "Sheba, I've got an important call to make. If you need something, call me."

He hung up with Sheba and called Delilah. Delilah didn't answer her phone as it rang and rang. "Pick up. Why aren't you answering your phone?" he yelled.

Trisha walked into his office. "Everything okay? I could hear you all the way outside," she said.

David replied, "It's okay. Look, I need to get to Shreveport. Call my pilot and tell him to meet me at the airport pronto."

While on the way to the airport, David attempted to reach Delilah. Each call was unsuccessful. Since Sheba couldn't handle getting her man in the bed, David would need to intervene.

Chapter 31

Sheba would have been happy to see Delilah outside her door if she and Uriah weren't having problems. Delilah was the source of their problems, so she opened the door but didn't invite her in.

Delilah said, "I want to see if I can make things right with my brother-in-law. We are family."

"I don't think this is a good time. Maybe later." Sheba stood with her hands on her hips.

"Sheba, you look a little flushed. He hasn't hit you, has he?" Delilah eyed Sheba curiously.

Sheba shook her head. "No, of course not. Uriah would never raise his hand at me."

"My legs are a little tired, so if you don't mind, I'll come in and sit down." Delilah walked closer to the door.

Sheba sighed. "Come on. Since you insist. Uriah's in the den. Might as well get this over with."

Delilah looped her arm through Sheba's arm. "Let me throw on my Baker girl charm. Uriah will come around in no time."

Sheba wasn't too sure about it. She plastered on a fake smile and led Delilah into the den. "Dear, look who's here."

Uriah looked up and then looked back down at the television without saying a word.

Not good, Sheba thought.

"Yuaruh, I'm glad you're home," Delilah said.

"It's Uriah," Sheba said, correcting her.

"I need to go to the restroom. I'll be right back," Delilah said.

Uriah still didn't say anything. He turned the volume up on the television. Sheba had to do something. She walked over to where Uriah sat and took the remote from him. She clicked the off button.

"I was watching that," he said.

"I've never known you to be rude before. So what's the deal?"

"I've heard about the problems she caused at that church, and I told you I don't want that woman in my house."

"That woman is my sister. Like I told you before, it's something you will have to deal with. She's family."

"Her being your family is still questionable. I don't have to deal with her. Now, hand me back the remote."

"Uriah, come on. She looks just like my mom. That's all the proof I need right there," Sheba responded.

"I don't trust her, and I don't have to like her."

Sheba sat down next to Uriah and started rubbing his leg. "She's not as bad as you think. Sure, she can be a little obnoxious, but beneath all of that, she's really a nice person."

Uriah looked in her eyes. She batted her eyelashes and pouted. "Okay, I'll try, but I can't make you any promises."

Sheba grabbed his head and planted kisses on his cheeks. "Thank you. That's why I love you so much."

Uriah laughed. "Don't get carried away just yet."

"So is it safe to enter?" Delilah asked.

Sheba responded, "Have a seat. I want my two favorite people to get to know each other better. While you two are doing that, I'll go put dinner on."

Sheba thought it was best to let them talk things out among themselves. Hopefully, by the time dinner was ready, they would have come to terms with their differences, and they could be one big happy family.

Laughter filled the room as Delilah entertained them over dinner. The doorbell rang.

"Were you expecting anyone?" Sheba asked Uriah.

"No, so let me go see who it is." Uriah got up from the table.

"So, little sis, you like how I worked that Baker girl charm on him?"

"For a minute, I was feeling a little jealous. I haven't gotten Uriah to laugh like that since he's been back." Sheba meant it, too. She could feel the green-eyed monster rearing its ugly head when she noticed how Uriah seemed to be entranced with every word that came out of Delilah's mouth. She and Uriah had yet to sleep together since he'd been back, and she was beginning to wonder if being pregnant had taken away her sex appeal.

Those doubts were erased when she looked up from her plate and into the eyes of David. David's eyes seemed to pierce right through her soul. The heat scorched her to the core. She unconsciously picked up her napkin and fanned herself.

"David, nice to see you again," Delilah said.

"Same here. Sheba, how are you?" David asked.

Sheba cleared her throat. "Fine. And you?"

This was the first time they had seen each other since the morning David dropped her off after their tryst. He seemed more buff than before. He wasn't in one of his stuffy suits. He was wearing a shirt that showed off his biceps and triceps. Sheba forgot that Uriah was in the room.

Uriah stepped from behind David and addressed Sheba. "Looks like you can set an extra plate. Mr. King, you came just in time."

"Uriah, we're off the clock now, so call me David."

Delilah patted the table next to her. "He can sit right next to me. Two good-looking men. Now this is the life."

"I'm sure David would rather eat at one of the five-star restaurants than eat my cooking," Sheba said as she cast her eyes downward. She hoped her eyes, filled with desire for David, wouldn't betray her.

David sat down next to Delilah. "I'm sure you're an excellent cook, so bring me a plate."

Sheba wanted to wipe the smirk off David's face. She had made amends with Uriah, and now here David was, throwing another monkey wrench into her seduction plans.

Sheba couldn't enjoy her meal. She spent the entire time watching David and Delilah. Delilah was flirting with David a little too much, in her opinion. She caught Uriah watching her, so she flashed him a smile. She went back to picking over her food.

Toward the end of the meal, she excused herself and went to the bathroom. She held her head over the commode, but nothing came out. It was a false alarm. She walked right into Uriah when she exited the bathroom.

"I decided to leave those two alone. I think I see a connection there," Uriah said.

Sheba wanted to say "I hope not," but instead she remained silent. She welcomed Uriah's embrace with open arms. She closed her eyes, with her mind on David and Delilah.

Chapter 32

David was enjoying the cat-and-mouse game he and Delilah were playing. Delilah was a beautiful woman, but she didn't have that special something that Sheba had. He chuckled to himself because it appeared that Sheba couldn't keep her eyes off of them. She needed to be careful, though, because she didn't want to raise any suspicions with Uriah.

David removed Delilah's hand from his. "You can stop with the act now. They're gone."

"Who said it was an act? I find you very attractive," Delilah replied.

David leaned back. "Most women do. It's hard to resist my charm."

"You're conceited, too, but I like that." Delilah smiled.

"I think you know that I have feelings for your sister, so anything between us would never work."

"Let me make you forget all about her." Delilah moved her chair closer to him.

David moved his chair farther away. "That's just trifling. Trying to hook up with your sister's baby daddy."

Delilah's mouth flew open. "Oh my goodness. She's pregnant."

David placed his hand over her mouth. "Shh. Keep it down. Yes, she's pregnant, but you don't have to broadcast it."

Delilah raised her hand and counted with her fingers. "Ooh. Wow. Wait until he finds out. He's going to kick your behind from here to Afghanistan."

"You need to chill out. He's not going to find out from me or from you."

"Y'all going to hell, and I don't want no part of it."

David eyed her curiously. "If that's not the pot calling the kettle black . . . all the dirt I've heard you've done."

"Rumors, David. Just rumors. But what you're saying is fact." Delilah pushed away from the table.

"Where are you going?" he asked.

"I'm going to find Sheba. She and I need to talk."

"Stay out of it, please. We're going to work this out."

Uriah stepped back in the room, with Sheba on his heels. Uriah said, "A lovers' spat already. Delilah, stop giving this man a hard time."

Delilah looked at David and then back at Uriah. "David will be all right. Won't you, David?"

David cleared his throat. "Uriah, why don't we go to the casinos and hang out? I would love to get a face-to-face report on what's going on overseas."

"Well, Sheba and I were about to—"

Sheba interrupted him. "Go with David. We can handle our business when you get back."

David and Uriah left, and about thirty minutes later, they pulled up in front of one of the city's casinos. They found a table near the bar, and David went to get their drinks. David noticed a woman all up in Uriah's face when he returned to the table.

"Dear, I don't think his wife would appreciate you pushing up on her man like that," he said.

"Whatever," the woman said as she rolled her eyes. She grabbed her drink and left their table.

"Thanks, man. I was trying to let her down nicely, but she wasn't taking the hints."

"When women are that aggressive, I've found the best approach is the direct approach," David said as he handed Uriah a drink.

"I haven't had any liquor in months," Uriah said. "I'm really not a drinker."

"You've earned it. So bottoms up." David held up his drink. What Uriah didn't know was that David's drink was straight cola. David rarely drank.

Uriah downed the bourbon and Coke. They played a few rounds at the roulette table. David made sure Uriah kept a drink in his hand for the next few hours. Satisfied that Uriah was good and drunk, David felt his mission had been accomplished. Now all he had to do was get Uriah safely back home to his adoring wife.

Uriah said, "I'm sorry. I normally can hold my liquor better than this." He staggered a little bit. "Sheba, can't see me like this. She'll freak out."

David had second thoughts. Maybe he should have Uriah sleep it off a little and then take him home. "Uriah, hold on. Let me get a room, and you can chill there before I drop you off at home."

"That sounds like a plan. 'Cause I really don't feel like hearing Sheba moan about me getting drunk."

David didn't want to hear her complain, either, but he sure would love to hear her moan. Moan out his name. David checked himself real quick. The hotel clerk recognized him and gave him the electronic keys to his usual suite.

Uriah leaned on him as they made their way to the room.

Once they were inside the room, David said, "Sit here and I'll get you a cold compress."

"Man, I'm fine." Uriah plopped down on the sofa.

David went to the bathroom and wet a hand towel. When he returned to the living room area, Uriah was laid out on his back with his mouth open, snoring.

"What in the world?" David said.

He walked up to Uriah and shook him. Uriah didn't budge. "Uriah, man, wake up."

Nothing.

Uriah was stiff as a board. David took the wet towel and placed it on Uriah's forehead. Uriah stirred, but he didn't wake up. A moment later he shifted his body and turned over, with his back now toward David. Uriah was out cold, and David's nudging didn't affect him at all.

David called Sheba. "Hate to tell you this, but Uriah won't be coming home tonight."

"What do you mean, he won't be coming home? What have you done to my husband?" Sheba screamed.

David moved the phone away from his ear. When he didn't hear Sheba's voice, he put the phone back up to his ear. "He sort of had a little too much to drink. We came up to my room for him to get himself together, and he passed out. I mean out cold. He won't wake up."

"That's why I don't like him drinking. He can't hold his liquor."

"Well, how was I supposed to know that? I'll bring him home as soon as he wakes up," David said.

"Whatever. Oh, and another thing, I don't appreciate you flirting with my sister."

"Are you jealous?" David asked.

Sheba hung up on him.

David laughed. *She's jealous. I know it.*

Chapter 33

"So it's just you and me for the night. We can have a sleepover," Delilah said.

Sheba hated that Delilah had overheard her conversation with David. "I'm fine by myself."

"I wasn't going to say anything, but I think you better decide what you're going to do about the baby you're carrying."

Sheba felt exposed. "What baby? What are you talking about?"

Delilah stood up and placed her hand over Sheba's stomach. "I can see a little pouch developing. You're pregnant, dear. And if I do the math, Uriah's not the daddy."

Sheba let the floodgates open. Delilah wrapped her arms around her and let her cry on her shoulder.

"What am I going to do? I can't have this baby unless Uriah's the father," Sheba said.

Delilah handed her a tissue from the box on the nearby table. "You're not going to be able to pull it off, so you need to come clean with Uriah. Do it while you still have a chance. Don't let him find out another way."

"He'll never forgive me. I need for him to think this baby's his."

"Sheba, how can you expect the Lord to bless you and this child if you keep living a life of dishonesty? Don't be like me. Be better."

Sheba pulled herself together. "I think you better go home."

"Tsk, tsk. You're treading on thin ice right now. This game you're playing with David is going to blow up in your face. I'm only looking out for you . . . for the baby."

Sheba rolled her eyes. "Delilah, I'm warning you. You need to mind your own business."

Delilah grabbed her purse. Before she left, she reached into her purse and handed Sheba some literature. "Looks like you'll have to learn things the hard way. This is the kind of woman I want to be and the kind of woman I thought you were," Delilah said.

Delilah left Sheba alone with her thoughts and the literature. Since she was far from sleepy, Sheba held on to the paper and read it as soon as she got back on the couch after seeing Delilah out. Tears streamed down Sheba's face as she read a familiar passage from Proverbs 31. She was far from being a virtuous woman. She had allowed lust and a bout of temporary insanity to cause her to break her wedding vows.

She held her head down in shame. She was an adulterous woman. She wondered if she would ever be able to redeem herself in the eyes of God. She rubbed her belly as she thought about the sin she'd committed. The little one growing inside her belly was the reminder of her one-night lapse of judgment.

She closed her eyes and prayed. "Lord, please forgive me. I know that I haven't been going to church like I should. That I haven't been praying like I should. But I'm so sorry. If you could get me through this, I promise you, Lord, that I will do better. Please don't let me lose my husband. Uriah's a good man. He doesn't deserve to get hurt. If he finds out about this, he's going to leave me. I don't know if I can live my life without him, Lord. Please, God. Please fix this situation."

By the time Sheba stopped praying, her face was covered by tear-stains. After praying, she curled up into a little ball and fell asleep on the couch. She remained there until the next morning, when she heard the front door open.

She yawned and stretched. "What happened to you?" she asked Uriah.

"Baby, I'll explain later. First, I need to take a shower." Uriah headed toward the master bedroom.

She didn't notice David until he spoke. "How's it going?"

"I've had better mornings," Sheba replied coldly.

"Your man is going to need peace and quiet for a few hours. He has a slight hangover."

If looks could kill, David would be dead. Sheba bore into him with her eyes. "I blame you, you know."

"He's a grown man. If he couldn't hang, he should have stopped drinking."

"He looks up to you and is always trying to impress you."

"I'm a likable guy. I wish you liked me," David said as he walked near her.

"Good. You're still here," Uriah said, startling them both.

David turned around to face him. "What's wrong?" David asked.

"I got a call from the satellite office. I need to get back there as soon as possible."

"Nooo," Sheba wailed. "You haven't been here a week yet. You told me you were going to be here for two weeks." She ran up to Uriah.

He looked at her. "I know, baby, but duty calls. I'm responsible for the satellite office, and with things not going well, I need to get back there pronto. They thought they could handle everything without me, but something's come up."

Sheba turned to face David. "Can't he handle the problem from here? Can you send somebody else?"

David looked at Sheba and then back at Uriah. "I'm afraid not, Sheba. He's been handling this phase, and if something's not going right, he's the one I trust to fix it."

"Fine. Then go." Sheba pouted.

A moment later she stormed out of the room, went to their bedroom, and lay across their bed. Ten minutes later Uriah entered. He lay across the bed, too, and placed his arm around her.

"I'm sorry, baby. I wish I didn't have to go."

Sheba cried and cried while Uriah held her tighter and tighter. She cried because she was going to miss Uriah. She cried harder when she realized that there was no way in the world she would be able to pass off her child as Uriah's unless they did it before he left. Sheba did her best to seduce Uriah, to entice him into having sex with her.

Uriah's body wouldn't cooperate. "Baby, it's the stress. You know I want to, don't you?"

"But I need to feel you inside of me," Sheba said, pouting.

"I can't make it do what it won't do," Uriah said as he got up and started packing some of his clothes.

While he packed, she watched. She refused to help him pack to leave her. The doorbell rang.

"That's probably David's driver. I'm not getting the door," she announced.

"Come on, Sheba. Don't be like this. Do you love me?" he asked.

"Yes, of course I do," she responded.

"Then let me see that big, pretty smile of yours before I go."

Sheba tried not to smile.

Uriah said, "Come on. Is it coming? There it goes."

Sheba smiled. She stood up and gave Uriah a tight hug. "I'm going to miss you."

"I'm going to miss you, too, baby." Uriah bent down and kissed her.

Their tongues tangoed. The doorbell rang again.

"I better go answer that," Uriah said.

Sheba didn't want to let him go.

When he returned to the room, he said, "That's the car service. Baby, these next few months will fly by. Just wait and watch."

Sheba walked with him to the door. He hugged and kissed her once more. She stood in the doorway until the car drove away.

She rubbed her belly. "That's who should have been your daddy."

Chapter 34

David wrestled with the guilt he had brought upon himself. Uriah was a good man. David thought of ways he could make it up to Uriah before drifting off to sleep. During the night, David's private line rang, jerking him out of his sound sleep.

Simon, with a shaky voice, said, "Uriah's been killed. He was on his way to meet some government officials to finalize the plans for the building and . . . well, he was killed."

"No!" David shouted. Then Simon could be heard sniffling from the other end of the phone.

David had felt guilty about sending Uriah on a mission he knew could possibly end his life. Now that Simon had broken the news of Uriah's death to him, David regretted ever sending Uriah to work in the Afghanistan office.

Simon asked, "Mr. King, are you okay? I've never heard you sound like this before."

"I wasn't expecting this. Uriah was a good man. Don't know why this happened," David rambled.

Simon said, "I tried to get him to wait until we could get more protection for him to go into the city, but he insisted on going today."

"Have you called his wife?" David asked.

"No. I didn't know how you wanted to handle it."

"Well, let me go. I need to tell her before she hears about it through other channels."

David called his pilot. Two hours later they were landing at the private airport in Shreveport. The starless sky made the night seem even gloomier than it already was. He eased out of the car after his driver parked in front of Uriah and Sheba's house. The walk up the stairs seemed to take forever. He knocked on the door. No answer.

He pulled out his cell phone and called Sheba's number. "Open up. I'm outside," he said when she answered.

A few minutes later, looking sleepy, she opened the door. She was wearing a satin robe, and he couldn't tell if she had anything on under it or not. With squinted eyes, Sheba said in a sleepy voice, "It's two o'clock in the morning. I know you can afford a hotel, so why are you here?"

"I need to talk to you," David said.

"Can't it wait until tomorrow, when I'm awake? I have a seven o'clock shift, you know."

David pushed his way past her and walked inside. "Close the door. Come sit. There's something I need to tell you."

Sheba grudgingly did as she was told. She sat down on the couch and crossed one of her legs under the other. "This better be good, or else you're going to be on my S list."

David didn't want to prolong telling her the news any longer. He grabbed her hand. She jerked it back. "Bathsheba, I hate to be the one to tell you this, but I thought it best that you heard it from me. Uriah went to meet some government officials, and while on the way there, the truck he was in was ambushed by some rebels."

Sheba started shaking. "How bad is he hurt?"

David bit his bottom lip. "I regret to have to tell you this, but Uriah didn't make it. He was killed during the ambush."

Sheba screamed, "Noooo!" right before passing out.

David tried not to panic. He patted her on the face. "Wake up, baby. It's going to be okay. Wake up."

Sheba slowly came to. "This is all my fault. He only went over there to make money so we could get a bigger house. If I hadn't been so demanding as a wife, he wouldn't have ever taken the job you offered him and he would still be alive."

David tried to think of a way to console her. "No, it's not your fault. You did nothing wrong. It's those rebels' fault. They are the ones who killed him."

Sheba wrapped her arms around herself and rocked back and forth. "I can't believe he's gone. Tell me this is all a bad dream."

"Sheba, I'm afraid it's not. Uriah's not coming back. He's gone."

"We didn't even have a chance to say good-bye. He's been busy ever since he got back there. We were supposed to talk tonight. I thought he was just busy when I didn't hear from him. I should have known when he didn't call me that something was wrong. Oh, Lord, help me please."

David reached out to Sheba, and instead of pushing him away, like he'd expected, she allowed him to comfort her. He rocked her in his arms and said a silent prayer. "Lord, forgive me."

Chapter 35

Sheba didn't remember getting in bed. The last thing she recalled was David rocking her back and forth after he told her the news of Uriah's death. She glanced at the clock, and it was after eight in the morning. She was supposed to be at work at seven. She was surprised no one had called her from work to see why she wasn't there yet. She reached for the phone and checked the caller ID, just in case she had been asleep and hadn't heard the phone ring, but there were no missed calls.

Her mind was in a million and one places. What would she do about Uriah? She had so many things to do. She had to find out where Uriah's body was. She had to notify his relatives. Some of those same relatives had never liked her, but they were his family, and they needed to know.

The first number she dialed was her job. Annette answered and immediately offered her condolences.

"David King called and told us what happened to Uriah. We are so sorry. Your supervisor said you can take off as much time as you need," Annette said over the phone. "And if there's anything you need me or anyone else to do, please call me, okay?"

"Okay," Sheba said as she went through the motions. She thought she could make the calls, but she couldn't. She needed help. Where was David? When did he make that phone call?

Her questions were answered when he appeared in the doorway of her bedroom. "You were sleeping good, so I didn't want to disturb you."

She listened to David as he told her what had happened. He had carried her in the bedroom and laid her down on the bed after she had cried herself to sleep on the couch. Looking at David now reminded her of the sin she had committed against her husband.

"Thanks for calling my job. I have so many other calls to make. I really just feel like crawling back in the bed and dying myself."

David looked sad. "Don't say that. I called Delilah, and she's on her way."

"You did? Thank you. I really don't want to be alone right now."

"You'll never have to be alone. I'm here."

Delilah rushed through the unlocked front door and into Sheba's bedroom. "And your big sister's here." Delilah hugged her, and Sheba found herself crying again. She thought all the tears had dried up, but they hadn't, and she wet Delilah's shoulder with the hurt and the pain she was feeling. Delilah patted her on the back. "Let it out. Don't hold it in."

"We never got a chance to hold each other again. I miss him already," Sheba said.

Delilah held Sheba. "David, I know this may be asking too much, but can you help with the funeral plans? I don't think Sheba's up to it."

"I'm fine. He was my husband, and that's the least I can do. This will be the final thing I do for him, so I have to." Sheba sat up and dried her eyes with the back of her hand.

Delilah placed her hand on top of hers. "You don't have to do this alone. You have me."

"And you have me. Working together, we'll make sure Uriah has a good home-going service," David said.

Sheba wanted to handle everything on her own but knew she didn't have the strength. She welcomed their help. One thing she would do on her own was pick out the suit and the casket. No one would have a say in that.

She looked at David. "I need for you to find out when I should expect to get Uriah's body."

"Sheba, I'm not sure."

"David, please. That's all I'm asking you to do now."

David pulled out his phone. "I'll do what I can."

She got up and retrieved a gold-looking day planner. She handed it to Delilah. "I need for you to call people and tell them that Uriah's gone. Can you do that for me? Tell them I'll get word to them about when the funeral will be."

"I got this. Why don't you take a long hot bath and try to relax a little?"

Sheba's whole body seemed to shake. "It'll be a while before I can relax. Believe that."

Delilah put the day planner down, grabbed Sheba by the hand, and gently led her toward the bathroom. "Come on. You sit, and I'll run the water," she said once they reached the bathroom. Sheba sat there with her legs curled under her as Delilah ran some bathwater.

"I love Moonlight Path," Delilah said as she poured in the liquid bubble bath. She put her finger in the water. "Ooh, now that's just right."

After Delilah left the bathroom, Sheba stripped naked and dipped her body in the hot water. Every muscle in her body seemed to need the feel of the water as the tension released itself. Sheba leaned back in the tub and shut her eyes. She wished what she was feeling would go away, but she knew it wouldn't. The guilt on top of grieving was not healthy for her. She wished she wasn't pregnant, because she wanted to drown out her feelings with liquor. Instead, she was alert and sober and was left to deal with the pain head-on.

Chapter 36

David's only task right now was to deliver Uriah's body to Shreveport. He was having a hard time getting to the right person. He yelled at Wade. "Get Uriah's body here, or someone will be looking for another job."

"Yes, Mr. King," Wade said.

Thirty minutes later David received a call informing him that what remained of Uriah would be shipped to the air force base in Bossier City the following day. Once he got that taken care of, he went into the living room.

"Where's Sheba?" he asked Delilah, who was sitting on the couch alone.

"She's taking a bath," Delilah informed him.

"Do you think she's going to be okay?" he asked as he sat in a chair across from the couch.

"She's going to need folks who care about her to help her."

"I'm here. I will not let her go through this by herself," David said.

"David, let me be honest with you. I think you're the last person who should be here. I mean, if it wasn't for you, her husband would be safe and sound. He would be here."

David knew there was some truth in Delilah's words, but he felt enough guilt. He didn't need someone else accusing him. Delilah seemed to see right through him. She talked as if she knew he had set Uriah up to go speak with the government officials.

Sheba entered the room, looking fresh. Her hair was up in a bun, and she was wearing a jogging suit. Her face was without makeup. David couldn't recall a time when he had seen her without makeup. She didn't need any. She had a natural beauty. Being pregnant with his child made her skin glow. He wanted to reach out to her but knew that now was not the time to do so.

"Sheba, your husband's body will be flown to the air force base tomorrow. I have to take care of some things in Dallas, but I will be back tomorrow, before his body arrives."

Sheba hugged him and said, "Thank you, David. Thank you for everything. Thank you for getting my husband back to me."

David squeezed her before leaving the room and walking out her front door. Guilt weighed him down as he got in the back of the waiting car. He hoped Sheba never found out the truth about him purposely sending Uriah to set up his Afghanistan's office when he could have easily sent someone in Uriah's place. This was a secret he planned on taking to his grave.

When David got back to the office in Dallas, it was in disarray at the news of what had happened to Uriah. He was the first casualty the company had experienced at any of its foreign locations. Uriah's death also made the national news.

Trisha said, "Nathan's waiting for you in your office."

David turned to walk in another direction. Nathan came out of his office at that moment.

"David, there you are. I came to check up on you."

Not wanting Trisha in his business more than she had to be, David turned back around and followed Nathan into his office. He closed the door. "Have a seat," David said. Nathan sat. David went and sat behind his desk.

Nathan said, "I've been waiting to hear from you, but when I didn't, I thought I would just drop in. You haven't been returning my phone calls."

"Well, as you know, I've been busy. I have reporters and a grieving widow to deal with." David nervously tapped a pen against his desk.

"I have a question for you." Nathan had a serious look on his face.

"Man, now's not the time." David's forehead wrinkled.

"Please. Answer this question, and I won't bother you anymore."

David twisted his neck from left to right. "I'm listening."

"What would you do if one of your employees, who you've paid a nice salary to, purposely stole from one of his or her poor relatives?"

"If I found out about it, he would be fired and, I would hope, prosecuted for being a thief."

"My beloved friend, the Lord has placed this on my heart to tell you, but, David, you are that man. God has given you an empire. You are the CEO of one of the largest media conglomerates in the world. Women flock to you, beautiful single women, and yet you had your eyes on one woman. Another man's wife. God showed me in a vision what happened to Uriah. I saw it before I heard about it on the news. You didn't bomb his truck, but you might as well have. David, you killed Uriah, and God is not pleased with you."

David's head wanted to explode. He felt naked and ashamed in front of the Lord and in front of Nathan. His head dropped into his hands. "God is going to punish me. What have I done? I'm going to lose it all."

"God is a God of grace and mercy. Repent now, my friend," Nathan pleaded.

Nathan left David alone with his thoughts. Once alone, David cried out to the Lord. "Oh, my Lord, my soul is in despair. I have sinned against thee and have broken several of your commandments. Have mercy on me, my Lord. I've been disobedient. I humbly bow down before you and ask that you please let your wrath pass me by. "

David prayed until sweat dripped from his forehead.

Chapter 37

"I don't know if I can do this," Sheba said as Delilah helped her get dressed the day of Uriah's funeral.

"You can and you will," Delilah said as she buttoned up Sheba's black dress.

"What if I can't cry? People will be talking about that."

"Baby girl, don't worry about 'people.' You grieve in your own way. If you feel like crying, cry. If you feel like laughing, laugh. Do you, and don't worry about everybody else."

Sheba looked at herself in the mirror. She was dressed in a new knee-length black dress. She slipped on the silver sling-back slippers with three-inch heels. She debated about whether or not to wear a hat. She opted not to, and her hairdresser wrapped her long hair up in a bun. She grabbed her huge black shades and followed Delilah into the living room.

A knock was heard at the door.

Delilah said, "That's probably the driver. You got everything?"

Sheba looked around. She inhaled one deep breath and then exhaled. "Ready."

The ride over to the church was solemn. Delilah had been her backbone these past few days by being by her side, filtering calls, and being the loving sister she had always wished she had.

Sheba knew Uriah had known a lot of people, but she wasn't expecting this many people. There was not an empty space in the church's parking lot. She thought that since a lot of people came to show their respects at the wake the night before, there wouldn't be a large crowd at the church today. She was wrong.

The cameras flashed as she and Delilah exited the limousine. Some of the local news media, along with the station that Uriah had overseen, had cameramen filming. Delilah tried to shield Sheba as they walked toward the front of the church and followed the preacher's instructions.

"Ma'am, we're going have to ask you to get behind the family," one of the funeral home attendants said to Delilah.

"I am family. I'm her sister," Delilah responded.

"Oh, I'm sorry. Someone told me that you weren't a part of this family," the funeral home attendant said.

"I don't know who could have told you that, but Bathsheba's my sister, and I'm staying with her." Delilah's temper flared.

The attendant backed away. Sheba heard murmurings but didn't care. Delilah was more welcome there than some of Uriah's family. Some of the people who stood in the funeral processional line neither she nor Uriah had seen in years.

The pastor of the church started reciting scriptures. Sheba tuned out everything around her. She held her head up high and followed behind the preachers. Thankfully, Delilah was on her right side, holding her up, because her legs were beginning to feel like jelly.

The closer they got to the front, the more Sheba wanted to run the other way. Fortunately, the bomb hadn't blown up the top half of Uriah's body. That was still intact. She stopped in front of his casket. The tears she had been holding in all morning streamed down her face. She leaned down and kissed him on the lips one last time. "I love you, baby. I'll always be your pumpkin." She removed the necklace he had given her with the half heart pendant and placed it in his hands.

She could hear people whispering, but this was her moment with her husband, so she didn't care. She kissed her fingers and placed them on his lips one last time before taking her seat.

Her head hung low as she waited for the rest of his family to be seated. She was handed a funeral program. She looked at the picture of Uriah on the front. It reminded her of happier times. Of when they didn't have a care in the world. She had two regrets in her life. One was that she cheated on him, and the second one was that they would never have a child together.

About midway through the service, Sheba felt the funeral was getting to be too long. She sat impatiently, waiting for the sermon to be over. People were laughing, but she couldn't find anything humorous in what the pastor had said. She knew Uriah was in a better place, but he had left her alone. Alone to deal with the world. Alone to deal with raising a child that should have been his.

"Do you want the casket opened up again?" the funeral home director asked her.

Sheba shook her head.

Delilah answered for her. "No. If they didn't get a chance to see him yesterday or before the service, too bad."

Sheba had been doing well, but now she found herself crying uncontrollably. As the funeral home director and the attendants got ready to roll the body down the aisle, Sheba and Delilah stood up to walk behind them. Sheba's feet were planted in one spot. She rocked back and forth and said, "My baby. There goes my baby."

Delilah wrapped her arms around Sheba's waist and tried to get her to walk, but she wouldn't move. David approached them and assisted Delilah with Sheba. Sheba fainted, and she would have hit the floor if David hadn't caught her in his arms. When she woke up, she was in the back of the limousine. David was on one side of her and Delilah on the other.

"Tell me I didn't miss the burial." Sheba felt her heart drop again.

Delilah said, "No. We're on our way there now."

Sheba was relieved. "David, thanks for catching me back there."

"Yes, sis, you almost hit the floor. Now, that would have been a sight," Delilah said, trying to lighten up the situation.

Sheba laughed a little. "Delilah, thank you for helping me this week. Lord knows I wouldn't have been able to get through this week without you."

Delilah winked her eye. "That's what older sisters are for."

After Uriah's casket was lowered into the ground, Sheba remained seated for a while. People walked up to her to offer their condolences. Then David walked up to her, and standing next to him was a man almost as handsome as he was.

"Ladies, I want you to meet my best friend, Reverend Nathan McDaniel."

Sheba shook Nathan's hand.

Then Delilah shook Nathan's hand and said to David, "Your best friend is a preacher, and you're like you are." Delilah looked at Nathan. "I bet you use up a whole bottle of holy water on him."

Nathan laughed. "Well, dear, I can tell I might have to sprinkle a few drops on you, too."

David said, "He just calls it likes he sees it."

Delilah rolled her eyes.

Sheba, tired of the display, stood up. "I'm ready to go home."

"The repast is back at the church's fellowship hall," Delilah said.

"Y'all can go. I think I just want to go home," Sheba sighed.

Joyce, one of Uriah's cousins, walked up to her at that moment and said, "That looks like a baby bump. Are you pregnant?"

"Joyce, now is not the time for this," Sheba said as she turned and walked toward the limousine.

Joyce shouted, "Don't walk away from me."

Sheba threw her hand up in the air and waved and got inside the limousine. The tears flowing down her face were not only from the grief of losing her husband, but also for her and David's betrayal.

Chapter 38

"Being at that funeral was one of the hardest things I've had to do in a while," David confessed to Nathan over lunch the following week.

"You're going to have harder days than that unless you did what I told you to do. Did you repent? Did you go to God and ask him to forgive you for the things you've done?"

David stopped eating. "Yes, but he's been whipping me. I haven't had a good night of sleep since I sent Simon that e-mail about having Uriah handle the issues with the government officials there."

David just realized that it was the first time he'd confessed what he had done to anyone. The only other person who knew was Simon, and Simon treasured his job too much to mention to anyone that sending Uriah to meet with the officials had been David's idea. David waited for Nathan to berate him again.

"The Lord is not through with you, David. Don't think that because He's punishing you that He has taken His hand off your life. You're still His child, and He will never leave you or forsake you."

It was reassuring to know that God was still in his midst, although lately David hadn't felt His presence.

They were riding in the back of David's limousine after lunch when Nathan asked, "What are you going to do about Sheba?"

"I really don't know. I've been giving her time to grieve, but she's having my child, and I want her and the baby to move in with me."

"But do you think that's wise?" Nathan asked.

"I've made so many bad decisions as of late, but I think asking Sheba to move here so I can take care of her and the baby is the right thing to do. I am the father."

Nathan didn't voice his agreement or disagreement. He allowed David to make his own decision. "Be prepared for the aftermath."

"I'm used to people talking," David said.

"Up until now, the media has portrayed you in a positive light. Know that this move may change the public's opinion about you."

"I don't allow the public to dictate my moves. I'm David King. Only God can dictate my moves."

Nathan said, "Don't say I didn't warn you."

The limousine dropped Nathan off at his house. David waited until Nathan was gone and then dialed Sheba's number.

"How are you doing?" he asked.

"Better, but not good at all," she responded.

To David, Sheba sounded really depressed. He wished he could make her feel better. Contrary to what Nathan and Delilah thought, he really did care about Sheba. He wanted the best for her. Right now, with Uriah gone, David felt he was the best.

"Why don't you pack a bag? I'll have a driver come pick you up, and my pilots will fly you into Dallas."

"David, you can't be doing that. What are people going to think?"

"Does it matter? You're having my baby, and I just want to make sure my baby's mama is relaxed."

"Well, I didn't want to say anything, but I went to the doctor today and he put me on bed rest. I'm off work until I have the baby."

David and Sheba went back and forth in a friendly banter of conversation. David tried his best to convince her to come to Dallas for the rest of her pregnancy. "Delilah can watch your house. I'm pretty sure if you ask her, she'll do it for you."

"Delilah has been great. I'm going to miss her if I move out there," Sheba said.

"She's welcome to come out here anytime she wants. My house is big enough for the three of us."

"As crazy as it sounds, I'm thinking about taking you up on your offer. Let me think about it and get back with you."

"You got my number," David said. He had to handle the situation with her delicately because he was close to getting her to move in with him. If he could get her to Dallas, he knew she would succumb to her feelings for him.

He could tell she liked him more than she let on. He recalled the night he and Delilah flirted with one another. She had the look of a jealous woman, and if she was jealous, that meant she had some feelings for him.

He didn't have to wait long for her to respond. A few days later Sheba called him back. She said, "Delilah's agreed to watch my house, so if you, not your driver, can come and get me this weekend, I'll come back to Dallas with you."

"You drive a hard bargain, but I will be there. Can I ask what helped you make up your mind?"

Sheba responded, "Joyce has been telling everyone I'm pregnant and that there's no way that Uriah is the father."

"How did she find out?" David asked.

"She's just speculating. As you know, she approached me at the grave site, but I ignored her. I guess that pissed her off, so she's been gossiping about me ever since to anyone who will listen."

David could hear the tension in Sheba's voice. "Getting upset isn't good for the baby."

"I know. That's why I need to get away. I can't stand to be around Uriah's family right now."

"Where's Delilah?"

"She's been screening the calls, because if one more person calls me with some mess, I swear I'm going to snap."

"Calm down, Sheba. Breathe in and out." David could hear Sheba doing as he instructed. "Better?" he asked.

"I will be. Let me take care of some business here, and you'll see me soon."

David was glad that Sheba was coming, but hated that she had to endure ridicule from Uriah's family. He hoped the stress wouldn't affect her or the baby much. He would make sure when she arrived in Dallas that she was well taken care of.

David was supposed to be going out of town during the weekend, but he would juggle whatever he had to because he was bringing his woman home. Well, she wasn't officially his woman yet, but she would soon be. He had to convince her that he was all she needed. Her and their baby would be one big happy family.

David could control a lot of things, but time wasn't one of them. The week seemed to drag by. He was up bright and early Saturday morning. For one, he still wasn't sleeping well, and two, he was anxious about his soon-to-be houseguest.

He gave his maid strict instructions on how he wanted Sheba's room. He had noticed she liked peach and had painted her bathroom that color, so he had an interior decorator come in and redecorate one of the rooms across from his bedroom in peach. His ultimate plan was to have her move in the master bedroom with him, but until then, he wanted her room to be her personal sanctuary.

He was glad he did redecorate, because ten hours later, when he arrived back at the house with Sheba, her eyes lit up when she saw her room.

"David, thank you. This is absolutely beautiful."

His butler placed her bags near the closet. "Mademoiselle, I'm not sure where you want your things. When you're ready to unpack, let me know and I will send Celia upstairs to help you unpack."

Sheba said, "No need to. You've done enough. I can handle it from here."

"But, mademoiselle, we've had strict instructions that you are not to lift a finger."

David said, "Bentley, I'll help her. Thank you. That'll be all for now."

"Yes, Mr. King." The butler turned and walked away.

"Wow. You really are living large. You're like the king of Dallas."

David laughed. "You can say that."

Having Sheba around had brightened up the lonely mansion already. David now had a queen for his castle.

Chapter 39

Sheba lounged around in bed. The door opening startled her. She had been at David's for two months, yet she still wasn't used to having someone available to her to help her do everything.

"Ms. Bathsheba, you have a guest downstairs. She says she's your sister," one of the maids said.

"Send her up please," Sheba said.

She hadn't told David that Delilah would be visiting, so she hoped he didn't mind. He did tell her prior to her moving to Dallas that she could have visitors. Besides, David had been out of town for the last few nights and their conversations over the phone had been brief. She slid out of the bed. Her hand automatically went to her belly. She had more than a pudge. It was obvious to anyone looking at her that she was pregnant.

Sheba went to the bathroom to freshen up. When she returned, Delilah was sitting in the long chaise near her window. They hugged and exchanged greetings.

"You're glowing," Delilah said as she pulled back from her to get a good look.

"Dallas air agrees with me."

Delilah looked around the room. "You were not lying when you said this place was like a mansion."

"David didn't spare any expense."

"To think he was living here all by himself. I knew he had bank. From now on, I'm calling him King David."

Sheba laughed. "His head is already big enough, so please don't call him that."

"Doing good, li'l sis. You're doing real good."

Sadness swept across Sheba's face. Delilah apparently noticed, because she said, "What's wrong?"

They each sat on the chaise.

Sheba said, "I feel bad about my pregnancy. I'm excited about this baby. David's been a sweetheart, and I'm enjoying his company."

Delilah placed her hand over the top of Sheba's. "Uriah's gone. There's no sense in you sitting around in Shreveport, moping, when you can be here and be treated like a queen."

"But I don't deserve all of this. I cheated on my husband, and I'm having another man's baby."

"A man who seems to adore you. Do you know how many women wish their baby's daddy would set them up like this? You're living the life of royalty, so, Sheba, stop complaining."

Sheba heard what Delilah said, but it still didn't make her feel comfortable to enjoy life after losing her husband only a few short months ago. "Things would be so much different if Uriah was alive."

Delilah reached her hand out and gently rubbed her belly. "You would have had to tell him about this little one. This may sound morbid, but at least he was spared the pain of knowing you were bearing another man's child."

Sheba could always count on Delilah to keep it real with her. "I think I'm cursed," Sheba admitted.

"Why do you say that?" Delilah asked.

"This pregnancy is wearing me out. I thought the morning sickness should have subsided by now, but it hasn't. It's like the baby is playing tug-of-war in my belly."

"What does the doctor say?" Delilah asked.

"He's confined me to bed rest, like the one in Shreveport did. I can't take too much more of it. I'm just having to bear with it. I look at it as my punishment, so I'm trying not to complain."

"Oh, Sheba, don't look at it like that. Having a child should be a joy. There are plenty of women who wish they could have children."

"I wish you were having this one," Sheba said.

"You don't mean that. Give it some time."

"Lord, forgive me. I love my baby. I really do. I just hate that Uriah's not the father."

"How's David been treating you?" Delilah asked.

"Like a queen. He's giving me my space, but he's attentive to my needs at the same time. I've actually gotten a chance to know him, and if the memory of Uriah didn't stand in the way, I could see myself falling in love with him."

Delilah placed her hand on top of Sheba's again. "I see me coming here was perfect timing. Let's look at your situation. If David wants to be more than just your baby daddy, give him a chance. Look around you. Do you really want to give up all of this?"

"I'm not into material things." Sheba knew that was a lie the moment she said it.

Delilah did, too, and that was why she laughed. "Not Ms. Got-To-Have-It-Even-If-It's-Not-On-Sale. I'm Delilah. You can keep it real with me."

Sheba whispered, as if someone else could hear them. "Okay, I have to admit that I love the fact that I can buy any and everything I want without having to worry about how much it costs. Since I'm really not supposed to be on my feet much, guess what happens? David sends personal shoppers here, and I just tell them what I want."

"Say what? So someone actually has a job to shop. I need to apply for that position."

Delilah and Sheba laughed.

"Check out my walk-in closet."

Delilah got up and went into her closet. She walked out, holding a nice evening gown. "This would make me feel like a princess—correction, a queen—because you know I'm the queen in my world."

"That you are, sis. But I wore it only once, because the next week my stomach had grown."

Delilah twirled it around. "You don't mind if your older sis borrows this, do you?"

"You can have it. In fact, the clothes on the left side, you're welcome to them if you want them. It'll be a while before I can fit into them again."

"I feel like a kid in the candy store. I want them all," Delilah said.

Sheba and Delilah spent the rest of the morning talking and laughing. David called to alert Sheba that he wouldn't be returning until next week, so the two sisters were home alone.

Over dinner one night, Delilah said, "I hate to bring this up, but I think you should know that your in-laws are all convinced that you're pregnant and the child isn't Uriah's."

Sheba shrugged her shoulders. "It's that Joyce. If she had kept her mouth closed and had stayed out of my business, folks wouldn't be talking."

"You leaving Shreveport when you did didn't help the situation, you know," Delilah said.

"Right now the most important thing to me is my baby. Those gossiping heifers can say what they want."

"That's the spirit. I've never cared about what folks say about me. Most of the time, it's just jealousy, anyway. So what if Uriah's not the father? He's gone on to glory now. You just worry about your baby and yourself. Let them deal with the aftermath."

Sheba wished it was as simple as Delilah thought it was. The truth was, she did care what folks said. She didn't want them to look at her in a negative light. She wanted to hold on to her upstanding position in everyone's eyes. She didn't want Uriah's memory marked by the shame of her infidelity.

Delilah and Sheba didn't discuss the rumors floating around Shreveport anymore and enjoyed each other's company for the rest of Delilah's visit. Sheba felt sad when it was time for Delilah to return to Shreveport. She had been there a week, but now it was time for her to return home.

"I wish you could stay longer," Sheba said after hugging Delilah.

Delilah and Sheba hugged one last time before she left. Sheba watched her get in the car. The house now felt empty. Delilah's visit had made her see that she had to move on. She would never forget Uriah, but she had to provide a family for her unborn child. It was time she moved on and gave David a chance.

Chapter 40

David eased his chair into the upright position after his pilot announced over the intercom that they were about to land in Dallas. He had purposely kept his distance from Sheba these past two months. It was becoming harder and harder to do so as he watched his baby grow in her stomach. He loved Sheba and the baby more than anything else in the world.

His butler had alerted him that Delilah had been there for a week. He was glad that Sheba hadn't been home alone. He sometimes wondered how she coped when she was there alone. They had developed something of a friendship. Sheba rarely gave him attitude, like she had when she first moved there or before. Now they had civilized conversations and spent time not just talking but also laughing together. Sheba had introduced him to a world of reality TV, and he had introduced her to his world. She had adapted to the life of the rich quite well.

He hadn't seen her in two weeks, so he couldn't wait to get home to at least hug her. She did allow him that luxury. He had been tempted to kiss her so many times, but he didn't want to ruin their newfound relationship.

About an hour later, his driver pulled up to his house. After showering, David went to Sheba's room. He called out to her but got no answer. Her door was ajar, so he walked in her room.

David panicked when he saw Sheba passed out on the floor next to the bed. He rushed to her side and scooped her up. "Sheba, oh no! What happened? Somebody call nine-one-one!" David yelled.

The maid rushed in. "Mr. King, what happened?"

"I don't know. Have the driver come back out front. I'm rushing her to the hospital myself. We don't have time for an ambulance to come." David rushed downstairs while carrying Sheba in his arms.

On the way to the hospital, David prayed. "God, please don't take the two most important people away from me."

The driver broke all the traffic laws but got them to Presbyterian Hospital safely.

"I found her passed out, and we need to see a doctor right away," David explained to one of the emergency room nurses. He watched as they placed Sheba on a gurney.

"Does she still have a pulse?" the nurse's aide asked another nurse.

She has to be all right, David thought to himself. "She's pregnant," David told the nurse.

"Sir, just stand back," one of the nurses said.

"Does she have insurance?" one of the hospital staff asked.

David pulled out his Visa Black Card. "This should take care of any expenses."

The clerk took David's card and handed him some papers. "Fill this out please."

After David filled out the papers and got his Visa Black Card back from the clerk, he went to the waiting room. Unable to sit still, he paced back and forth. He checked his watch every five minutes. He was impatient. He walked up to the nurses' station.

"Can you give me an update on Bathsheba Richards?"

"Let me check." The nurse scanned through the computer. "She's been taken to a room. You can go straight through those doors."

David didn't breathe until he saw Sheba. By now she was awake. He rushed to her side. "Sheba, I was so worried. I found you passed out by your bed."

She looked at him with sleepy eyes. "I don't know what happened. I felt queasy, and when I got up to go to the bathroom, I got dizzy. I tried to make it back to the bed, but I guess I must have fallen before I could."

David reached for her hand. His eyes filled with tears. "I thought I had lost you and the baby."

Sheba said, "I'm fine. But I don't know about the baby."

The doctor came into the room at that time. "Mrs. Richards, your sugar dropped. That's why you passed out."

"My baby?" Sheba asked.

"Well, things aren't looking too good. You were dilating."

"I can't be. It's too early." Sheba started crying.

David squeezed her hand to let her know he was there.

"Mr. Richards, she's going to need round-the-clock care."

David looked up at the doctor. "I'm David King, and I'll make sure she gets it. In fact, I would like to find out how I can get a private nurse."

The doctor said, "Are you *the* David King?"

"Yes." David was annoyed. It wasn't about who he was. Right now he needed to make sure that his child, whom Sheba was carrying, was going to be okay.

"I'm sure I can get someone reliable to come out to your house and check on her daily."

David looked at the doctor. "No, you don't understand. I need someone to come stay with her until the baby is born. I'm willing to pay whatever it costs."

The doctor pulled out a card and wrote a number down. "Then, this is who you need to call. She'll be able to get you someone."

"Thanks. I'll make sure I leave a sizable donation to this hospital," David said.

"Thank you, Mr. King."

David's attention was now back on Sheba. He wished he could wipe the sadness from her face. "Sheba, I know I said I wasn't going to pressure you, and this is the last place I had planned on doing this, but in light of almost losing you and our baby . . . I want to know if you would do me the honor of being my wife. Bathsheba, will you marry me?"

Sheba squeezed David's hand. She blinked her eyes a few times. "Yes, David."

David had to ask her to repeat herself, because her response surprised him. "What did you say?"

"David, I'll marry you," Sheba said, with a gleam in her eyes.

David didn't realize he had been holding his breath. He exhaled loudly. "Sheba, I promise you will never want for anything. You and our child will be well taken care of."

Sheba said, "All we need is your love."

David touched his heart. "You already got that. I love you, Sheba. I always have. From the moment I laid eyes on you."

David planted a kiss on her mouth. Sheba kissed him back.

The nurse walked in. "Sorry. Didn't mean to interrupt anything."

David smiled. He was finally getting the woman he wanted. Sheba would be his, and now he had to make it official. While the nurse helped Sheba get dressed, David sent Nathan a text message, informing him of his upcoming nuptials. David wanted Nathan to marry him and his queen.

David said a silent prayer to God, thanking him for saving Sheba.

Chapter 41

Sheba looked at her reflection in the full-length mirror. She was nervous as she thought about her rash decision two weeks ago to marry David. She had grown to care about David, but was now having second thoughts about marrying him. She turned in front of the mirror. The white wedding gown she wore did little to hide her big pregnant belly. Delilah's reflection appeared next to hers.

"You make a beautiful bride."

"But white? I should have chosen another color," Sheba said.

"Girl, forget tradition. You look beautiful. Don't you agree?" Delilah turned to face the wedding coordinator, Georgia Vanguard, one of the best in the country.

Georgia said, "I do agree. Especially since she chose the wedding dress I preferred." Georgia had had to rush and put together a wedding in a short period of time. The nice sum that David was paying her was enough for her to forgo normal protocol and drop everything to handle the wedding of David King to his beautiful bride-to-be, Sheba.

Sheba moved her body in different directions to view herself in the mirror. "You ladies are correct. It does look good. Baby bump and all."

They all turned in the direction of the door when they heard the knock.

Georgia said, "It's time. Are you ready?"

Sheba looked at Delilah and then back at Georgia. "If I wait any longer, we'll be having the ceremony at the hospital."

"I'll let everyone know we can get started," Georgia said as she turned and walked away.

Delilah and Sheba were now alone in the study. A lone tear threatened to fall from Sheba's eye. She could feel a crying session coming on. She sniffled.

Delilah said, "No, we are not having this. Not today. Today's a happy occasion."

"But I feel so guilty. I'm not supposed to be happy. I'm not supposed to be in love with another man so soon after losing my husband."

Delilah patted the tears flowing from her eyes. "Baby girl, let the dead bury the dead. You have to live your life."

"The people back at home are talking about me. You know it, and last night Annette told me what folks at the hospital are saying about me."

"Annette can go back and tell them to kiss your you-know-what. They are all just jealous. They wish they were in your shoes. Women all around the world today will be in mourning because you, my dear, are becoming David King's wife. Many have tried, but they all failed. They don't have that Baker girl charm."

Sheba laughed at Delilah's last comment. "Well, this is it. I just need a few minutes alone and I'll be ready."

Sheba would do her best to push the negative thoughts to the back of her mind. She had to live her life and stop worrying about what other people were saying about her.

Delilah said, "Don't make us wait too long. As your maid of honor, I want the first dance with the best man."

"Nathan is not your type."

"Oh, I thought you knew. I love a man of God." Delilah winked at her and walked out of the room.

Sheba closed her eyes. She rubbed her stomach. "Father God, thank you for sparing me and my child's life. Thank you for having his father be a part of our life. I never would have dreamed of a day like today. Thank you for your grace and mercy as I prepare to walk down the aisle."

Sheba heard the music. She said out loud before leaving the room, "Uriah, just because I'm marrying David, it doesn't mean I don't love you. You were my first love, and I'll never stop loving you."

Georgia returned to the room. "It's time."

Sheba followed Georgia out into the foyer, and the small, intimate crowd of guests, who were sitting in the white chairs outside of David's and now Sheba's mansion, all stood. The pianist played the customary bridal music, and Sheba seemed to float down the aisle.

She had wanted something small and intimate, and David had obliged her. The hundred guests she saw standing up were mostly David's closest friends or colleagues. The only people in attendance that Sheba knew personally were Delilah and Annette, and they both were part of her small wedding party.

David's smile was a mile wide as he reached for her hand and they stood face-to-face with the minister. Nathan had decided not to officiate over the wedding, because he still had misgivings about how David and Sheba ended up together. After David pleaded and begged him, Nathan finally agreed to be David's best man.

They exchanged vows. David planted a long kiss on Sheba's lips as the crowd cheered. He whispered in her ear as he embraced her, "Bathsheba Marie King, I promise to love, cherish, and honor you all the days of my life."

"I love you, David," Sheba said right before kissing him again.

"Ladies and gentlemen, I present to you David and Bathsheba King."

They walked down the aisle as husband and wife. David insisted that Sheba sit as the wedding processional took place and they personally greeted each guest.

Sheba kept hearing, "You make a lovely bride." She wanted to believe them, but she knew they were all wondering why David was marrying a pregnant woman, since they all thought the child belonged to another man. David appeared noble by marrying her.

Everyone assumed it was her late husband, Uriah's child, but she, David, Nathan, and Delilah all knew the truth.

Chapter 42

David wanted to surprise his bride with a honeymoon, but she was on bed rest, so he promised to take her somewhere exotic as soon as the baby was old enough to travel. He thanked God again for allowing Sheba to be his bride. He knew that he still had a lot of making up to do for how he had set things up with Uriah, but today he felt that the favor of the Lord was upon him.

"Baby, are you tired?" he asked as he helped Sheba sit on top of his king-size bed.

He had her work with an interior decorator, and she had revamped the entire master bedroom. He didn't complain, because he liked the brown and maroon colors she had chosen. It was a room fit for a king and his queen.

"A little," Sheba responded.

"Here, let me help you." David eased her legs up on the bed. He propped the pillows up behind her. "Is that better?"

"Much. Thanks, David."

David sat on the bed next to her. "Thanks for making me the happiest man alive today."

Sheba smiled. David loved to see her smile. Her whole face seemed to light up. "A queen has to marry a king."

She leaned toward him, and they shared a kiss. The kiss started off slow, but David ended up ravishing her mouth with his. "Baby, I want to show you how much I love you, but I'm afraid to hurt the baby."

Sheba said, "Did you feel that? The baby just kicked me."

She took David's hand and placed it on her stomach. David's eyes teared up as he felt their baby move. "He knows his daddy's voice," he said. "Daddy loves you." He kissed Sheba's stomach.

"We love Daddy, too," Sheba said.

David felt loved. With his previous two wives, David hadn't felt like this. He had hoped and prayed that Sheba would love him, and she did. The child she was carrying had brought them together, and for that he was grateful.

They hadn't been this close since the night their child was conceived. This was the moment he had been dreaming about. Even after she accepted his proposal that night in the hospital, they had remained in separate rooms. He shifted in the bed as Sheba laid her head on his chest. He ran his fingers through her hair. He inhaled the peach scent.

"I love you," David said. He kissed her on the top of the head.

They fell asleep in each other's arms. It was the most peaceful sleep David had had in months. If he were to be honest, it was the most rest he'd had since Uriah was killed.

David held Sheba in his arms the entire night. The sun beaming through the curtains the following morning woke David up. Sheba shifted her body and squeezed him tight. David would enjoy waking up next to her every morning.

He smiled. "Good morning, my queen."

"Good morning, King David," she responded.

David and Sheba stayed in bed most of the morning. They entertained some of David's friends for lunch. When Sheba was taking her afternoon nap, David decided to go outside and enjoy the nice, cool spring air. He found Nathan and Delilah enjoying each other's company on the patio.

"You two look a little chummy out here," David said as he sat in one of the patio chairs.

"Delilah's been keeping me entertained," Nathan said, smiling.

"Better watch out. You don't want to get caught up in her web," David said.

"I can handle Delilah."

"Boys, I'm sitting right here. I don't need to be handled, okay?" Delilah held both of her hands up in the air.

"What goes on between y'all is none of my business," David said as he poured himself a glass of lemon iced tea.

Delilah stood up. "I'll be inside. Nathan, come see me before you leave."

David watched Nathan watch Delilah as she twisted back into the house. David said, "Nathan, don't get caught up."

"Oh, she's harmless." Nathan grinned.

"I don't think Samson Judges would agree with you," David said.

"Touché."

"Mr. King, would you like me to bring you something to eat?" asked the butler, who had just come outside.

"No, I'm fine. Nathan, would you like anything?"

"I'm still full from lunch."

"You can check with Ms. Delilah. Otherwise, we'll be fine until dinner."

Nathan had a pain-stricken look on his face. "David, man, I don't know how to say this. I've been trying to avoid telling you, but God won't let up on me, so I have to."

"What? Spit it out." David was sure that God had forgiven him and that he was back in God's good graces. He was curious to know what Nathan had to say.

"Remember when I told you about how God felt about you sending Uriah overseas so that you could get access to his wife?"

"Yes, but that's not exactly how it happened."

"David, we both know you sent that man out into a war zone. and it was just as if you had pulled the trigger yourself."

David turned beet red. Nathan was ruining what was a beautiful day. "Spit it out, man. Tell me. What did God reveal to you?"

"Your baby is cursed. Your baby was conceived in a way that wasn't pleasing to God, and I hate to say this, but Bathsheba will not deliver a healthy baby."

"So are you saying something is going to be wrong with him? The doctors said he should be fine. We just have to keep Sheba calm and relaxed."

"No, David. God has shown me that your son will not live. I didn't want to tell you, but I didn't want you to be surprised when it happened, either."

"Get out. Get out of my house now. You just can't stand me being happy. You're just jealous that God continues to bless me." David stood up, knocking the glass on the table over, and the tea fell on to the patio.

Nathan stood up. "You can kick me out, but it still doesn't change the facts."

David watched Nathan walk away. In the doorway stood Delilah. Their eyes locked. Had she heard their conversation? David would figure out a way to find out. He had to. He couldn't risk Sheba ever learning of his past plans that resulted in Uriah being sent to Afghanistan.

Chapter 43

Sheba sensed the tension between David and Delilah. She had hoped that her sister would get along with her current husband. Up until the past few days, they had. She wondered what had happened to cause the rift.

"David, why are you and Delilah always going at it?" she asked when Delilah left to go shopping.

"Delilah has to realize I'm the king of my castle, and if she wants to take over something, she needs to go back to Shreveport, to her own place."

"But, baby, having Delilah here helps me out a lot."

"I know that, and that's the only reason why I haven't asked her to leave." David went inside the master bathroom.

Sheba sighed. *Not déjà vu. First, Uriah and now David.* Her baby kicked. "Little man, what are we going to do with your daddy and aunt?"

Sheba's stomach felt like a knot. She doubled over in pain. "David!" she yelled.

David ran out. "Sheba, hold on, baby." He pulled her up in his arms, but Sheba couldn't sit up straight. David yelled, "Where's your nurse? I'm paying her all this money, and she's nowhere to be found."

"I heard you down the hall," the nurse said as she entered the room.

"What's wrong with her?" David shouted.

The nurse asked Sheba, "Were you experiencing pain prior to this?"

"It came all of a sudden. I feel like someone hit me in the stomach with their fist," Sheba said and cried out in pain.

"We should get you to the hospital," the nurse advised.

Sheba looked at David. Fear was written across her face. She could feel something wet in between her legs. "Yes, get me to the hospital now."

"What's wrong, baby?" David asked.

"I think it's time."

An hour later Sheba had her heels in the stirrups. Due to the medical complications and David's overbearing personality, which seemed to irritate the hospital staff, the doctor had convinced David that it would be best if he waited in the waiting room. The pain shooting through Sheba's body had subsided some, but not completely, after they gave her a shot in her spine.

The doctor said, "I need for you to concentrate on something good and close your eyes and do as I tell you."

Sheba's mind was only on her baby. She couldn't think of anything else. "God, I know at first I didn't want this baby, but now I do. I love him more than life itself. I love him. Please don't let anything happen to him. Take me, if you have to, but please spare my baby's life," she pleaded.

The doctor whispered, "He's not breathing."

His whispers weren't low enough that Sheba couldn't hear him. "No, please don't tell me my baby's dead," Sheba said as a bout of pain hit her body. A few seconds later she heard her baby's cry. "Let me see him. I need to see him."

The baby was cleaned up and then handed to Sheba. She cried as she held her five-pound baby in her arms.

The doctor said, "He's not breathing like I would want him to, so we're going to need to examine him and put him in an incubator."

"What do you mean, he's not breathing right?" Sheba asked as the doctor took her baby and began examining him more thoroughly. "What's wrong with my baby?" Sheba yelled frantically.

"Nurse, give her something to calm down," the doctor requested.

The nurse did as she'd been told. It took two of the nurses to hold Sheba down so they could administer the shot.

Sheba, calmer, said, "My husband. Where's my husband?"

David was escorted in. "Sheba, I could hear you outside, but they wouldn't allow me in."

Sheba held on to his hand. "Our baby's in an incubator. He wasn't breathing. I need to see him. I got to hold him only for a few seconds."

David said, "I'm going to check on him. You just get some rest, my queen. Little David is going to be okay."

Sheba didn't believe that her baby was going to be okay, and she could tell by the scared look in David's eyes that he didn't, either. She had to hold on to his words, though. Little David had to be fine. She'd already lost two people she loved; she couldn't lose another one. God wouldn't be so cruel as to let her carry him eight months and then take him from her. Not the God of Abraham, Isaac, and Moses. No, he wouldn't do that to her.

Sheba fell into a deep sleep. She woke up a day later and demanded some answers. "Where is my baby?" she asked David.

"Little David's not doing too good, Sheba." David's voice shook.

"I want to see my baby. They can't keep me from my baby," Sheba yelled.

"Mrs. King, we need you to hold it down. You're disturbing the other patients," one of the nurses said, peeking her head into the room.

David stepped in to intervene. "Can you get a wheelchair so I can take her to see our son?"

"I'm afraid we can't do that. We have strict instructions that she's supposed to remain in her bed."

"Please. If this was your child, you would want to see him," Sheba said.

The nurse showed compassion. She looked at Sheba and said, "Fine. Don't tell anyone I did this. If you feel dizzy at all, let me know." The nurse then looked at David. "Mr. King, I'm going to need your help."

David assisted in getting Sheba in the wheelchair. He took a blanket out of the closet and placed it around her. The ride down the hallway didn't take long. The nurse showed them little David. Sheba wasn't allowed to hold him in her arms, but she was able to touch him.

"Your mama is right here. I love you. I love you so much. You're going to get stronger. You're going to grow up and be just like your daddy."

David said, "And you're going to marry a woman just as beautiful as your mama."

Sheba didn't know she could love a man as much as she did at that moment. Watching David being gentle with their baby touched her. "Little David, you have to get better because Mama needs you."

The nurse reappeared. "I have to get you back. The doctor's making his rounds, and I don't want him to find you here."

David said, "You go on, baby. I'll stay here with little David, and then I'll meet you back in the room."

"Okay."

Sheba squeezed his hand. David leaned down and gave her a peck on the lips. Sheba looked back at David, who stood by the incubator, rubbing little David's leg. She loved them both.

Chapter 44

David didn't care who was around. He kneeled down next to the incubator. He closed his eyes. With one hand on little David's small leg and the other on his forehead, David prayed silently. "Father God, I know that I've been disobedient. I know that I don't deserve to ask you to spare my child's life, but, Lord, I've done what you asked. I've repented. I've made amends. I'm trying to do right by providing for my wife and child.

"Lord, if it is your will, please let death pass us by. I give my son to you to do with what you may. I promise to bring him up in a way that's pleasing to you. Lord, have mercy on your humble servant."

David was ending his prayer when he felt an arm on his shoulder. "I was told you were down here."

David stood up. "Nathan, he's not doing too good."

David rarely cried in front of anyone, but at this point, he didn't care. He turned and cried on Nathan's shoulder. Then David pulled himself together and followed Nathan out of the room. He kept looking back at little David.

"Sheba told me you were here. Delilah's in the room with her."

"I can't face Sheba right now. Tell her I will be back later. I need to get out of here," David said and hurried down the hallway.

"David," Nathan called out to him.

David rushed past everyone and out the hospital doors. "Why, Lord? Why now? I thought you forgave me. You let me believe that things were going to be all right. Now this."

David threw his fist up in the air in anger. His driver saw him and tried to calm him down, but it didn't do any good.

David heard a woman's voice say, "I got him."

He looked up into the face of Delilah. "You're the last person I want to see."

Delilah grabbed him by the arm. "Get in the car, David."

He was in too much pain to argue, so he got in his car, and Delilah got in right behind him. She said something to his driver. David's driver closed the car door, and a minute or so later, he pulled off.

"Where are we going?" David asked.

"You tell me. You were the one running out on my sister when she needs you."

"Look. My baby's dying, and I don't have time for your attitude."

"Woe is David. I'm trying to get you to deal with this so you can be with Sheba. Sheba needs you right now. You say you love her. Then act like it. Don't bail on her right now."

"I'm not bailing. This is just too much. My baby's being punished for something I did."

Delilah said, "Don't beat yourself up."

"Oh, you're not going to gloat. I know you overheard me and Nathan talking."

There, David had said it. Everything was out in the open. No more pretenses between him and Delilah.

"David, I figured out what your plan was long before I overheard your conversation. I don't fault you, because—believe me when I say this— I've done some things I'm not too proud of."

"So you're not going to tell Sheba?" David asked.

"Sheba's not a stupid woman. If you think that, then you don't know the woman you married."

David wasn't satisfied with her response, so he said, "Promise me you won't tell Sheba what you overheard. As her sister, I'll ensure that you are always well taken care of."

"Really? I was going to keep the secret for free, but since you insist on sharing some of your wealth. . . ." Delilah looked around the back of the town car. "Share it with me, brother-in-law. I'm not even going to give you a dollar amount. Whatever your heart desires to give me, I'll accept."

Delilah had to be one of the sneakiest, most underhanded women, besides his ex-wives, that David had come across. He had fallen right into her trap. If it would keep her big mouth closed, then he would do it. He would call his accountant as soon as he could and would have a nice amount of money transferred into Delilah's bank account.

"Let's do monthly installments, so the government won't be suspicious," Delilah said. David looked at her like she was crazy. She went on to say, "I'm thinking about all those taxes I'll have to pay."

"It'll be the same amount regardless if it's monthly or one large sum."

"Oh, in that case, give me all you got, King David."

David called his accountant and set up the transfer. Delilah seemed pleased. David had to hand it to Delilah. She had accomplished one thing. He had momentarily forgotten about his son and his wife, but now it was back to the issue at hand. He needed to convince God to spare his son's life. How? He had no idea.

Chapter 45

Sheba demanded to see the doctor. The nurses were calling her the patient from hell, but she didn't care. It had been seven days, and her baby was still hooked up to machines. He didn't appear to be getting better.

"Where is David? He was supposed to meet me here!" Sheba shouted.

Delilah replied, "He said he had to make a quick stop at the church and then he would be here."

"He needs to hurry up. They must not know I'm David King's wife, or they wouldn't keep me waiting."

"Calm down, sis. They are doing everything they can for little David."

"It's not enough." Sheba was a nurse. She knew they were providing him with the best care, but as a mother, she felt like there was more they could be doing.

The doctor had released her from the hospital four days ago, but she had yet to go home. Delilah or David brought her clothes to change into and food to eat. The food she barely touched, because since having little David, she hadn't had an appetite. How could she think of food or anything else when her baby was fighting for his life?

The doctor finally came into the waiting room. "Mrs. King, sorry to keep you waiting."

Sheba didn't bother with the formalities. She didn't reach out to shake his extended hand. "What's the prognosis on my baby?" she asked.

Dr. Philips said, "Do you want to wait on your husband?"

"No. I'm standing right here. I need for you to tell me when you expect my baby to get better."

"Mrs. King, his little heart is fighting, but I'm not sure of how long his heart will last. He was born with a defective heart, but I want to assure you that we're doing all we can."

Sheba plopped down on the chair. Her hands flew to her face. "Lord, please. Take me, not my baby."

Delilah sat in the chair next to her. She patted her gently on the back. "It's going to be okay."

"No, it's not. It'll never be okay."

The doctor continued, saying, "I'm sorry, Mrs. King. I wish I had better news for you."

Sheba wiped some of the tears from her face. "Dr. Philips, thanks. What should I do now?"

"Do you have a pastor who can come pray over your son?" he asked.

Delilah pulled out her phone. "I'll call Nathan."

"Thank you, Doctor," Sheba said, barely above a whisper.

"I'm so sorry. I wish there was more I could do."

Sheba heard Delilah deliver the bad news to Nathan. She hung up with him. "He's on his way."

"Where's David? I need my husband," Sheba said as she bent down and wrapped her arms around her knees. She rocked back and forth as Delilah patted her on the back. Sis, it's going to be okay," Delilah said.

Sheba wished Delilah would stop saying that. If she lost little David, it would never be okay again. Her world was crumbling all around her, and there was no sign of David. She needed him here with her.

By the time Nathan arrived, Sheba and Delilah were in the nursery. The nurses allowed Sheba to hold the baby one last time. She sat in the rocking chair, with him in her arms, and she rocked him back and forth.

She heard Nathan tell Delilah, "David's on his way. We were at the church, praying. His car had a flat, but he'll be here soon."

Delilah responded, "I hope he hurries up. Bathsheba needs him."

"How are you holding up, dear?" Nathan asked, turning to Sheba.

"The doctor says my baby's dying, Nathan. His little heart's not holding up. I don't know how I'm supposed to deal with this. Look at him. He's so innocent in all of this."

Nathan kneeled down beside Sheba. She stopped rocking as Nathan placed one of his big hands on little David. "Father God, we ask that if it is your will, you heal David and Bathsheba's child right now, Lord. Put your arm of protection around this child. Let him know that he's loved not only by his parents, but also by those of us who have had a chance to be in his presence."

Nathan looked in Delilah's direction. Delilah was wiping her face with a tissue. He continued his prayer. "I know that this is not what we would have for little David, but you know best. Lord, be with his parents, and let them know, regardless of the outcome, that you are still in their midst. That you will never leave them or forsake them. That you will never put more on your children than they can bear. If you put them through it, they can make it through it."

The alarm that was hooked up to little David went off. The nurses ran over to where Sheba sat and took him away from her. Sheba didn't want to release him.

Sheba yelled out, "No! Not my baby," as they unsuccessfully attempted to revive him.

Chapter 46

David could hear the commotion going on in the nursery. He rushed inside. He knew from the expression on Nathan's face that he was too late. Little David was gone. He saw a doctor wrap him up in a blanket.

"I need to hold him. Can I hold him one last time?" David pleaded, choking on his tears.

The doctor saw the pain in David's eyes and motioned for the nurse to hand little David to him. The nurse did as instructed.

David unwrapped the blanket. He kissed little David on the forehead and on the cheek. "I love you so much. I'll never forget you, son."

Nathan walked up to David. "Man, they need to take him. Give little David to them."

David said, "I know. Look at him. He's so little. He looks helpless."

Nathan placed his hand on little David's body and took him away from David. He handed the baby to the nurse. He placed his arm around

David. "Come on, man. Your wife's over there. She needs you."

When David had first entered the nursery, he had eyes only for little David. He didn't even think to look for Sheba. He saw her tear-stained face. She stood up, and as soon as he reached her, she fell into his arms.

"Our baby's gone, David," Sheba wailed.

The nurses and doctors around them allowed them their time to grieve. David motioned for Nathan to come near him. Sheba could barely walk.

David said to Nathan," Can you take care of whatever needs to be taken care of? I need to get Sheba home."

"Don't worry. Delilah and I will take care of everything," Nathan assured him.

David used one arm to hold Sheba up and the other to dial his driver, alerting him that they would be coming downstairs. They left the nursery and got on the elevator. Sheba kept her head on David's shoulder as people getting on and off the elevator looked on.

"Can you give us some privacy please?" David snapped.

The driver had the car parked out front. David helped Sheba inside. Silence kept them company. The only sounds that could be heard were their sniffles as they each dealt with the death of little David in their own way.

The driver had alerted David's staff of the bad news. They were all waiting for him and Sheba when they pulled up in front of the house. David accepted their condolences.

"Mrs. King, I've drawn you some bathwater," one of the maids said.

"I don't feel like doing anything but getting in the bed," Sheba responded.

David said, "Help her up the stairs. I'll be up shortly."

The butler and the maid assisted Sheba up the stairs. David headed to the kitchen. On the way, he said a silent prayer. *The Lord giveth and the Lord taketh. Your will has been done. I ask now that you comfort my grieving wife.*

When he saw David, the cook said, "Mr. King, again, I'm so sorry about your baby."

"Thank you, Jorge. I wanted to ask you to prepare some of the missus's favorites."

"B—but . . ." the cook stuttered.

"Prepare some of my favorites, too, while you're at it. We'll be having dinner at our regular time."

The cook couldn't understand David's commands. "Mr. King, I would hate to cook all this food and no one eats it."

"What we don't eat, you can take home to your family." Without saying another word, David left the kitchen to go check on his grieving wife.

He stood in the doorway of the bedroom. The nurse had given Sheba a sedative, so she was sleeping. He sat in the chair and watched her sleep. He cried until he couldn't cry anymore. Not wanting to wake her up, he quietly exited the room.

By now Nathan and Delilah were waiting downstairs.

"David, we'll need to talk about funeral plans. But that can wait until later," said Nathan.

Delilah asked, "How's Bathsheba?"

"She's sleeping, but you can go check on her again for me, if you like," David told her.

"I'll do that." Delilah walked away and headed toward Sheba's bedroom.

David led Nathan into his study, and they both sat down. "I know Sheba's not going to be up to making the plans, and truthfully, neither am I. If you can handle this, I will be grateful. We want to have the funeral as soon as possible. Tomorrow even. The sooner we have it, the quicker we can start the grieving process."

Nathan asked, "Where do you want him buried? I know your family is buried back in Louisiana."

"Never thought it would be used for this purpose, but there's a spot near the garden out back. I would like for him to be buried there."

"You sure?" Nathan asked. "You'll have to get approval to have that done."

"Yes. I want him buried out back, and I will take care of the legal aspects of it, trust me." David stood up. "Follow me. I'll show you the exact spot."

Chapter 47

Sheba allowed David to make the funeral plans for their baby. She knew it was the cowardly way, but she could barely breathe. She felt an emptiness inside that left her feeling sad. Even when she lost Uriah, she didn't feel this much despair, and losing him had taken its toll on her.

Delilah pinned Sheba's hair up for her.

"Thank you."

"Sheba, you know you don't have to thank me."

Sheba turned her seat around. "This is what family is about."

Delilah bent down and gave her a hug. "Look at me. I'm about to mess up your hair."

"I don't even care." Sheba stood up.

David entered the bedroom. "Baby, it's time to go."

He reached his arm out, and Sheba grabbed his hand. Delilah left the room before them, and they followed right behind her. There was no funeral-home limousine, since David owned his own.

Sheba looked out the window as they proceeded to Church On the Way Missionary Baptist Church. A small crowd was there, only because David had insisted that he didn't want a lot of people around.

The walk up the middle aisle seemed like déjà vu for Sheba, except this time it was her baby she was burying, instead of her husband. There he was, little David, dressed in a little baby blue suit and in a small baby blue casket. She had had no idea they even made caskets that little. Seeing him there made her weak in her knees.

"Baby, I got you," David said as he held her up.

She cried out, "My baby," as she fell on top of the casket and sobbed.

David grabbed her. "Come on, Sheba. There's nothing more we can do for him. Come on. Let's go take our seats."

"No. I want my baby."

Nathan walked up to them. "Sheba, little David is with the Lord. He's no longer in pain. He doesn't want to see his mother in pain, so come on. Let me and David walk you to your seat."

Sheba loosened her grip on the casket and stood up. "Thank you," she heard David tell Nathan.

She was seated. David wrapped his arm around her shoulders. Her head fell on his shoulder and stayed there throughout the funeral. Nathan presided over the funeral. He said a special prayer for the parents of little David. Sheba couldn't recall much else as she sat in a zombie state.

The organist played "Amazing Grace" as they were getting ready to walk out of the church. Memories flooded Sheba's mind. That was the song her mother had loved to sing. Ironically, it was being sung today. David had no idea that was her mother's song. The pain and all the memories were too much for Sheba to bear. She cried out and couldn't stop weeping. David had to carry her out of the church.

"I'm okay," Sheba said over and over as he placed her in the back of the limousine.

Sheba had noticed that David had remained quiet during most of the service. She seemed to be his main concern. She loved David beyond a shadow of a doubt. No one, not even Uriah, had ever been as attentive to her needs as he was.

David had told her earlier where he wanted to bury little David. She had agreed that that would be a good place, but she couldn't watch as they buried her firstborn in the plot David had had dug right next to the gardenias in the garden. It was a place she had found comfort in when she was able to walk around outside the house.

She went to her bedroom but looked out one of the windows as they lowered her baby's body down into the ground. David, who normally stood straight and tall, was hunched over. She watched as Nathan's hand patted David on the back.

Sheba closed the curtains and slowly walked back down the hall to the master bedroom. She removed her clothes and slid under the bedcovers. Sleep wasn't her friend. She wished she had a sedative so she could sleep. Maybe if she could sleep, she would feel better.

She heard a knock on the door. She yelled, "Come in."

Delilah walked in, holding a plate of food. "I brought some of your favorites."

"I'm not hungry."

"Come on. You need to eat something."

Sheba took a small bite of each item. "Satisfied?" she asked.

"It is better than nothing." Delilah took her plate and placed it on the side of the bed.

"Where's David? Where's my husband?" Sheba asked.

"He's downstairs. I'll go get him."

"Tell him I need him. I can't make it through this day without him." Sheba pulled the covers up over her body and once again attempted to go to sleep.

Chapter 48

David was going through the motions. He talked and laughed at some of the jokes being told, although he didn't feel like it.

Nathan said, "Man, you don't have to put up this front like everything is okay. People will understand if you don't want to talk."

Nathan was referring to some of the colleagues who had stopped by to show their respect. David knew they didn't think it was his child, so that was why he was able to stand there and be strong. And he was able to be strong because he and the Lord had had a one-on-one. David knew that his child's death was predestined because of his own sins.

Delilah walked up to him and whispered, "She's asking for you. She says she needs you."

David attempted to get everyone's attention. "I want to thank you all for coming out and paying your condolences. Me and my wife appreciate all that you've done for us. You're all welcome to stay, but my wife needs me, so I'm going to retire for the evening."

Ten minutes later David was upstairs. He discarded his tie before he made it through the bedroom door. Sheba was under the covers.

"David, is that you?"

"Yes, baby. I'm here."

She peeped over the covers. David's heart skipped a beat as he made his way to the bed. She reached her arms out to him, and he embraced her. He wiped the tears from her face. Their eyes locked, and his mouth ravished hers.

Were those moans he was hearing coming from Sheba?

It had been a couple of months since David had felt a woman's body. He hadn't cheated on Sheba once since he moved her here from Shreveport. His body responded to her, but he tried to refrain himself. Sheba's hands roamed over his body.

"Baby, it hasn't been six weeks. Normally, you're supposed to wait six weeks."

"I don't care. I need to feel you inside of me," Sheba said.

David could not resist his wife. Sheba could have whatever she wanted from him. He gave in to her demands, and the day that they buried their son was only the second time they slept together.

The love he felt for Sheba poured out of him and into her. He held her close to his heart as they drifted off to sleep.

The next morning, when David woke up, he found Sheba sitting up on the side of the bed. He rubbed her back. "Lay back down with me. It's still early."

"I'm fine. I needed you last night, and I thank you for being there for me."

"I love you. I will always be there for you," David said.

Sheba turned around to face him. "You have a good heart, David. I know you don't like to show it much, but you do."

David felt a little emotional. "I can't help but love you. You and I have been through a lot, Bathsheba. If we can make it through all of this, I think we can make it through anything."

"You're right. This past year has been hard on me, but with you by my side, I feel that everything is going to be all right." Sheba leaned down and kissed him on the lips.

David got out of the bed. "I'll go run you some bathwater. You shouldn't be getting around too much."

"I'm fine, baby."

"Let me take care of you." David wondered if Sheba could hear the fear in his voice. He almost

said, "Let me take care of you, because I don't
want to lose you, too," but he caught himself.

"Use the French vanilla bubble bath that I
love."

David ran the bathwater and helped Sheba get
in the tub. He washed her body and dried her off
afterward. After he made sure she was okay, he
went and took a bath himself. He drifted in and
out as he meditated in the tub. He thanked God
for another chance. He vowed to live upright
from that day forward. He thanked Him for the
love of a good woman.

The temperature of the water dropping
prompted David to climb out of the tub. Sheba
wasn't in their bedroom. David called out for
her.

One of the maids said, "Mr. King, she's out on
the patio."

David rushed out on the patio, but she wasn't
there. He could see her off in the distance. She
was near the place where they had buried their
son. He walked to where she stood.

Before he could say anything, Sheba said, "He
was so handsome. He looked just like you."

"He had your eyes." David reached for her
hand, and they stood there and held hands.

David stood out there until Sheba was ready
to go back in the house. Inside, the couple had a

quiet brunch. After eating, Sheba left the dining room and left David alone. He took the time to get caught up on the news. He was fine until he saw one of the headlines in the morning paper belonging to one of his competitors: RUTHLESS MEDIA MOGUL BURIES HIS STEPCHILD. Several question marks followed the word *stepchild*.

He proceeded to read the article. It read: *Sources close to David King reveal he was more than the stepfather. Could the nation's King of Media be tied to a love-child scandal? He married his wife only a few months after she buried her husband of over ten years. Who says money can't buy you love?*

David's face turned beet red. He stopped reading the article and hid the paper under his arm. He didn't want Sheba to find out about the article.

Chapter 49

David's attempt to shield Sheba from the paper was not successful. Sheba grabbed the paper from under David's arm before he could object. She read some of the article out loud.

"His wife's husband was one of his employees. He was working in one of the most dangerous areas in the world. What kind of man would send an employee to a death trap? David King is ruthless."

Sheba couldn't believe the hateful words written in the article. "They are the ones who are ruthless. We just buried our son, and they are writing stories like this."

Sheba was livid. Although it was true that little David was David's biological son, only two other people knew it besides themselves, so the reporter was just speculating.

"I'll call someone and get them to retract the story," David said.

"Don't bother. I'm just overreacting. We both know that little David was yours, and it'll only make them try to dig into our past more. What's that saying? 'Let sleeping dogs lie.'"

David said, "The reporter who wrote that story is as good as fired. The owner of the paper owes me a favor."

"Oh, you got it like that?" Sheba smiled.

"Baby, I'm the king, so you better know it."

"Well, as soon as your queen is up to it, she can't wait to hit the malls. I need some retail therapy, something to keep my mind off all this."

David got up and returned with an iPad. "In the meantime, let your fingers do the shopping."

"Do I have a limit?" Sheba asked.

David looked up at the sky through the window. "The sky's the limit." He winked his eye at her and then left her alone.

Sheba scanned several sites and had a difficult time making a purchase. Things were different now that she was able to buy whatever she wanted and never had to worry about money. But she would give it all up if she could have her son back.

"I'm going to think happy thoughts," she said out loud.

She clicked on several Web sites and made purchases with the credit card David had given her when she first moved to Dallas. She chose clothes that were just a few sizes larger than her regular size, since she had gained weight from her pregnancy. Surprisingly, some of the baby weight had already started to drop off her body.

Her hand went to her stomach, to the empty place that used to house her baby. "Lord, please look after my little baby."

After shopping, Sheba turned on the television and was appalled at some of the comments coming from someone who was supposed to be a well-respected journalist. Why were they concerned about David's love life? So what if he had fathered her child? It was their business and their business alone.

She was grieving and shouldn't have to deal with the foolishness of these reports, which seemed to be the talk of the town. The phone rang, so she turned the volume down on the television. Delilah's number displayed on the caller ID.

Without saying hello, Delilah blurted out, "I thought I was scandalous, but, girl, you got me beat."

"Not you, too," Sheba said, frustrated beyond belief.

"I saw it on my favorite talk show this morning. I started to call you then."

"Glad you didn't."

"Well, I think you should know that I've been contacted by several reporters wanting the scoop."

"Delilah, you didn't? Please tell me you're not the source."

"Of course not, dear sister. I would never betray you like that."

Sheba sighed. "It would hurt me to find out that you are the one leaking information. Tell me now, because the truth always comes out."

"Sheba, I promise you, I'm not the one. But if you ask me, it is probably Joyce. I wouldn't put nothing past her. I saw her in a new ride last week, and didn't you tell me she lost her job?"

"Yes," Sheba responded.

"Well, I think she's the link and someone paid her to tell her story," Delilah speculated.

"Glad you told me. I have a phone call I need to make." Sheba was livid.

"What are you going to do?" Delilah asked.

"Let's just say I'm about to handle some business." Sheba clenched her teeth.

"Don't do anything I wouldn't do," Delilah said.

"No need to worry about that."

Sheba disconnected the phone call with Delilah and dialed Joyce's number from memory.

"Hello," Joyce answered.

"This is Bathsheba Baker King, and I advise you to keep my name out of your mouth." Sheba didn't try to hide her anger.

"Sheba, so now you want to talk," Joyce said, with sarcasm in her voice.

"For someone who claims to have loved their cousin, you sure are going about it the wrong way."

"I loved Uriah. He was like a brother to me. You're the one who didn't love him. While he's off risking his life, working, you're whoring around with his boss. That's scandalous." Joyce raised her voice.

"No. What's scandalous is you telling lies to reporters for money," Sheba responded. Joyce remained silent. Sheba continued, "Yes, you thought I wouldn't find out. You're the source. Uriah would be appalled that you're tarnishing his image the way that you are."

"Oh no, sister, don't blame me for your mistakes."

"What goes on with my body is my business and mine alone. Not yours or anyone else's in your nosy family."

"See? That's why I never liked you. You always thought you were better than us."

Sheba responded, "You better be glad I'm a Christian, or I would purposely drive to Shreveport and commence to whupping your—" Before Sheba could finish, she heard the phone click. "Oh no, she didn't just hang up on me." Sheba pressed REDIAL. This time she got Joyce's voice mail.

She waited for the tone and said, "Don't think this is over. If you talk to another reporter, I will sue you for slander, and that new car you just got will be mine."

Chapter 50

David's attempt to get the article retracted was met with opposition. "What do you mean, you can't retract it?" he asked Phillip Jingles over the phone. Jingles was the CEO of the newspaper company that had printed the scandalous article about David and Sheba.

Jingles responded, "Our reporter writes opinionated pieces based on information from what are deemed reliable sources."

"Phillip, you owe me, and I'm cashing in the debt."

"David, I wish I could, but what's done is done. There's nothing I can do. You should know once it hits cyberspace, it takes off like the wind."

David, not satisfied with Jingles's response, hung up without saying another word. He could care less what folks were saying about him. He didn't want this to affect Sheba. Dealing with the death of their son was enough for her. She shouldn't have to deal with people voicing their unwanted opinions about a situation they had no details about.

"Mr. King, reporters are camped outside the office, and the phones are ringing off the hook with people wanting to speak with you," Nancy, one of his receptionists, said, while standing in the doorway.

"Continue to screen the calls. Tell everyone I have no comment. There are more important matters they should be concerned with than my personal life. My personal life is just that—personal. And you can quote me."

"Yes, sir," Nancy said before walking away.

Before David could blink, Trisha walked in. "David, you're one of the greatest bosses a girl could ever ask for, but if I get one more reporter calling my desk, I'm quitting."

"Trisha, I need you. Don't quit on me. I don't know why this has been blown out of proportion, but for now tell them, like I told Nancy, no comment."

"David, regardless of what's being said, I just want you to know that I got your back," Trisha assured him.

"That's good to know, because everyone else seems to want to crucify me in the media."

"You know how people are. You deliver the news, and now you're part of the news. Tomorrow it'll be someone else."

"I'm hoping tomorrow comes sooner than later." David chuckled for the first time that day.

"Mr. King, your wife's on line two," Nancy announced over the phone.

"Tell her I'll be calling her," Trisha said before leaving David alone.

"Hi, baby."

"I found out who one of the sources is," Sheba informed him.

David listened to her as she told him about Uriah's cousin Joyce. David already had it in his mind to find out whatever he could about Joyce and make her pay for the humiliation she was causing Sheba. "I'm on it. She's going to hate the day she ever crossed us."

"What do you plan to do?" Sheba asked nervously.

"When I finish with her, she won't be talking is all I'm going to say."

"I'm going to pretend like this conversation never happened," Sheba said.

For the second time that day, David chuckled. "Baby girl, I'm not going to kill her, but she's going to wish I had when I let her see how it feels to have her business put out on Front Street."

"I would say be gentle, but I wouldn't mean it."

"Bathsheba, you're supposed to talk me out of doing these things."

"She better be glad you're handling it, because the way I feel right now, I want to call her sister and tell her to be prepared to dig a grave right next to Uriah's."

The mention of Uriah's name put David back in a solemn mood. "Don't worry about a thing. I'm going to handle this, okay?"

"It's out now. Got to deal with the consequences."

Sheba was handling the situation better than David had expected. He loved her and would do anything to protect her. As soon as their conversation ended, he called his head of security and gave him all the information he had about Joyce. He gave him twenty-four hours to come up with everything he could about her. Everyone had skeletons in their closet, and David would find out hers. If that didn't work, then he would have to come up with a plan B. One way or another, she would be personally apologizing to Sheba.

David's eyes flared as he caught a glimpse of himself in the mirror on his desk. He hated to resort to under-the-table antics, but Joyce had left him no choice.

Garrett Morgan, head of DM King Media's security department, took a seat across from David.

He handed him a manila folder. "Everything you need to know about Joyce Johnson is there. Up until recently, she was on the verge of losing her house. The information shows that she made a huge deposit a few weeks ago."

David scanned the information. He looked Garrett in the eyes and didn't blink. "I need you or one of your men to make a personal visit to Ms. Johnson. Let her know that under no circumstances should she talk to anyone else about me or my wife. Make it clear that if she does, she will lose absolutely everything, including her two children to her ex-husband. I see that's the only thing that seems to matter to her."

"Consider it done," Garrett responded.

David watched Garrett as he left the room. Garrett provided security at the office, as well as David's personal security. He trusted Garrett to handle the situation without any legal repercussions. Satisfied that the situation with Joyce would be taken care of, David finally left the office. He was never one to have a regular workday. His days started before six and might not end until after ten at night, seven days a week.

His schedule had slowed down a bit since he married Sheba. His first two wives had complained that he was a workaholic. He didn't want to make the same mistake with Sheba. Although tonight he was getting home after ten, he tried to be home at least by eight or nine when possible. With Sheba not working, he would make it a point to include her in some of his business trips that were more than two days long so they could spend more time together.

He couldn't wait to get home to the comfort of her arms. Knowing she was waiting for him made all his hard work seem worth it. He longed to see her truly smile again. David was determined to figure out a way to make that happen. Maybe sharing the news about Joyce would do it.

Chapter 51

Sheba paced back and forth. It was after ten, and David still hadn't made it home. She had left a few messages on his cell phone, but she knew that if he was in a meeting, he wouldn't be able to return her call unless she specifically stated it was an emergency. Her nerves were jittery from all the unwanted attention from the press. She willed herself to finally stop looking online.

Every news feed talked about her and David, and hardly anyone had anything nice to say. She turned off the television set after one of her favorite news shows chimed in on the subject.

"Uriah, I'm sorry, baby, that your name is being pulled through the mud," Sheba said out loud as she looked out her bedroom window. The moon cast a glaze on the well-manicured lawn below.

"What in the world?" Sheba said as she saw a shadowy figure approach the house. She pressed the panic button located next to the bed.

A male voice was heard over the intercom. "Mrs. King, is everything okay?"

Sheba responded, "There's someone lurking outside, in the front, near the bushes."

"Mrs. King, lock your door. I'll go check it out," was the security guard's response.

Security turned the high-beam lights on outside. Sheba watched from the window as a slim white male was apprehended in no time. She could see David's car approaching from the distance. The security guard approached David's car when it pulled up. Sheba could tell David was angry from the way he jetted toward the man, who now stood with handcuffs on. She wasn't sure what was being said, but she couldn't wait to find out. Less than ten minutes later, David was entering the bedroom with his key.

He walked directly to her and embraced her. She held on to him tight. The day had been eventful, and just the feel of his arms around her eased the tension.

"Baby, I'm so sorry. It was an overzealous reporter. He's going to be arrested for trespassing." David ran his hand over her hair to soothe her.

"I'm okay. Just scared me. Good thing I was waiting up for you, or else there's no telling what would have happened."

"He wouldn't have made it inside, because security has a silent sensor that goes off anytime any of the doors or windows are opened," David assured her.

"Well, that's good to know."

David led Sheba to the bed, and they both took a seat. "Sorry, I didn't call. I had to put out some more fires."

"Who would have thought our relationship would make headline news?"

"It's the price you pay for fame," David said.

"Keep the fame. I want things the way they used to be." Sheba looked away.

"Joyce will no longer be a threat. I've taken care of it," David assured her.

"Thanks. But everything's spiraled out of control now. The damage is done."

"I wish I could erase these last twenty-four hours," David said as he reached out and grabbed her hand and squeezed it.

"It's not your fault. If I was truthful to myself, I really can't blame anyone but myself." Sheba stood up and walked to the window. David got up and stood behind her.

"Sheba, you have to stop beating yourself up about what happened. We're human. We make mistakes."

"Our mistake was costly. I lost my husband, and we lost our baby. That's a high cost for one mistake."

David didn't have a comeback for her last comment. He wrapped his arm around her waist as she leaned her head on his shoulder. They stood in that position for what seemed like minutes before retiring to bed.

The next morning David was gone before Sheba woke up. She retrieved a note from where he had laid. *I forgot to tell you I had an early flight to New York. I didn't want to wake you. I will call you.* It was signed, "Love, David."

"I love you, too," Sheba said out loud.

Sheba got up and got dressed. She looked in the mirror at her long, flowing hair. With everything that had happened, she felt like she was in need of a change. She called the driver David had hired for her and told him to meet her out front. An hour later the driver dropped her off at a local salon.

"I don't have an appointment," Sheba told the receptionist.

The receptionist responded, "We can get you in as a walk-in. Just sign in and have a seat."

Sheba signed in and then found an available seat in the busy waiting area. She thumbed through several hair magazines as she waited.

"Mrs. King, you can come back now," Dawn, one of the beauticians, said, as she approached her.

Sheba handed Dawn the magazine and showed her the hairstyle that she wanted. "Do you think you can do this?"

"I can, but are you sure?" Dawn asked as she looked at the picture and then at Sheba's radiant, long, flowing hair.

Sheba thought about it for a few seconds. "I'm sure. It's time for a change. Do it."

Dawn relaxed Sheba's hair and gave her the style that she wanted. Sheba looked in the mirror once Dawn was finished. Satisfied with her new short hairdo, she left Dawn a generous tip.

"Thank you."

"No, thank you," Sheba said. "I love it."

Sheba took mental notes as Dawn explained to her what she could do for daily maintenance. "When do you want to set up another appointment?" Dawn asked.

"I'll be in here every week, same time and day, unless something comes up," Sheba responded.

Dawn wrote her in her digital appointment book.

Sheba found herself looking in the mirror in the car on the way home. The driver looked up and smiled. Having a short hairdo would take some getting used to. When she arrived back home, several of the house staff complimented her.

David arrived home the following day. He stared at Sheba, but his facial expression was blank. Sheba didn't know what to make of his silence. He then flashed his pretty smile. "It's going to take some getting used to, but I love it. You're a beautiful woman. I'm lucky to have you in my life."

Sheba agreed. He was lucky. Truth be told, she loved David, too. Their relationship didn't start out like an ideal relationship, but they had been through some tragedies together and that had brought them closer, establishing a strong bond.

Six weeks later Sheba found herself standing over the toilet, releasing that morning's breakfast. *Could I be . . . ? No, I can't be,* she thought. She and David had just started being intimate again. But there had been one time. The night of the funeral. Sheba didn't want to get her hopes up too high.

Sheba picked up the phone to call David but changed her mind. Instead, she called the driver and told him to take her to the nearest drugstore.

She walked briskly inside and bought several pregnancy tests, just in case one was wrong, or she messed up or something. When she got back home, she rushed up the stairs and into the master bedroom. She removed the tests from their packaging and took them all.

She waited a minute before checking all the sticks. Each one of them came back with a plus sign. She wondered how David would feel about her getting pregnant this soon after losing little David. But she knew how she felt—alive again.

"Thank you, God, for this baby. I promise to take good care of it," she said out loud.

Sheba took a long hot bath and later dressed in a slinky red dress. She had instructed the cook to make one of David's favorite meals. The aroma of dinner filled the air. She greeted David with a kiss as soon as he came through the front door.

He looked at her. "You smell good."

Sheba had sprayed on the expensive perfume he had given her as a gift from one of his trips. It was her first time wearing it, so she was glad that he loved it. "Wash up, because dinner's ready."

Sheba flirted with David all throughout dinner.

"I love this playful side of you," David said as they looped their arms together and retreated to the living room.

David sat down on the couch. Sheba stood behind him as he sat on the couch, and massaged his shoulders. She kept looking for the perfect opportunity to tell David the news, but each time she opened her mouth to tell him, she would lose her nerve.

Before long, they were upstairs, in the master bedroom. She changed into sexy lingerie while David went to the bathroom.

He came back out, holding a box. "Is there something you want to tell me?" he asked.

She smiled and turned around, revealing her lingerie, and said, "We're having a baby."

David's face was expressionless, so Sheba didn't know if he was happy or mad about it.

She said, "David, did you hear me? We're having a baby."

"Thank you, Lord, for giving us a second chance," David said, right before dropping the box and running up to her. David grabbed Sheba around her waist and swung her around. "Oops. I shouldn't have done that."

"That's okay. I'm fine."

"We need to call the doctor. Set up an appointment."

"Done that. We have one set up for next week."

"Next week? No, he needs to see you tomorrow."

"Tomorrow's Saturday, David."

"I don't care. My wife is having a baby." David stopped and looked at her. "You're okay with this, aren't you? It's only been a few weeks since . . ."

Sheba placed her finger over his lips. "Shh. I'm fine. I'll never forget little David, but God has blessed us with another child, and I'm going to enjoy the blessing. This time we did things the right way."

David embraced her. She closed her eyes and thought that although she went through heartache and pain, she was right where she belonged—in the arms of David King.

Chapter 52

David leaned back in his chair and thought about the joy he'd heard in Sheba's voice the previous night as they cuddled. With the news of Sheba's pregnancy, David felt like his life was turning around in a positive direction. That is, until Wade walked in his office.

"Mr. King, our stock has dropped ten points," Wade regretfully informed him.

"What are the reports saying are the reasons why?"

Wade paused. "The media frenzy with your personal life is more than likely the reason."

"I pay you to do damage control, so do your job," David snapped.

"Yes, sir. I'm on it. I think you should do a press release."

"My personal life has nothing to do with DM King Media, so you need to come up with another solution."

"Talking to one of our own reporters will help squash some of the negative rumors. You can put your own spin on it," Wade insisted.

David hesitated before responding again. "I'll think about it. In the meantime, set up a videoconference with all my VPs for this evening, please."

"Yes, sir."

Once Wade had left, David dialed Trisha's number. "Please have the masseuse come to my office ASAP."

"Will do, Mr. King."

David had made several international phone calls by the time the masseuse arrived. An hour after getting a full-body massage, he felt relaxed and was able to go through the rest of his day without being tense. The videoconference with his vice presidents was a little uncomfortable at first—for them, but not for David—as he addressed the rumors.

"I'm sure you've heard how the media is trying to tarnish my name. I think it's ironic because I am the media, but that's life. We can't let their comments stop us from reaching our ultimate goal, and that's to be a part of everyone's household in some form or fashion—whether it be via their television screens or the printed material they bring into their household. In fact, we want to be their one source for information."

He hit buttons on his computer screen so he was able to see the expressions on their faces. Satisfied that they were all on the same page, David continued, "Our stock has fallen ten points, so that's a challenge to us. I want to see it rise back up to its normal level by this time next week. Any suggestions on what we can do?" he asked.

Floyd Williams, one eager vice president, responded, "I'm on it, Mr. King. I guarantee it'll be up by this time next week."

David didn't doubt it.Williams had proven in the past that there was nothing he wouldn't do to succeed. David overlooked some of his antics, as long as they didn't affect his bottom line.

"Mark your calendars for another videoconference. Same time next week." David announced, then signed off and called Sheba. "How are you and the baby?" he asked.

"We're doing just fine. Glad you called. I'll need to go to Shreveport to handle some business tomorrow. I've decided to sell the house, and I need to meet with a Realtor."

"Can't you set that up from here?" David asked.

"I could, but I want to go through the house and pack up some more personal items. I'll also determine what I want to keep or give away."

"You shouldn't be doing too much strenuous work. I'll have a mover get your stuff."

"David, that's fine, but I still need to be there to tell them what to pack or discard."

"When do you want to go?" David asked as he scanned his e-mails.

"Tomorrow morning."

"If you can wait until Friday, I can go with you."

"David, this is something I think I should do by myself."

David wasn't too happy about her going to Shreveport without him, but he didn't want to press the issue. "I'll have the jet fueled and ready to take you tomorrow morning, whenever you're ready."

"Thank you, dear."

David held on to the phone a little longer than necessary before placing it back in the cradle. Out of all his wives, he loved Sheba the most. There wasn't anything he wouldn't do for her.

He called one of his pilots and a moving company. With Sheba out of town for the next few days, he would attempt to figure out how to stop his stock from dropping. He only knew one recourse and that was to pray. Pray to God for divine intervention.

It had taken David years to build up his empire, and he didn't want to lose it due to the public's opinion of him. It wasn't his fault they had all put him on a pedestal. It was true that those who loved you today could easily turn around and hate you tomorrow. His competitors had all jumped at the chance to smear his name even more now that he was in the spotlight. Thanks to the school of hard knocks, he had a thick skin.

David kneeled down at the side of his desk. "Father God, my enemies are camped up around me, waiting for me to fall. Have mercy on me, Lord, and shield me from the accusations hurled my way. Once again, I ask you for forgiveness for my part in seducing a woman who was married. I know you're a forgiving God and that your mercy endures forever. I promise that now that Uriah's gone, I will love and cherish Bathsheba for the rest of my days here on earth.

"Please protect our unborn child and let it be born healthy. If it's a boy, let him be the man that I could not be. Let him be as wise as Solomon. Let him have my friend Jonathan's heart."

David prayed until sweat dripped from his forehead. He got off his knees and retrieved a handkerchief from his desk drawer. He felt at peace as he wiped his face.

Chapter 53

Sheba waved at her neighbors through the un-tinted window as the driver of the town car drove down the street, heading toward the house she'd once shared with Uriah. Some of her neighbors waved back only after realizing who the woman in the car was.

Delilah had been stopping by her house to make sure it was secure. Sheba could tell that she had been getting the lawn mowed as well, because everything was just as she had left it. She was eager to start packing so she could close this chapter of her life for good and move on.

Sadness swept through her spirit as she entered the house and recalled how she had convinced Uriah that it was the perfect house for them. She closed her eyes as she was transported back in time.

"This is perfect. I can have the big walk-in closet. You can have the closet in the guest bedroom to put all your stuff in," she recalled saying.

Uriah's infectious laugh filled the room. "As much stuff as you have, you'll probably need that one, too."

She agreed. "You're right. I'll take that one, and you can put your stuff in the hallway closet."

A knocking sound on the front door snapped Sheba out of her memory. "Those were the good ole days," she said out loud.

She walked to the front door and opened it without asking who it was. She welcomed Delilah in with a sisterly hug.

"I'm glad you're selling. You need to put the past in the past," Delilah said as they both walked toward the living room.

"You're right. I can't keep holding on to yesterday." Sheba picked up one of the African figurines on the mantel and held it.

"I'm surprised your hubby isn't here with you," Delilah said as she stood nearby.

"He wanted me to wait. I thought it would be best if I handled this myself."

Delilah said, "I'm looking at you, and there's something different about you. It's like you have a special glow."

"I'm pregnant." Sheba wanted to wait at least another month before telling anyone she was pregnant, but now that she was face-to-face with Delilah, she decided to tell her.

Delilah held up her hands and counted off the months on her fingers. "One, two, three. You two didn't waste any time, did you?"

"So what?" Sheba responded.

Delilah's hand flew to her mouth. "Oops. I'm always putting my foot in my mouth. I'm happy for you. I really am." She looped her arm through Sheba's arm.

"I'm on an emotional roller coaster. What if . . ." Sheba's eyes watered.

Delilah interrupted her thoughts. "No what-ifs." Delilah placed her hand on top of Sheba's stomach and told her, "This is going to be a healthy baby." Then she spoke directly to Sheba's unborn child. "Aunt Delilah is going to do what-ever she can to help out your mommy."

"If you mean it, then I need you to help me pack."

"Anything but that." Delilah laughed. "Besides, you're filthy rich. Where are the movers?"

"They'll be here tomorrow. In the meantime, I need to go by and see the Realtor."

"Well, I just wanted to swing by and see you, since you called. Call me later, and I'll come pick you up and treat you to dinner," Delilah said.

"You mean no home-cooked meal?"

"Please. Don't get me wrong. I can be domesti-cated when I want to be, but why be so when you can afford to eat out on occasion?"

"I sort of miss cooking. David has a cook who takes care of all our meals."

"You're the queen of the house, so if you want to cook, tell her so and do it."

"You have a point. I have to admit, though, that I've gotten spoiled. I love having people wait on me. It's like a fairy tale come true. Well, it was up until I lost little David." Tears started forming in Sheba's eyes. She grabbed tissue from a nearby tissue box and wiped her face. "I'm sorry. I didn't mean to get sentimental."

Delilah wrapped her arm around Sheba's shoulder. "Let it out."

Sheba did just that. She cried a river of tears as she leaned on her older sister's shoulder. A few minutes later she regained her composure and acted like the moment had never happened. "I'm fine. I better get out of here before I miss the Realtor."

Later on that night, Delilah picked her up, and they went to one of the local restaurants. After they were seated, the waitress took their order and then reappeared fifteen minutes later with heaping plates of seafood.

"I love their stuffed shrimps," Sheba said as she devoured her fourth one.

"Me, too, but I'm not eating for two, so I have to watch my girlie figure." Delilah winked her right eye.

Delilah and Sheba continued to talk over dinner.

"That's her. I know that's her. I saw her on that blog," a young woman blurted out to the woman she was with as they passed Delilah and Sheba's table. They stopped and stared.

Delilah said, "Excuse me, but do you two have a problem?"

One of them rolled her eyes. "No."

"Then I suggest you keep it moving," Delilah advised.

"This was a free country the last time I checked. I can be where ever I want," the woman retorted.

One of the restaurant workers walked over to the table. "Is everything okay over here?"

Sheba responded, "Everything's fine. Those young ladies were just leaving."

The two women walked away in a huff, but not without Sheba overhearing one of them say, "She's not all that. I thought she would be prettier than what she is."

Delilah shook her head. "Haters. Can't live with them."

"But I could sure live without them," Sheba said as she attempted to enjoy the rest of her dinner.

Chapter 54

David missed Sheba but knew that going back to Shreveport to handle the sale of her house was something she had to do on her own. He felt that once she was able to close the door to her past, they could truly move forward in their relationship.

David looked at the folder on Joyce that Garrett had given him earlier. He picked up the phone and dialed the number written in big red letters on a page inside the folder. "Joyce, I understand we've come to an agreement."

She sounded muffled on the other end but said, "Yes, we have."

"Good. Well, my wife's in town, and she would love it if you would make a special point of apologizing to her personally about what you've done. She would appreciate it, and so would I."

"But that wasn't part of the agreement," Joyce responded.

"Consider it a bonus on my part. Now, she's there for a few days, and I hope to hear from her soon that you apologized. Got to go." David hung up the phone.

Garrett's man had convinced Joyce to stop talking to reporters by offering her a substantial amount of money, but what really did the trick was when they confronted her about her past drug use, which could possibly be the information her ex-husband needed to win custody of her two kids. Once she realized her back was in the corner, she quickly signed the papers stating she would keep silent from that day forward. David stared at her signature and closed the folder. He filed it away in the filing cabinet located near his desk.

David could have wrapped up his work and called it a night, but since Sheba was out of town, there was no need for him to try to get home early.

"I was hoping I would catch you," Wade said as he walked through the door.

"Have a seat." David pointed to the chair across from his desk.

"We need for you to do an interview for *Business Week Today*. Can you do it as early as tomorrow?" Wade asked.

"The purpose of this interview?" David asked.

"Our investors need to know that DM King Media is solid. There's no need to focus on anything personal. State the facts, and that'll reassure our investors and advertisers that we're solid."

"Fine. I can do that. But tell me, what do we do about that?" David stood up and walked to the window and looked down.

Although he was on the top floor, he could still see people standing outside his office building. "They have been out there all day, holding signs and talking to anyone who will listen. I'm trying not to cause too much of a ruckus, because it'll only bring more bad publicity, but, Wade, I need for you to make sure they are removed from the premises pronto."

Wade said, "It's eight o'clock at night. You would think they would have gone home already."

"You would think. But since they are still here distracting others, get them removed. I don't want to see them when I get here tomorrow. Understood?" David said as he grabbed his laptop and placed it in the case.

"Yes, Mr. King."

"Now that we have that understanding, you have a good night. Don't work too late."

David locked his office right after following Wade out into the hallway. He dialed his driver. "Meet me in the back. I want to avoid the crowd out front."

"Yes, Mr. King," his driver replied.

David took a long hot bubble bath after he got home. The heat helped ease the tension in his muscles. He moved his head from side to side as he exercised the pressure out of his neck.

He was drying off when his cell phone rang.

"Guess what just happened?" Sheba said from the other end of the phone.

"What?" David responded as he used the big towel to dry off.

"Joyce stopped by the house and apologized for everything. I don't know if she was sincere, but she sure groveled. I don't know what you did, but thank you."

"You're welcome, my dear."

"It won't erase the pain she's caused, but to see her apologize really caught me off guard. She's never liked me."

"I'm sure she won't be a problem for us ever again."

"I hope not. Because I haven't always been saved. I would sure hate to resort back to my school training and knock her out."

David laughed. "I can't see you hurting anyone."

"Please. I can fight. I don't like to fight. I never looked for a fight, but if one found me, I did what I had to do. See, growing up, some girls were jealous of me and were always trying to pick a fight with me. One girl tried to slash my face with a razor, and I beat her like her whole family stole something from me."

"I better sleep with one eye open. Don't want you having a flashback moment and hurting a brotha." David laughed.

"Ha-ha. I'm just saying. I'm glad she apologized, because now maybe, just maybe, some of this mess will die down."

David sighed. "Well, dear, I didn't want to say anything, but earlier today and well into the night, there were some people outside my office building, picketing. They were saying that they won't buy the products advertised on my stations."

"They are taking this too far. It's just not right."

"I've dealt with picketers before. It'll all go away."

"There has to be something we can do. You know what? I've been avoiding the press, but maybe it's time that I come out of the background and set some stuff straight."

"Sheba, you have to think about the baby. You're not to be put under any kind of pressure."

"It's more stressful trying to avoid reporters. If I talk to the press, it'll be my pick who I talk to."

"I still don't think it's wise," David responded. "You don't know them like I know them. They can be cutthroat. My competitors have found an opening, and that's through you, my dear."

"David, let's get something straight. You didn't marry a weak woman. Yes, I let some stuff get me down, but that's life. I'm not going to sit back and let these people continue to talk about me without doing something."

In a shaky voice, David said, "I'm just worried about you and the baby. I don't want anything to interfere with your health."

"I think this is best. Otherwise, I'll feel like I have no control. This way, I have some control. Then they can take what I say and do with it whatever they will."

David still didn't agree but would support Sheba on her decision. "Fine. Let me know who you want to interview with, and I'll have it set up. But there's only one condition."

"And what's that?" she asked.

"If the reporter asks you something and you feel uncomfortable about it, I want you to take the liberty of getting up and walking away."

"David, I got this. You just set it up. Now, dear, this baby and I are tired, so I'm going to get me some sleep. I suggest you do the same."

David prayed that Sheba doing the interview wasn't a bad call. Sheba was new to the spotlight. He wanted to please her, but maybe he should follow his gut and forbid her from doing the interview. He laughed out loud. Sheba had a mind of her own, so she would get her interview with or without his help. It would be a smoother transition if he helped.

Chapter 55

Sheba recited Joyce's apology to Delilah the next morning, as they ate breakfast at Sheba's old kitchen table. "She shocked me," Sheba confessed. "I almost didn't open the door when I saw she was on the other side of it."

"You're better than me. I would have still kicked the heifer's behind," Delilah said.

"It's over with. Now it's up to me to work on forgiving her. It's going to take a lot of praying for me to do that. I'm nowhere close to forgiving her yet," Sheba said.

"The Bible does say we're supposed to forgive as God has forgiven us."

Sheba couldn't argue with Delilah on that point. "I'm trying to do the right thing. Lord knows I have a lot of wrong I need to make up for."

"Sheba, have you prayed and asked God to forgive you? If you have, then forgive yourself. Sometimes we can be our own worst enemy."

Sheba thought to herself, *Who would have thought Delilah would be the voice of reason?* She responded, "I'm working on it, sis. I'm working on it."

"Well, work a little harder. I had to forgive myself for what transpired between me and that preacher I told you about. Although I was wrong for pursuing him relentlessly, he still had control over his own actions. I don't own his actions. I only own up to mine."

"Delilah, it sounds like you've had an epiphany."

"Let's just say God is working on me. Boy, does He have His job cut out for Him," Delilah said as she drank her orange juice.

"Well, at least you admit it."

"Never professed to be a saint, like some holy rollers," Delilah said.

A knock at the door interrupted Sheba's thoughts. "That must be the movers." She got up and let them in.

Six hours later she was tired and ready to take a nap. "Everything I want to take with me is on the truck, and the other stuff, well, whatever you don't want, I'll see if someone at the church needs it before donating it to a shelter," Sheba said to Delilah as she plopped down on the sofa.

Delilah responded, "My friend Keisha might want some of your furniture. You have good taste, and I know she is looking to get a new living room set."

"She can have whatever she wants," Sheba replied.

"Cool. I'll call her."

"While you're doing that, I'm taking me a long hot bath."

The following day Keisha stopped by and confirmed that she wanted the living room set and one of the bedroom sets. Sheba made a list of the other items she had left to donate, while Delilah took pictures with her digital camera. Delilah assisted her with her inventory list and printed it out so they could take it with them to church the following day.

Sheba got up bright and early the next morning to get ready for church. She eyed herself in the mirror as she got dressed. She opted to wear a purple suit with a matching hat. Although she probably shouldn't wear high heels, she rounded off her ensemble with some purple snakeskin heels. She wanted Delilah to go with her, but Delilah had planned on going to her own church.

The driver waited for Sheba as she locked up. The closer the driver got to her old church, the more the palms of her hands sweated. She wasn't sure how the church members would act toward her, with all the rumors that had been floating around locally as well as in the national news. The driver pulled the town car up to the front of the church and, without waiting for him to get out and open her door, she exited.

She had purposely arrived a little late, so she wouldn't have to converse with too many people. Songs of praise could be heard as she walked up the steps leading into the sanctuary. One of the ushers handed Sheba a program as soon as she entered the door. The ushers used their hands to direct her to the right side of the sanctuary.

Sheba looked until she saw an empty spot on one of the middle pews. She heard whispers as she walked down the aisle. "Isn't that Bathsheba?" she heard one lady say.

"She looks a little different," she heard another one say.

"I can't believe she's showing her face here," she heard a familiar voice say.

Before sitting down, she looked back in the direction of the voice and saw that it belonged to one of Uriah's cousins.

When the announcement clerk asked if there were any visitors, all eyes were on her. Sheba tried to scoot down in her seat. She wished she could disappear. The clerk said, "We have our sister Bathsheba back in our midst. Sister, would you like to say anything?"

Sheba took a few deep breaths and stood up. "First, give praises to God, to our wonderful pastor and other members of the clergy, and to my church family. I'm grateful to be able to walk through these doors again. Life has dealt some hard punches, but by the grace of God, I'm here today. I want to ask you all to keep me in your prayers." She heard some amens, and she heard a few people mumbling, as she took her seat.

The topic of the sermon was forgiveness. "Peter asked Jesus how many times he should forgive. Peter thought forgiving someone seven times was plenty. We would be in terrible trouble if our Heavenly Father gave us only seven times to mess up. Can you imagine going through life and being allowed to make only seven mistakes?" the preacher asked.

Sheba had probably fumbled seven times before hearing the sermon, let alone in the course of a lifetime, she thought as she continued to listen.

The preacher continued, "Brothers and sisters, God has a word for you today. As I talk about forgiveness, I'm reminded of the parable that Jesus told Peter of the shocking servant. Turn with me to the eighteenth chapter of Matthew, verses twenty-one through thirty-five. You can remain seated."

Sheba located the scripture and read it silently as the pastor read it out loud.

The pastor went on to say, "If someone has done you wrong, let it go. Stop holding on to something that happened yesterday. Some of y'all are holding on to stuff that happened twenty years ago. Look at your neighbor and say, 'Let it go.'"

Sheba looked at the woman sitting next to her, and they said in unison, "Let it go."

"I can't stand here in this pulpit and tell you that forgiving someone is easy, because it isn't. That's why you need to take the issue to God, and when you take it to Him, leave it with Him. Ask Him to help you get past the hurt, the pain, the resentment. With God in the mix, you can let it go. Colossians three, thirteen reads, 'Forbearing one another, and forgiving one another, if any man have a quarrel against any: even as Christ forgave you, so also *do* ye.'"

Sheba felt that the message was just for her as she wrote down notes from the sermon. As the pastor continued to speak about forgiveness, one other point stood out to Sheba.

"As I come to a close, I want you to forgive yourselves. God is a God of mercy and grace. He gave His only begotten son so that we all could have access to eternal life. So whosoever will, let him come now and be saved. God forgives you, my child. Let go and open up your hearts and receive God's precious gift."

Tears streamed down Sheba's face as she released the guilt and pain from the past year.

Chapter 56

David stood in Nathan's pastor study, waiting for him to finish talking to one of the members of his congregation. He thumbed through one of the books Nathan had on his desk. The title caught his attention: *Letting God Take Center Stage in Your Life*.

He was on the third page by the time Nathan walked in the room. "You can take that copy if you want it."

David closed the book and said, "I might just do that. I'll have it replaced."

"No need to. Consider it a gift."

"Thank you, my friend."

"Where's your beautiful wife?" Nathan asked.

"She's still in Shreveport. She'll be home tomorrow."

"Good. I'll treat you both to dinner sometime this week."

"I think it's funny that I have more money than you but you're always treating me to dinner."

"Me too. What's up with that? I think I need to reevaluate this friendship of ours." Nathan laughed.

"Your sermon on compassion was what I needed to hear. So many people have been coming after me verbally that my spirit has been vexed," David said as he sat down in a chair across from Nathan's desk.

"I've been hearing and reading about it. You know how I feel. There's always a price to pay when we sin."

"But when do we stop paying? First, I lose my son, and then this. My stock price is dropping, and the vultures are trying to take advantage of the situation by buying up as much of my company's stock as they can."

Nathan stood up and placed his hand on David's shoulder. "Let us pray. Father God, your servant David is asking for a word from you. Let him know that you are the only judge, and that because of your grace and mercy, although we fumble, you're right there to pick us back up.

"David's heart grieves, and only you, Lord, can fix the hole that's in his heart. Work a miracle in his life. Search his heart and find what's true. Allow the compassion you've shown him to manifest itself in his life, where he's able to show compassion to others. Forgive us all as we fall short of living up to the blueprint you left for us to follow. Be with us as we travel this journey called life. You promised to never leave us or forsake us. If it is thy will, O Lord, fix David's situations.

"Through it all, let him know that it is you, O Lord, that is in control and that you want a center stage in his life. Not just when things are going bad, but every day of his life. Bless him and his wife, Bathsheba, as they prepare to welcome a child into the family. Bless the child so that he will be all that you will have him be to help further your kingdom. Amen."

David opened up his eyes and looked up into Nathan's face. "How did you know that Bathsheba was pregnant?"

"I knew before you did." Nathan's eyes twinkled.

"She told you?" David asked.

"No. I dreamed it. I was just waiting on you to tell me," Nathan admitted.

"I was going to tell you but was afraid you were going to have bad news for me."

"David, you know I love you like a brother. I speak the truth and will never tell you anything that I haven't already discussed with God first."

"I know. I should listen to you more."

"Yes, you should, but we're not going to harp on that right now." Nathan and David both laughed.

"I don't know about you, but my stomach is growling," David confessed.

"Mine too. I normally don't eat Sunday mornings, before my sermons, so you know it's way past chow time for me."

"Since we're both steak-and-potato men, let's go to the Roadhouse."

"Let me lock up here, and I'll meet you there."

"If I get there before you, I'll wait in the lobby," David said.

David and Nathan spent the time together at the restaurant getting caught up. David couldn't help but express his excitement about Sheba's pregnancy. He felt more hopeful that she would have a healthy pregnancy after talking with Nathan.

Later on that night, after talking to Sheba and preparing for bed, David got on his knees beside his bed and prayed. "Lord, thank you for showing me mercy. I know brother Nathan prayed for me earlier, but I wanted to talk to you, Father God, for myself. I want to thank you for showing me mercy. Even in my sinful state, you've protected me from my enemies. Lord, put up your shield of protection as I continue on this battlefield."

David prayed until his eyes got weary. "Lord, thank you. If I had ten thousand tongues, I couldn't thank you enough. Be with me, Father, all the days of my life. And when it's time, Father God, allow me a place in your kingdom. Amen."

Chapter 57

Sheba knew this would be the last time she saw the house she'd once shared with Uriah. A lone tear streamed down her face as she closed and locked the front door for the very last time. "This is it." She placed her hand over her heart. "No matter where I'm at, you'll always be in my heart. Love you, Uriah."

She turned the knob to make sure the door was locked, and with a slow pace walked down the walkway to the waiting car. She looked back one last time and waved as if someone were going to wave back.

The driver held the car door open for her, and she climbed in. "Good-bye," she said as the driver got in the front seat and drove away. Less than four hours later the jet she was on landed at Addison Airport.

To her surprise, David greeted her as she exited the plane. "I've missed you," he said as he held on to her.

"I've missed you, too," she responded. She honestly had missed him. David had weaved his way into her heart, and she was not ashamed to admit it.

The driver retrieved her bags and placed them in the limousine. David waited for Sheba to step in the limo and got in right behind her.

"Your eyes look puffy," David said.

"I'm just a little emotional right now," Sheba confessed as she pulled a small compact mirror out of her purse to look at her eyes. "Oh my. I do look bad."

"You're home now. If you need to talk, you got my ear."

"I'm fine. Just a cleansing process that I should have gone through long before now."

"All things happen in their designated time," David said.

"Wise words," Sheba said as she looked out the window.

David reached over and took her hand. He squeezed it a few times. They rode the majority of the way home in silence. Both were lost in their thoughts.

"It's good to be home," Sheba said as they entered the front door.

"I'm glad you think of it as home."

"It took a while, but I think I'm accustomed to it now." Sheba flashed a smile.

David helped her unpack her bags. "I've been all around the world, and no woman can match your beauty. I'm not just speaking of your outer beauty, either," David said.

"That's sweet of you to say." Sheba turned and faced David.

David bent down and kissed her on the lips. "Your lips taste like sweet nectar."

"Mr. King, you're mighty tasty yourself," Sheba said as she smiled.

"I love you, Bathsheba," David said.

"I love you." Sheba meant it. She had fallen in love with him. She couldn't pinpoint the moment, but she had. Uriah would always be special to her, but now she could finally let go of the guilt that she had been holding on to about betraying Uriah and give her all to David. She looked into David's eyes and said, "I love you, and I'm ready. I'm ready to give you my all."

David's hand rested on top of her belly. "Having my child is the best show of your love."

Their lips locked, and two hours later they were both sound asleep in each other's arms.

The alarm clock woke Sheba out of her sound sleep. She couldn't remember setting the alarm. David was still asleep. She shook him. "David, wake up. The alarm went off." She glanced at the digital display. It read 6:45 a.m.

David jumped up. "I can't believe I overslept. I normally wake up before it goes off, and cut it off so it won't wake you."

She rubbed her sleepy eyes. "Well, this time it beat you up."

Sheba slid back under the covers as David got up and got ready for work. While he was dressing, she said, "Did you set up the interview?"

"No. I was hoping you'd changed your mind."

"I haven't. Set it up. I need to tell my side, or should I say our side of the story."

"Okay, I'll set it up today. I promise."

Later on that day, Sheba received a call from a popular national talk show host, Kandie Washington, confirming an interview for two days later. Sheba thought that would be perfect. She called Dawn to confirm her hair appointment and also made appointments to get a manicure and a pedicure. "What was I thinking? I could have had them all come out to the house. I'm rich. I can afford it," she said after making the appointments. She called them all back and gave them her address. *Yes, being rich comes with benefits.*

Now that she could get out more, she refused to use the personal shoppers David had on standby for her. Sheba found the keys to the Jaguar David had given her and ventured out toward the Galleria. Dallas traffic was backed up on the interstate. She wished she had called the driver after being stuck in traffic for over an hour.

She finally reached the mall and found the perfect outfit at Neiman Marcus. It was a cream-colored pantsuit. She would wear the pearls David had given her as a wedding gift, and with her new cropped hairstyle, she would look great for the camera.

Sheba needed to look good, because she was nervous about opening herself up to an interview. She had never done anything like this before. She hoped she didn't stutter or say the wrong things. She needed to protect Uriah's memory, as well as help David preserve his image.

Chapter 58

David seemed more nervous about Sheba's interview with Kandie Washington than Sheba did. He wiped his brow several times as he coached her. "Don't look directly at the camera. Try to be natural. Whatever you do, don't get upset."

"I can do this," Sheba assured him.

David gave her a tight hug and watched from the sidelines as she went to sit on the interview couch. Kandie Washington had decided to film her show from the Dallas location since she was able to get the exclusive interview with Sheba. The promotions for the show would send her ratings through the roof when the show aired.

Kandie walked out onstage wearing a black skirt and a gold blouse. Sheba stood and shook her hand.

"Thank you for agreeing to do this interview. You don't know how much this means to me."

"You were my only choice," Sheba said.

"I will ask the questions the public wants to know. I just don't want you to be caught off guard."

"I'm ready. I have nothing to hide."

"In that case, let's do a sound check, and we're ready to tape." Kandie tested her microphone. She looked at the show's producer. "Are we ready to rock and roll?"

"On three," the producer said.

Sheba held her hands tightly together as Kandie did her opening monologue. "Welcome to another edition of *Set the Record Straight*. I'm your host, Kandie Washington. Today it's my pleasure to introduce you to Bathsheba King, the wife of David King, the CEO of DM King Media. Welcome, Mrs. King."

"Call me Sheba."

David smiled. She remembered. *Make it personal.*

"Mr. King is such a private person. So many are curious about how you two met."

Sheba looked at Kandie. "I met David for the first time at a gala held at the Ritz Carlton Hotel right here in Dallas. Of course, he was charming."

They both laughed. "Would you like to address the rumors that have been floating around?"

Sheba said, "Kandie, I doubt if there's anyone out there who hasn't done something they've regretted. I'm no different."

"Did you leave your husband for David? is the question that's been on the mind of a lot of my home viewers."

"No, I didn't. I loved my husband. David and I did not get together as a couple until after Uriah died. David was there for me when I needed him. As he would tell you, I did my best to resist falling in love with him, because of my loyalty to my deceased husband."

"We're going to go to a commercial and be right back with Bathsheba King," Kandie said, looking directly into the camera.

One of the workers rushed over and freshened up their makeup. The producer counted down to the end of the commercial.

Kandie continued the interview. "Welcome back. I'm here with an exclusive interview with Bathsheba King." Kandie looked in Sheba's direction. "I've read reports that the child you recently lost was David's and not that of your deceased husband. Are those allegations true?"

Sheba sniffled. She took a tissue from the box on the table that sat between her and Kandie. She wiped one of her eyes. "Kandie, losing a child was one of the hardest things I've had to go through. Even more so than losing my husband."

"I have kids of my own, so I can sympathize with you," Kandie assured her.

"David went beyond the call of duty and, knowing that I was pregnant, asked me to marry him, anyway. I don't know too many men who would do that. Do you? You've seen the pictures. I was well along before David and I marched down the aisle and said 'I do.'"

"So, was the child David's?" Kandie asked.

"If you asked David, he would say that he was. David loved him even before he was born."

David wanted to give her a high five for how she was answering the questions. He tried to rein in his excitement until after the interview was completely over.

Kandie turned toward the camera. "Well, ladies and gentlemen, there you have it. Bathsheba King has set the record straight." Kandie smiled and looked at Sheba. "Any final thoughts before we bring on our next guest?"

Sheba looked directly at Kandie and said, "In honor of the son I lost, I would like for your viewing audience to consider donating funds to the March of Dimes. Their Web site is www.marchofdimes.com. Thank you."

"We'll have more information about the March of Dimes on our show's Web site. We'll be right back after the commercial with one of the star players from the Dallas Mavericks," Kandie added. Once the cameras were off, Kandie turned to face Sheba. "You did great. Thank you for being so candid in the interview."

Sheba stood up and shook Kandie's hand. "Thank you. I watch you all the time. Keep up the good work."

"If you're ever in New York, give me a call."

"Will do."

Sheba walked over to where David stood. He kissed her lightly on the lips and led her out of the studio.

As they walked, David said, "Bathsheba, you did better than great. You were outstanding."

"So, did I sound believable?"

"You told the truth, but in a way that the audience is still left to come up with their own conclusions."

"Great. Because I really didn't want to lie, and I wanted to protect Uriah's memory."

They hopped in the back of the limousine. David directed the limousine driver to take them home. While enroute, David poured two glasses of grape juice. He handed one to Sheba and toasted her. "Mission accomplished."

Chapter 59

Seven months later . . .

David sat behind his desk, thinking that life couldn't get any better than it was at that moment. After Sheba's interview, she received many requests to speak. People were still curious about the wife of David King. They all hoped to learn more about him by talking to her. Sheba was able to turn a negative into a positive.

He picked up the picture of Sheba on his desk and smiled. She held her hand on her round belly. David prayed daily for a healthy baby.

"Mr. King, Reverend McDaniel is on the line," Trisha said over the intercom.

"My main man, where you been?" David asked.

"I was in Shreveport, doing a revival at Reverend Adam Marks, Sr.'s church. I wish you could have been there to see the miraculous things that the Lord did this past week."

"God's been working some miracles out here, too, brother."

"Tell me about it."

"Why don't you meet me at the Four Seasons for lunch and I'll do just that?"

"Sounds like a plan. Our regular time?"

"Yes," David responded, while admiring the other pictures of Sheba that he had on his desk.

After the call with Nathan, David went to Wade's office. Wade was there but had his back toward the door. David eavesdropped from the doorway rather than alerting Wade of his presence.

He heard Wade say to the caller, "He doesn't have a clue." There was a pause as he swiveled his chair around. His face turned white when he saw David standing there. "Look, I have to go. Will talk to you later."

David strolled into the room. "Hi, Wade. I came by to see if you got the final papers we need for the deal in Tulsa."

Wade stuttered, "I—I did, but we didn't get all the signatures needed to make things official. My contacts at the FCC wouldn't approve them."

David now stood near Wade's desk. "I wonder why. You normally have no problems getting approval. Is there something going on that I should know about?" David looked down at Wade.

Wade seemed to cower. "No, sir. I just need to go over their heads and make it happen."

"That's right. Make it happen. That's what I've been paying you to do."

Wade's phone rang. He looked down at the number and then back up at David.

David asked, "Aren't you going to get that?"

"They can wait," Wade responded.

"Get the Tulsa deal approved. I'll talk to you later." David did an about-face and walked out of Wade's office.

David pulled out his phone and called Matthew, the head of his IT department. "I need a report on the incoming and outgoing phone calls and e-mails of Wade."

"Yes, sir. When do you need it?"

"I need it yesterday. And, Matthew?"

"Yes?"

"I need you to handle this yourself. Don't let anyone, especially Wade, know that you're doing this." David's instincts told him that Wade was up to no good, but he wanted proof before deciding how to deal with him.

"Do I need to alert security about anything?" Matthew asked.

"No. I'll handle that if need be. Just get me the information, and have it to me by the end of the day. I'll be out of the office for the next few hours, so if you need me, you can reach me on my cell phone."

David ended the call and headed to meet Nathan for lunch. Nathan was waiting for him when he arrived at the Four Seasons Hotel and Resort restaurant.

"You're late," Nathan said.

David sat down across from him. "Dealing with a traitor. But I hope I'm wrong." David told Nathan his suspicions about Wade.

Nathan said, "Follow your gut instincts. In this case, I don't think you are wrong. I wasn't going to say anything, but I had a dream last week, while in Shreveport, about this. I just didn't have a chance to call you."

"I wish you would have. I probably could have done something sooner."

"God's been beating me up because I've been slacking in some areas. Even I, a man of God, get too busy to do the Lord's work." Nathan looked up. "But I hear you, Lord. I'm going on a monthlong sabbatical. I need some alone time with just me and the Lord."

"I hope your sabbatical won't start until after Bathsheba has the baby. You're supposed to be the godfather."

"When she gets ready to have the baby, you just call me. I'll be there," Nathan assured him.

"Well, that could be any day. She looks like she's about to pop right open."

"My friend, don't worry. I will be there. I wouldn't miss it for anything."

David looked down at his phone and read the text message that had just come through. He looked up at Nathan. "Looks like your sabbatical will have to wait."

Chapter 60

"Breathe in and out," Sheba heard the doctor say as she pushed.

David held her hand. She squeezed his hand tight and yelled. David's face turned red. "Baby, you can do this," he said.

Sheba felt this sharp pain from her head to the tips of her toes, and then, just like that, she heard the most beautiful sound she had ever heard. The cries of her baby.

The doctor said, "You have a baby boy."

In between tears of joy, Sheba said, "Let me hold him."

The doctor handed her baby to her.

David said, "The Lord has told me we should name him Solomon."

Sheba looked down into his beautiful face. His skin was David's beige color, and he had David's sandy red hair. He had her eyes. "Solomon Zaid King, welcome to our world," she said and kissed him on the forehead.

The nurse reached for Solomon. She said, "Mrs. King, we promise to take good care of your little man."

Sheba did not want the nurse to take Solomon from her, so she held on to him tightly.

David intervened. "Baby, they have to clean him up some more and give him a thorough checkup."

"But I don't want to be without my baby." Sheba feared she would lose Solomon, just like she'd lost her other baby.

"Mrs. King, as soon as we get him in the cute little blue outfit your husband brought for him, we'll bring him down to your room," the nurse assured her.

Ten minutes later Sheba and David were waiting in her private room for the nurse to bring Solomon to them.

"Do you think something's wrong? What's taking them so long?" Sheba asked. She did her best not to panic.

"Baby, the doctor has assured us that Solomon is fine. I even went over his head, and the king of doctors assured me he would be fine."

Sheba had a quizzical look on her face.

David continued, "God, baby. God's assurance that Solomon will be fine is all that we need. So stop worrying, okay?"

Before Sheba could respond, the nurse wheeled Solomon into the room.

David said, "Can I hold him?"

Sheba gave the nurse an approving nod. A huge smile spread across Sheba's face as she watched David and his son bond. She asked the nurse, "Can you hand me my purse please?"

The nurse handed it to her. Sheba got out her cell phone and took a picture. She wanted to capture that moment on film, although it would forever be planted in the memory banks of her mind.

A knock was heard on the door before it opened. Nathan walked in, carrying balloons and a stuffed animal. "I came to check on the mother and my godson." Nathan bent down and gave Sheba a hug and a kiss on the cheek.

"We're doing just fine," she responded.

David glanced up. "Look at my little man."

Nathan walked over to them. "He's going to do great things."

Solomon started crying.

The nurse said, "He's probably hungry. Have you decided if you're going to breast-feed, give him formula, or both?"

"I'm breast-feeding," Sheba replied.

Nathan said, "That's my cue to go. I just wanted to check on you before I left to go out of town."

"We're fine," Sheba said as David handed her Solomon.

David walked Nathan out. When he returned, Solomon was breast-feeding. Sheba rocked him back and forth.

"Look at his little hands and his little feet." Sheba couldn't stop admiring her little baby.

"He's perfect. Just like his mama," David said as he stood near the bed.

"He's a greedy little something, though, because every time I think he's through feeding, he won't let go."

"I guess he gets that from his daddy." They both laughed.

After they were assured that both mother and child were in good health, the doctors released Sheba and Solomon from the hospital. David had hired a nurse to watch them both, and she was waiting for them when they arrived home.

The butler helped Sheba up the stairs, while David held Solomon.

"We're glad to see you and the baby," the butler and other staff declared once they had reached the top of the stairs.

David said to the staff, "No one is to come around Solomon if they are sick. Even if you have a slight cough."

"Yes, sir," was heard from all the members of the house staff.

Sheba sat on the bed and had David lay Solomon in her arms. She couldn't keep her eyes off her little bundle of joy. She felt something wet coming from his diaper. She laughed out loud. "The joys of motherhood."

Chapter 61

David had prayed daily for hours during Sheba's entire pregnancy. God had heard his cry and had answered his prayers. He thanked God silently for blessing him with a healthy son. There was nothing more beautiful than the sight of Sheba changing Solomon's diapers.

His love for his wife grew daily. Women continued to flock to him, but they were all left feeling disappointed when he shot their advances down. Some of his colleagues were amazed at his faithfulness to his wife, since they took every opportunity to cheat on their spouse.

His vibrating cell phone pulled him out of his trance. Matthew was on the other end of the phone, with information about Wade.

"I got the information you wanted," Matthew said.

David had pushed the situation with Wade out of his mind over the past few days. Sheba and Solomon had been his top priority. Now that Sheba and Solomon were safely at home, he had to get back to the business at hand. "Matthew, I'm working from home today. Ask Trisha for the directions, and meet me here at my home in an hour."

An hour later David kissed Sheba on the top of the head. "Baby, I'll be downstairs if you need me."

Sheba said, "David, I told you, you don't have to watch me. I'm fine. Solomon's fine."

"I know, but I need to spend this time with the two of you. Can you give me that please, darling?" David smiled.

"Just another reason why I love you." Sheba blew him kisses as he walked out of their bedroom.

Matthew was seated in the living room when David entered. Matthew stood up.

David said, "You can sit." Matthew handed David a folder before sitting back down. David took a seat across from him and said, "So give me the specifics." David scanned the papers in the folder as Matthew talked.

"I'm afraid Wade has been undermining some of your projects, sir."

"It's apparent. No wonder we didn't get the bid for that station in Springfield, Illinois." David placed the folder down on the table in front of him. "Matthew, you've done a great job. I got it from here. Remember to keep this under wraps."

"Yes, sir. I promise."

"And thank you for respecting my family time, but you could have called me about this sooner. This was important."

Matthew said, "But Trisha said—"

"Next time do exactly as I tell you. Not what Trisha tells you."

"Yes, sir." Matthew hung his head down low.

David got up and went to a cabinet. He turned around and handed Matthew a cigar. "Smoke one of these with me. Help me celebrate the birth of my son."

Matthew now felt at ease. "Congratulations on your son."

David and Matthew enjoyed a smoke together. After Matthew left, David got on the phone with his attorney.

"I want him to pay for crossing me," David said.

His attorney responded, "You must have proof that he purposely sabotaged the deals, David. Otherwise, we don't have a case."

"I have the proof. You just make sure you take care of him for me."

"Done," his attorney said.

David called Nathan but didn't get an answer. He left a message. "I know you're on your sabbatical, but, man, I need you. I need some spiritual guidance right now. Call me back when you get this message."

A few hours later David received a text message from his attorney. Done.

David's wealth and power yielded quick results. Satisfied by the text message, he turned on the television and watched the news. In one segment a reporter was trying to interview Wade, who had been placed under arrest.

The reporter placed a microphone in Wade's face and asked, "Is it true that you've been embezzling money from DM King Media for a year?"

Wade's stricken face turned red. "No comment," he said as he was led out of the building in handcuffs and then placed in the back of a police car.

"Wade should have known not to mess with me," David said right before turning the television off.

He eased back up the stairs to check on his wife and child. They were both sound asleep. He gently removed Solomon from Sheba's arms and placed him in the bassinet at the side of the bed. He then removed his clothes and got in the bed beside Sheba. Before closing his eyes, he vowed to do whatever it took to protect his family and his empire.

Chapter 62

Sheba woke up to find David on his knees, praying, at the side of the bed. She didn't want to disturb him, so she remained quiet. She closed her eyes, too, as he prayed.

"Father God, thank you for showing my family grace and mercy. Thank you for my son, whom I give to you to do with what you will. I know that he will do far greater things than I ever could. I praise you today for all that you've done in my life and in my wife's life, Lord. I praise you today because you didn't have to, but you forgave me and have blessed me with my family. I thank you for giving me another chance and another chance. I tried to go on this life's journey on my own and failed. I've learned that if it's outside of your will for my life, it will fail.

"Please, Lord, continue to watch over my family near and far. Grant them your unequivocal peace. Open their hearts and minds so that they, too, can benefit from the knowledge of knowing you personally. I thank you, Father, for the favor that you've shown me throughout the years. Lord, I thank you. I thank you. If I had a thousand tongues, I couldn't thank you enough. Amen."

Sheba said, "Amen."

David's face looked peaceful when he looked up into Sheba's eyes. She reached her hand out to him. He took it and rose up and sat next to her. "I feel redeemed."

"Me too," Sheba confessed.

"I wasn't around my other kids like I should have been, but I have vowed that Solomon is going to be raised the right way, with two loving parents. We're going to teach him the ways of the Lord so that he will have a clear understanding of who the Father is and how he should live his life."

Sheba agreed. "That means we both need to start going to church regularly."

"Nathan's going to love that," David said.

She and David had been attending church on a more regular basis. Although David didn't go every week, he prayed daily, and Sheba could see that he had a strong relationship with God, even if he hadn't been attending church regularly.

"Another thing we need to address is you not spending time with your other kids. I think you should see about having them visit at least once a month. I want Solomon to know his siblings," Sheba said, batting her long black eyelashes.

David paused a few seconds before responding. "You're right. It's time that I do. Their monthly allotment isn't an excuse for me not spending more time with them."

"Good. Now we can be one big happy family," Sheba said as she gave David a tight hug.

Solomon started crying. David got him out of his bassinet. "I think he wants his mommy." David handed him to her.

She looked at the clock. "Yes, he's hungry. It is about his feeding time."

Sheba fed him, and then David helped her give him a bath.

"I'm so happy right now. I feel like I'm going to burst," she told David as he followed her back into their bedroom.

"This is just the beginning, my love. There will be plenty more days like this one."

Sheba hoped so. Last year was tragic for her, so the happiness she was experiencing was long past due.

The bedroom phone rang. David answered it.

"Ms. Baker is here," the butler informed David from the other end.

David responded, "Thank you. I'll be down in a minute." David hung up the phone and faced Sheba. "Your sister's here."

"Tell her to come on up." David was about to leave the room when she stopped him. She said, "Nathan's going to be Solomon's godfather, but we never discussed who his godmother would be. Do you mind if it's Delilah?" she asked.

"Truthfully, yes, I do mind." David didn't give Sheba his reasons, because then she would know how he and Delilah had schemed behind her back. David compromised and said, "But she is your sister, and I'm going to leave that decision up to you." Before saying another word, David left her alone to make the decision.

Minutes later, Delilah entered the room, wearing vibrant colors, which complemented her bubbly personality. She was holding a bag. "There's my favorite sister. Where is my nephew?" Delilah rushed toward the bed. She stopped by the bassinet. She removed the blanket from around his little body so she could get a better view of him. "He's a handsome little thing. Looking just like his daddy."

Sheba agreed. He was the spitting image of David. "Don't wake him up. I just got him to sleep."

"I'm here to help you out, so he and I will get a chance to bond." Delilah sat on the edge of the bed. "So how are you holding up? I should be mad at you because Nathan got to see the baby before I did."

"You've been in contact with Nathan? The two of you talk like that?" Sheba asked with a puzzled look on her face.

"Of course. He's been a real good friend. He's trying to keep me on the straight and narrow."

"No wonder he needed a sabbatical, because doing that is a full-time job," Sheba teased.

"Ha-ha. You got jokes." Delilah handed Sheba the bag she had been holding. "There's something for you and Junior in there."

"He's not a junior. We've named him Solomon."

"He's going to be wise."

Sheba looked at her curiously.

Delilah continued, "Don't be looking at me like that. I read my Bible."

"I see." Sheba removed the tissue from the bag and took out its contents. "This is the cutest little outfit. Thanks, Delilah." She also had a matching bib with the words *I love my aunt* written across it and matching cloth shoes to go with the outfit.

"That little, handsome thing is going to look good in that," Delilah said.

"Let's see what you got for me," Sheba said. She retrieved a gold envelope from the bottom of the bag and opened it. She reached over and hugged Delilah. "Thank you, sis. I need this. I'll have to wait until after my checkup, but I can sure use a day at the spa."

"I know it's not much."

"Please. This is just what I need. And as much as I love my baby, I will be needing me some 'me time' soon enough."

Solomon woke up. Delilah surprised Sheba when she volunteered to change his diaper. Sheba wasn't going to argue with her. She laughed when Solomon squirted on Delilah. Delilah didn't find it funny.

Delilah left to go get herself settled into her guest room while Sheba fed Solomon. She sat in the rocking chair David had brought her. "You're going to be so spoiled, and I'm going to be the main one spoiling you," Sheba said as she rocked Solomon back and forth.

Epilogue

A month later . . .

"Look at our little man," David said as he played with Solomon's little hands and feet.

Sheba watched from the distance. "He's perfect."

"I'm the happiest man on earth," David said as he rocked Solomon in his arms.

"It's almost time to leave for church," Sheba said.

"I'll carry him downstairs."

"You don't want to let him out of your sight, but you'll have to go back to work sometime, David."

David knew Sheba was right, but after experiencing such a miracle after losing their other child, it was hard to leave him. He had taken time off from work to be with Solomon and Sheba.

Sheba carried his diaper bag as she followed them down the stairs to the waiting car. The driver held the door open and waited until David had the car seat secured in the back of the car.

"He looks just like his daddy," Sheba stated as she looked at Solomon and then back at David.

"He gets those dimples from his mother."

Sheba smiled. "I'm glad he got at least one of my features."

"Now, when we have a girl, I want her to come out looking like you. Perfect."

Sheba held up her hand. "Put the brakes on it. I think that's it for me."

"I have ways of changing your mind," David said.

Solomon stirred in his car seat. He started crying.

Sheba said, "What's wrong with mama's baby?" She rubbed his little hand, and Solomon went back to sleep.

Thirty minutes later they pulled up in front of the church.

"Let me change his diaper, and then we'll be ready," Sheba said.

David waited outside the limousine as Sheba changed Solomon's diaper. Nathan walked up to him.

"How are you, my friend?"

"Great. Words can't express the joy I feel," David told him.

"God deserves all the praise."

"Amen," David said. David reached for Solomon as Sheba exited the car.

"There's your godfather," Sheba said as she greeted Nathan.

Nathan peeked at him. "How's my man doing?" Solomon smiled at Nathan.

Sheba cleared her throat. "Aw, fellows. I'm glad you're bonding, but it's almost time."

Delilah rushed up the stairs behind her. "Traffic on I-Twenty was a mess. I tried calling you to let you know."

"I forgot and left my phone at the house. I thought you were already here. We're just getting here ourselves," Sheba said.

David had been hoping that Delilah wouldn't make it. He now understood why Uriah didn't like Delilah. Delilah had some devious ways, but he couldn't say anything to Sheba about them. For now, he would keep a watchful eye on Delilah and protect his wife and son if she dared to step out of line. David put his personal feelings about Delilah aside for his beloved wife.

They all entered the sanctuary and took their seats. Nathan prayed and spoke of the special occasion of Solomon's christening. David held Solomon as he and Sheba went to stand at the front of the altar, next to Nathan and

Delilah. Although he didn't like Sheba's choice, he reluctantly agreed to let Delilah be Solomon's godmother. Delilah had her issues, but she had grown to love her sister and she adored her nephew. That he could see.

Nathan had his friend Adam Marks, Sr., come in from Greener Pastures Full Gospel Baptist Church in Shreveport, Louisiana, to preside over the regular church service. Nathan took a seat on the front pew, right next to David.

Sheba whispered, "Delilah goes to his church. Maybe when we're in Shreveport again, we can go."

"He's good," David responded as he rocked Solomon.

After the church service was over, David, Sheba, Delilah, Nathan, and the baby posed for pictures.

"Everyone's invited back to our place to celebrate Solomon's christening," David said.

"I'll be there as soon as I take care of some church business," Nathan responded.

"I'll follow y'all," Delilah said.

David gave directions to the visiting minister and the other people who were interested in attending the celebration. Twenty guests showed up at David and Sheba's house for a Sunday feast. David watched as everyone seemed to be engrossed by Solomon. David stuck his chest out like the proud father that he was.

"He's already commanding an audience," Sheba said as she stood next to her husband.

"Just like his daddy." David leaned down and kissed her on the top of her forehead.

"Let's hope he's not conceited like you."

"I'm not conceited. I'm just confident. There's a difference."

"With you, they are one and the same," Sheba teased.

"You got jokes, I see." David embraced her.

"Love you, King David." She removed herself from his embrace and went to gather Solomon up in her arms.

"I love you, too," David said out loud, not caring who heard him.

Soon thereafter the guests left. Nathan lingered. Delilah followed Sheba upstairs with Solomon. When David and Nathan were alone, they sat down on opposite ends of the sofa.

Nathan said, "My friend, I've seen you transform into the man God wanted you to be."

David responded, "God left me no choice."

"Oh, you had choices."

"True. I just chose to do things God's way for a change. The last time he whipped me, it almost left me defeated."

"God's a merciful God."

"Thank God for that, because I would hate for Him to remove His hands of mercy from over my life ever again."

Nathan said, "Continue to do right by your son. God's going to bless him and the generations to come." On that note, Nathan got up, headed to the front door, and bade his friend farewell.

David stood at the door and watched Nathan leave. He looked out at the still sunny, cloudless blue sky. He thanked God again for his wife and his son. David couldn't help but smile. He smiled from the inside out. It felt good to know that God had redeemed him. He shut the front door, knowing that a new chapter of his life was about to begin.

Reading Group Guide

1. Uriah loved Sheba. Do you think he was too naive when it came to their relationship?

2. Sheba and Uriah seemed to disagree about her spending habits. She had her own job, so do you think it was fair of Uriah to make a big deal about her shopping?

3. Do you think Uriah was justified in feeling the way he did about Delilah? Do you think she had an ulterior motive for being around Sheba? Would you have trusted Delilah?

4. Why would Delilah agree to help David manipulate her sister? Do you think she was harboring resentment about being given up as a baby?

5. David was attracted to Sheba from the moment he saw her. David could have any woman he wanted. Why do you think he lusted after Sheba?

6. Do you think David really felt remorseful when he set Uriah up for the kill?

7. Do you think Sheba suspected David of any wrongdoing when it came to Uriah, and if so, do you think she just turned a blind eye?

8. If Sheba loved Uriah so much, why do you think she slept with David?

9. Nathan tried to warn David about his bad behavior.

10. Why do we ignore warnings when we get them?

11. David's lust for one woman caused a multitude of bad things to happen in his life. Do you think our behavior can cause our lives to spin out of control? How can we get them back under control?

12. God showed mercy for David in the end. When you do wrong, do you go to God and repent, or do you just expect your situation to change automatically?

About The Author

Shelia M. Goss is the *Essence* magazine and Black Expressions Book Club best selling author of *Delilah, My Invisible Husband, Roses Are Thorns, Paige's Web, Double Platinum, His Invisible Wife, Hollywood Deception,* and *Savannah's Curse,* as well as four titles in the teen series The Lip Gloss Chronicles, namely, *The Ultimate Test, Splitsville, Paper Thin,* and *Secrets Untold. Ruthless* is her thirteenth novel and second Christian fiction novel. Besides writing fiction, Shelia is a freelance writer. She is also the recipient of three *Shades of Romance* Magazine Readers' Choice Multi-Cultural Awards and is honored in *Literary Divas: The Top 100+ Most Admired African-American Women in Literature.* To learn more, visit her Web site, www.sheliagoss.com, or follow her on Facebook, at www.facebook.com/sheliagoss.

UC HIS GLORY BOOK CLUB!

www.uchisglorybookclub.net

UC His Glory Book Club is the spirit-inspired brainchild of Joylynn Jossel, Author and Acquisitions Editor of Urban Christian, and Kendra Norman-Bellamy, Author for Urban Christian. This is an online book club that hosts authors of Urban Christian. We welcome as members all men and women who have a passion for reading Christian-based fiction.

UC His Glory Book Club pledges our commitment to provide support, positive feedback, encouragement, and a forum whereby members can openly discuss and review the literary works of Urban Christian authors.

There is no membership fee associated with UC His Glory Book Club; however, we do ask that you support the authors through purchasing, encouraging, providing book reviews, and of course, your prayers. We also ask that you respect our beliefs and follow the guidelines of the book club. We hope to receive your valuable input, opinions, and reviews that build up, rather than tear down our authors.

What We Believe:

—We believe that Jesus is the Christ, Son of the Living God.

—We believe the Bible is the true, living Word of God.

—We believe all Urban Christian authors should use their God-given writing abilities to honor God and share the message of the written word God has given to each of them uniquely.

—We believe in supporting Urban Christian authors in their literary endeavors by reading, purchasing and sharing their titles with our online community.

—We believe that in everything we do in our literary arena should be done in a manner that will lead to God being glorified and honored.

We look forward to the online fellowship with you.

Please visit us often at:
www.uchisglorybookclub.net.

Many Blessing to You!
Shelia E. Lipsey,
President, UC His Glory Book Club

ORDER FORM
URBAN BOOKS, LLC
97 N18th Street
Wyandanch, NY 11798

Name (please print):_____

Address:_____

City/State:_____

Zip:_____

QTY	TITLES	PRICE

Shipping and handling: add $3.50 for 1st book, then $1.75 for each additional book.

Please send a check payable to:

Urban Books, LLC

Please allow 4-6 weeks for delivery